I0824033

CHRONICLES
of
ORI

CHRONICLES of ORI

AN AFRICAN EPIC

Harmonia Rosales

W. W. NORTON & COMPANY
Independent Publishers Since 1923

Printed in China
First Edition

For information about special discounts for bulk purchases, please contact W. W. Norton Special Sales at specialsales@wwnorton.com or 800-233-4830

Manufacturing by Asia Pacific Offset
Book design by Chris Welch
Production manager: Julia Druskin

ISBN 978-1-324-11111-5

W. W. Norton & Company, Inc., 500 Fifth Avenue, New York, NY 10110
www.wwnorton.com

W. W. Norton & Company Ltd., 15 Carlisle Street, London W1D 3BS

1 2 3 4 5 6 7 8 9 0

To Hilaria Rosales

(January 14, 1928–November 27, 2017)

CONTENTS

BOOK III
LINEAGE

BOOK IV
THE OGISOS

BOOK V
YORUBALAND

BOOK VI
THE ALAAFIN OF OYO

BOOK VII
THE LAND OF ORIRUN

BOOK VIII
EVE

BOOK IX
OLOKUN'S OCEAN

BOOK X
THE CHILDREN OF ORI

AUTHOR'S NOTE

"Cada cabeza es un mundo." That well-known Spanish proverb was one of my Afro-Cuban father's favorite sayings. I remember asking him what it meant, and he said, "Every mind is a world." At the age of twelve, I took those words to refer to the powers of my budding imagination.

But as I grew older, I came to understand its fuller meaning: that each person carries within them a world shaped by their unique experiences, beliefs, and thoughts. Every mind is its own universe, intricate and distinct, even if we share the same reality.

When I finally grasped it, the proverb became one of my favorites, too. I use it as my artistic foundation. After all, isn't this what art is—a perspective from and on a moment in history, whether captured in images, inked on pages, or spoken aloud? History itself is an ever-growing mosaic, each piece representing an individual story that adds something to the sweep of human experience. Recognizing that every voice, every perspective, has its unique place is crucial to seeing the entire masterpiece.

As you dive into this epic, you may encounter stories that feel familiar, or perhaps ones that depart from or challenge what you've heard before. Or this may be your first introduction to the myths of the Orishas, of Oduduwa, of Oranmiyan and Moremi, of Mama Onile, and many other mortals and gods. No matter where you're coming from, I hope you see these stories as pieces of a broader narrative—my own and my father's, but also African history, and even more so, human history.

CHRONICLES
of
ORI

Oya's Invitation

I have been on this Earth since before the cultivation of the soil. Before life took root, flourished, and asserted control. The world belonged to me and my kind alone . . . and then came the soil.

When I was tasked with scattering the seeds of life across this unmarked canvas, I could not fathom the transformation that would ensue. The soil became the land, the birthplace of diversity.

Then the great flood separated mortals, scattering them far and wide. It split the world, creating two realms, the physical and the spiritual. The emergence of new deities ushered in an era of competition and rivalry, as each god vied for influence over the ever-expanding creation. Our world, once unified, was fractured yet again—each spiritual realm a reflection of the divided land below.

Walk alongside me, as mortals and gods once walked together, and let me tell you the history of the Orishas: of our rise, our battles, our fall, and our persistence. Through my words, we can relive the moments that defined us and witness the enduring fight that propels us forward.

—*Orisha Oya*

BOOK I

CREATION

CHAPTER 1

Ashé

If you want to know the end, look at the beginning.

—African proverb

In the beginning, there was an endless void, an eternal darkness. The seeds of life lay dormant, awaiting the spark that would ignite the cosmic cycle of life and death.

From the dark emerged a force, as ancient and arcane as the universe itself. This self-birthed primordial being entered into existence. Its actions would set in motion transformations that would shape the fate of all who were to come.

The primordial being unleashed the earliest glimmers of light, like the blinks of fireflies. Stars burned bright and fierce, pulsing with tremendous energy, only to fade and perish in the cold darkness. From their ashes, new stars were born, giving rise to planets and entire galaxies, each a result of the endless creativity of the primordial being, the universe's architect.

Like a serpent devouring its own tail, the universe now moved through endless cycles of birth, growth, and decay, each a variation on the one that came before. All of this was guided by the primordial being, who was undergoing transformation itself, shedding the past and reemerging into the promise of new beginnings.

A humble fragment takes its place in the grand design. Like a single drop of rain in Olokun's eternal ocean, or a grain of sand in Olorun's desert, this minute element awakens, embracing its role in the ever-shifting movement of the universe. And this is where our story begins . . .

Olodumare, the reincarnation of the primordial being, was a divine force in constant motion, free from the restrictions of form and boundaries. Drifting from one galaxy to another, he collected the minerals and microbial remnants of long-deceased planets.

Within the belly of his ethereal form, Olodumare bore the seeds of life, each a thing of pure possibility poised to be nurtured and reborn. He was like a cosmic gardener tending to the scattered vestiges of creations long past.

Yearning to understand the complexities of life, Olodumare ventured farther into the uncharted depths of the universe, fueled by an unquenchable desire to amass more seeds. As he navigated infinite galaxies, his journey brought him to the very brink of creation. It was there, in the farthest reaches, that he chanced upon a fellow primordial being, the alluring Odua.

Odua existed in the cold embrace of the void, her essence attuned to the many potent forces that governed the universe. Composed of pure hydrogen, she was a vision of transcendent luminosity, her form a veil of incandescent light shimmering in the dark. Odua sensed the approach of the wandering scavenger who would forever alter their collective existence. Unlike the restless Olodumare, she remained rooted, anchored to the place of her genesis. There was no need to wander, nor to scavenge, for she was both the beginning and the end. She was the womb from which all things emerge and to which all things return. She had been waiting patiently, her purpose clear and unwavering.

The instant their paths crossed, the pair of primordial beings felt an irresistible pull toward one another. Against the flickering stars, they danced in tandem, their energies destined to intertwine and transform each of them. Olodumare, the eternal seeker of life, discovered within Odua the catalyst for transformation, the divine spark that would kindle a new child of creation.

As their destinies entwined, the universe lay still, anticipating the birth of something truly extraordinary.

Olodumare became enmeshed in Odua's divine power, his own strength diminishing with each passing moment as he spiraled helplessly into her web. As Olodumare succumbed to immense compression, doubt shrouded his ecstasy. The darkness around them crackled to life with brilliant arcs of energy, their dazzling force weaving a barrier that appeared impervious. Odua constricted around Olodumare like a vise, compelling him to whirl wildly within the confines of her celestial cocoon.

At last, Olodumare could no longer bear the torment. With a cataclysmic explosion that reverberated through the void, he ruptured, scattering his very essence into the seemingly infinite abyss. His seeds of life were stripped from him by Odua. From the smoldering remains of this cosmic detonation, Earth clawed its way into existence, and time itself began.

The birth of this new world had taken a terrible toll on Olodumare. Without his seeds—his life's work—the once-magnificent being was reduced to a mere husk of his past grandeur, leaving him yearning to take back what Odua had seized. Odua, for her part, now transformed herself into the great ocean, the lifeblood of the new planet. Earth, whom she affectionally called Onile, was her creation, and she would forever be the ruler of her fate.

In time, Olodumare was able to gather himself whole again. In a desperate bid to reclaim his possessions, he sought to pierce Onile's atmosphere, hoping to draw sustenance. But his attempts brought disaster, causing meteorite strikes that left a scarred landscape of craters and ash in their wake.

These collisions damaged the seeds of life on Earth, serving as a harsh lesson: Onile was fragile. And as Olodumare gazed upon what his desperation had wrought, he knew that he must find another way to restore his former power, or else risk the destruction of all the seeds he had collected.

Olodumare saw that he needed to divide what was left of his power in such a way that he would become small enough to enter Earth without harming her. In his final act of divine transformation, he fragmented himself into three mystical beings, each bestowed with a piece of his once-unfathomable power.

What remained of Olodumare was a deep cosmic silence. His once-overflowing essence was now scattered across the skies and rivers of Onile. Creation had drawn upon his divine soul, leaving him hollow; no joy, no sorrow, no love flowed within. Now he exists as a presence that watches without desire and listens without reaction, patiently awaiting the renewal of his cycle.

CHAPTER 2

Orirun

The Earth is a beehive; we all enter by the same door.

—African proverb

The three celestial beings that emerged from Olodumare were Eshu, Orunmila, and Obatala. They were the Irunmole, each embodying distinct elements of their creator's power. Eshu was granted Olodumare's restless desire to wander; Orunmila, his boundless wisdom gained from exploring the universe; and Obatala, the vast knowledge of the seeds he had sown.

The Irunmole pierced Earth's atmosphere, racing through the clouds to an unknown world. Yet, as they set foot upon the fertile soil of Earth, their memories dissolved, leaving them with no knowledge of their celestial origins or divine purpose.

As they uncoiled from the deep imprint they left in the burned soil, their now-Earthly forms stood tall, their elongated limbs lending an air of elegance to their already regal presence. Their blue-black skin shimmered with the iridescence of a thousand galaxies, each delicate curve and contour of their bodies reflecting the ethereal beauty of the midnight skies above. Their eyes, deep and tempestuous, mirrored the fierce storms that raged in the skies. As they moved their arms and legs with fluid grace, they seemed to float like the very winds that had carried Olodumare across the universe, every gesture an attestation to the primordial being that had birthed them.

Awakening their senses to Onile's realm, the Irunmole marveled at the garden of life in full bloom before them. The seeds Olodumare had once borne within his belly had been cultivated into a mosaic of colors and sounds.

As they explored the lush landscape, they were greeted by four Orishas, guardians of the blossoming seeds: Oya, who sent the wind that pollinates the seeds; Oko, who managed the soil's fertility and the transformation of the seeds; Ogun, the keeper of the mineral, iron, that retains waters for the seeds; and Yemayá the nurturing protector of the seeds that lived on the surface of the land. The Orishas referred to the land they so affectionally cared for as Orirun.

The meeting of the sky guardians, the Irunmole, and the Earth guardians, the Orishas, should have been a momentous occasion. The Orishas too had come from Olodumare, pieces of his divine soul that escaped during his fragmentation. Yet, unlike the Orishas, the Irunmole had not yet awakened to the knowledge of their ashé, the vital force that granted them mastery over their respective domains.

The Orishas explained to the Irunmole the effects of passing through Earth's atmosphere, which they called Mama Onile's waters. Mama Onile was the ruler of the lands, and her waters had the power to wash the spirit and transform the soul.

From the Orishas, the Irunmole learned that it was their passage through Mama Onile's waters that had cleansed them of their memories, leaving them lost. Stirred by an intense desire for purpose, the Irunmole embarked upon a quest to uncover their origins and awaken the slumbering ashé within.

Guided by the Orishas, the Irunmole ventured deep into Orirun's jungle, in search of the oldest baobab tree, for in its core resided the soul of Mama Onile herself.

For days they traveled. With each step they took, the jungle sprang to life, rich hues of flora welcoming them. Colossal trees stood as stoic witnesses, their roots delving into the depths of time, while their branches sprawled across the skies with divine reach. The air was heavy with a scent strangely familiar to the Irunmole.

The Irunmole had to be careful about what they brushed up against, for they were not used to such intense stimulation and visions. With just a single touch, every living element revealed its entire story to them. Each leaf was a page in nature's history, full of undiscovered knowledge. A broken branch showed the Irunmole a vision of a hungry predator chasing its prey. The aged bones of a long-dead creature told a story of a terrible death.

At last, the Irunmole, led by the Orishas, arrived at the ancient baobab tree, its wide trunk anchored to the soil as if it had existed before the land itself. The branches beamed with vitality as birds darted among them.

Mama Onile reigned supreme from her throne. At her feet unfurled a sprawl of life. The mountains bowed to her command, rivers danced to her heartbeat, and the jungles swayed to the swish of her hips. Nature itself blossomed under Mama Onile's tender care.

Her hair was loc'd and cascaded to the floor. She had the deepest brown skin; it matched the soil from which she ruled. Except for her feet, every inch of her body was adorned in the finest diamonds and gold. She sat poised as though she were always anticipating esteemed guests. Veiled behind a gold beaded mask that concealed her face, she locked eyes on the Irunmole as they approached. She beckoned them to come closer so she could get a better look. They knelt before her, pleading with her to restore their memories.

Mama Onile complied, though she told them that their ashé came with terms. Her voice, although soft as the kiss of a breeze, carried unfathomable weight: "You descend from the sky above, seeking solace in my Earthly kingdom . . . know this, to reside here, you must understand and respect my sacred laws."

Her first decree: "The gold that veins through my soil shall never be harvested. It is the material manifestation of our supreme creator, of Olodumare's sacrifice, scattered across the lands as a reminder of him."

Next, she addressed the balance between land and sea: "All creatures under my care may partake of the ocean's bounty. Yet, let it be known, the

ALETA ONILE ASASAYA
Harmonia

giants of the deep waters are granted the same privilege as those on land. This reciprocity maintains the harmony between the rhythm of the waters and the pulse of the land. Assault these giants, and you will incite a war you cannot win, a tempest that will ravage both the land and all things on it."

Finally, she spoke of the mortal inhabitants of Earth, the Enks: "Destiny is banned in the land. These creatures shall forever lead simple lives, unencumbered by the complex web of fate. They exist to live, procreate, and return to the soil. Unshackled by time, their lives flow like a river, carving its own path through existence. They are devoid of both ambition and regret; they do not dream of tomorrow, nor mourn the past. They epitomize life in its most primal form: raw, simple, and free."

After she recited her laws, Mama Onile felt a tremor of unease ripple up her spine.

Since the Irunmole's arrival from the skies, she knew they wielded ashé potent enough to upset the balance she had so carefully maintained.

Obatala, the sculptor of life, bore an ashé akin to hers, but with a twist. He possessed the ability not just to breathe life into existence, but to shape entirely new species.

For his part, Eshu, the divine messenger, boasted an ashé that allowed him to communicate with the gods above and the land below. Such a skill eluded Mama Onile, and it gnawed at her, for it meant another could weave stories outside her control.

Orunmila possessed the ashé of knowledge and prophecy. His was a power that threatened to shatter her foundation—to pierce the veil of time and reveal hidden truths of the future. With Orunmila's knowledge, the Enks could form their own destiny and become enlightened, and Onile's role as their ruler would be diminished.

Mama Onile knew that if she bound the Irunmole, like she had the Orishas, by her laws and also separated them from one another, she could offset their powers. So she offered Orunmila a place in her kingdom, and granted the other two Irunmole freedom, though within certain limits.

The union between Mama Onile and Orunmila would serve as an alliance between the universe and Earth. He would reside in the soil with her, his knowledge locked away like a precious treasure, never to be shared with anyone but herself. Together they would become even more powerful than each was alone. She believed she could forever preserve her order. The Irunmole had no choice but to oblige her, for they were in a foreign land and had to obey its rules.

And thus, the fate of Orunmila was sealed, entwined with that of Mama Onile, as she endeavored to protect Orirun from the shadows of uncertainty that his ashé might cast upon it.

Mama Onile proclaimed to the other two Irunmole, Obatala and Eshu: "Now, to reclaim your ashé, you must walk my lands in their entirety. Should you defy my decree, your time shall be sealed, and you shall perish."

Obatala and Eshu, under the tutelage of the Orishas, ventured forth into the world, their minds full of curiosity and wonder.

They soon encountered the Enks, diminutive creatures swathed in silken fur of brown, black, white, red, and colors in between. Though they rarely exceeded four feet tall, their short stature deceived, for they were mighty.

Their bodies, otherwise slender and petite, had strong shoulders forged for the arduous task of scaling lofty treetops to scavenge for food. Their profiles were distinctly flat, characterized by pronounced brows and wide cheekbones, though with noses that boldly jutted out. The Enks found havens in the intricate pathways of caves that sprawled belowground, a labyrinthine sanctuary that was not only their home, but a natural fortress, offering protection from the lurking predators above.

Living amid nature, the Enks were the embodiment of tranquility and goodness. The land flourished under their watchful eyes. They were more than Orirun's inhabitants; they were the epitome of peace, the true stewards of Onile's abundant splendor.

In stark contrast to the Enks were the carnivorous giants born from chaos who emerged from the deepest trenches of the ocean. They towered over the land, and over both the Irunmole and Orishas. They had a twisted fusion of Enk and animal features, their skin had the texture of rough, weathered stone, and it was adorned with grotesque scales that had an eerie luminescence. Their limbs were elongated, with sharp claws that ripped the soil beneath their feet. Their faces were monstrous, with eyes like black pearls that reflected the depths of the abyss from which they had risen. Their mouths, filled with rows of jagged, needle-like teeth, stretched into perpetual, ravenous grins. They were a nightmarish mockery of the Enks, distorted by the chaos that had spawned them.

As these behemoths scavenged the land, their massive forms cast shadows that swallowed sunlight, and the sound of their thunderous footsteps were like drums of war. They devoured all life that crossed their path, their voracious appetite a manifestation of Mama Onile's fears.

The Enks were nourishment for these titanic beings; they were plucked from the Earth like ripe fruit. They seemed to exist only to serve as food. Obatala and Eshu, moved by the plight of the Enks, wanted to intervene to protect them from the giants' vicious predation. However, they were bound by Mama Onile's law. They had to endure the suffering that unfolded before them, for they were not allowed to alter Earth's nature. Their hearts swelled with empathy for the Enks. But Mama Onile knew that the great alchemist of time would render Obatala and Eshu's pain a thing of the past.

Time entwined itself around the Irunmole's hearts, transmuting their souls and tempering their spirits. It casts its spell upon them, rendering them impervious to the waves of despair that crashed against their existence.

Within the jungle of time's domain, they discovered the secret to their own invincibility: the understanding that pain and loss are fleeting, transient as the passing clouds that obscure the sun. With each lash of emotion, they grew stronger, learning to navigate the unpredictable waters of life.

At the end of their hundredth year in Orirun, the Irunmole discovered that time had become their greatest teacher, their most cherished companion, and their fiercest protector. Through the transformational cycle of life, their souls evolved from innocence to knowledge. As promised, Mama Onile restored their memories, unlocking their ashé, the inner power granting them mastery over her elements.

Though they were once keen on taking back their seeds, they were now driven by their own individual purposes. They chose to abandon their original mission to reclaim the seeds lost during Onile's birth, realizing that they had already taken root and flourished on her lands. They recognized that Mama Onile needed their protection, and embraced their role as guardians of her lush world.

CHAPTER 3

Obatala

If you don't know where you are going,
any road will take you there.

—African proverb

Obatala and Eshu were crowned Orishas and began exploring their new ashé. Because all the Orishas were diligently tending to their duties, Obatala found himself alone. Despite possessing the knowledge of life, he had yet to truly create it. His hands, skilled in the art of craftsmanship, molded small flora and fauna, simple and fleeting, yet nothing too complex. He had tried and failed many times, yearning to breathe life into a masterpiece that would surpass all others, a magnum opus that would become the favorite of Mama Onile. It wasn't long until he was wandering Orirun in search of inspiration.

One day, he chanced upon three beings, each one a paragon of beauty and power. They seemed to be reservoirs of mysticism and mystery. They were Emi, Eleda, and Ojiji—the three sisters of existence. They usually kept to themselves and were rarely visible to the naked eye, but there was something about Obatala that intrigued the sisters, so they revealed themselves to him.

Emi, the first sister, fed off the wind, her breath stirring mortals from their slumber and guiding them toward life. With each exhale, she infused the world with vitality, her every word a thread of existence.

Eleda, the second sister, was an enigmatic force, her aura an array of emotions that crashed like the tides of the ocean. She was the keeper of dreams and desires, the wellspring from which passion and purpose sprang forth, nurturing the souls of the Enks and all other living things alike. Within her aura, life found meaning.

Ojiji, the third sister, was the most mysterious of the three, her visage an ever-shifting play of light and darkness that mirrored the complexities of life. She was the guardian of legacies. The eternal companion of the soul, she remained when a life's journey came to an end. She was the shadow of a life well lived, the lingering memory of a soul.

As Obatala conversed with the three sisters, his perception of creation was forever altered. No longer would his craft be confined to mere form and substance; he would now infuse his creations with the breath of life, the depths of emotion, and the enduring legacy that lingered in the wake of a soul's departure. His hands, guided by the divine sisters of existence, would mold works of art that would reveal, in the contrast, the simplicity of the dutiful Enks and the chaotic giants.

Obatala beamed with anticipation. The sisters, sensing the potential for greatness within him, decided to take him on a journey beyond the physical boundaries of Orirun, to the place where destiny itself was created. There, amid swirling mists, they introduced him to the exiled Ajala.

Ajala, the blind potter, devoted his days to the intricate artistry of shaping destinies, which he affectionately called Oris. Each Ori was a spiritual guide, a delicate masterpiece, imbued with honor, integrity, and respect for the ancestral spirits. An Ori helped the one who possessed it align their actions with their ashé, and thereby contribute to the harmony of the universe. Ashé was the life force; Ori was destiny. Together, they could create powerful change.

However, when destiny was banned by Mama Onile, so was Ajala. Yet Ajala refused to stand idly by and wither away, like any Orisha who no longer used their ashé, and continued to create Oris. To ensure they remained beyond the control of Mama Onile, Ajala carefully nestled each Ori within a crystalline sphere. These spheres served not only as protective vessels but would also allow the Oris to be admired in their full splendor, their shimmering hues jumping about like captured stardust. As they rested within these spherical homes, the Oris remained anchored in place, their boundless potential safeguarded until the moment they were called upon.

Ajala was an unusual figure; his appearance seemed as ancient as the Earth itself. He was tall as any Orisha, but a severe hunch left him half the size of the others. His skin had the texture of dried clay, cracked and creased from eons spent shaping destinies. Each wrinkle told a story of countless lifetimes and the many Oris he had crafted.

His milky eyes were windows to another realm, guiding his hands with a subtlety that defied his blindness. His unkempt hair was a tangled mass of silver clumps that nested on top of his head like a grand misshapen crown. His hands were callused from his tireless work, yet they possessed unparalleled grace and finesse. His fingers, long and slender, moved like those of the most skilled weaver.

Wearing simple garments over his stooped frame, Ajala exuded humility and dedication. The fabric of his garments, woven from the fibers of the sacred mutuba tree, bore the marks of time and the elements, much like the potter himself. As he moved, his every step was deliberate and measured, a reflection of the care and precision he applied to his art.

In the presence of Ajala, Obatala could not help but feel a sense of wonder. For within this seemingly unassuming figure lay the power to shape the destinies of Orishas and mortals alike.

Yet, for all his skill and craftsmanship, Ajala was powerless to bestow Oris upon the Enks of Orirun. He was bound by the law of Mama Onile, who felt threatened by the potential of the gift of destiny to the Enk race. This left him with a collection of thousands of untouched destinies, their potential untapped and waiting to be unleashed, like a library of untold stories.

Seeing an opportunity for a mutually beneficial partnership, Obatala approached the potter with a proposal: He told Ajala that he would create a new species of life within Ajala's domain and place the Oris crafted by Ajala's skilled hands into the beings, granting each a destiny that would guide their journeys through the labyrinth of life and help them build an advanced kingdom of their own. In return, Ajala could witness his destinies unfold within

Obatala's creations. Without hesitation, Ajala seized the chance to fuse his Oris into complex beings, giving them a destiny to pursue.

The sisters of existence, pleased with the alliance between Obatala and Ajala, solidified the union with divine gifts. Emi, Eleda, and Ojiji each bestowed upon Ajala's Oris a fragment of their own power, ensuring that the destinies would be infused with the breath of life, the depths of emotion, and the enduring legacies left behind in the wake of a soul's journey.

At last, Obatala's ashé came into full bloom. Under the curious gaze of the sisters of existence and with the guidance of Ajala, he set forth on his greatest endeavor yet. He took the clay of the Earth and placed it in a large pot. He mixed in blood from the Orishas, Enks, and the giants so that his creations would embody the balance of Earth, of peace, and of chaos. He took the blind potter's Oris and placed them in the heads of his molds, and with each stroke of his hands he fashioned beings that were not only complex and captivating but also imbued with the power of destiny. He called them the Children of Ori.

Obatala worked tirelessly. His fingernails, stained with the soil, were a badge of his dedication. Soon there were hundreds of Children, and then thousands. The union of the divine sculptor and the blind potter had given birth to a new species more advanced than any the Earth had witnessed so far.

Harmonia

CHAPTER 4

Oah and Dada

If you think you're too small to make a difference,
try spending the night with a mosquito.

—African proverb

Within Ajala's walled domain, known as the Garden, the Children of Ori and their descendants thrived. So much so that both Obatala and Ajala found it too arduous to shepherd them alone. They looked to the other Orishas for aid and chose the nurturing Yemayá to care for the Children, the cunning Eshu to sharpen their focus, Oko to nourish the crops, Ogun to safeguard the Garden, and Oya to aid them in governing this newly formed kingdom, which they called Edin. Together, these seven formed the first Council of Orishas. Soon more Orishas joined the pantheon in Edin, and their Garden continued to flourish.

Yet, some of the Children of Ori's descendants, driven by curiosity, dared to seek the forbidden knowledge within the *Book of Creation*, where Obatala recorded the formation of Onile and the origins of Ori, and other profound truths of existence. Others challenged the sacred laws of the Orishas themselves, acts that also resulted in their exile.

Cast out from Edin and its Garden, these inquisitive Children ventured into the lands of Orirun, where they encountered the peaceful and friendly Enks. Devoid of Oris, the Enks became loyal servants and disciples to the

Children. Despite their differences, an unexpected union occurred, birthing a new race, humans, who possessed dormant Oris. Unlike the meticulously woven fates made by Ajala, the Oris of this new race were obscured and obstructed, causing many to never find their true purpose. Born of both the Children of Ori and the Enks, each human carried a unique blend of lineages in varied proportions, leading to diverse forms that led to tribal rivalries.

Those among the humans who bore a striking resemblance to the Children of Ori, marked by their towering stature and smoother skin, were venerated as true carriers of the Ori. Conversely, those who mirrored the Enks' more rugged and hirsute appearance faced unjust prejudice, deemed inferior for superficial reasons. Conflict loomed over Orirun.

Yet a single voice rose above the prejudice. Oah, a young human who resembled a Child of Ori, dared to question his existence and purpose. After all, humans shared a common adversary: the giants. His voice strong and unwavering, Oah asked, "Why must we endure the wrath of the giants?" Oah's Ori had been awakened by his curiosity and that simple question, "Why?"

His question not only captivated the humans who resembled the Children of Ori but also beckoned to those who had Enk-like traits. He had stirred something deep within all of them, fostering a newfound unity among the warring factions. Dada, a human with distinctly Enk features, was known for exceptional skill and courage, and he formed an unbreakable bond with Oah. Their friendship broke the barriers that had kept their peoples apart.

Oah and Dada embarked on a daring mission: to hunt and vanquish the giants that had long terrorized the land. They knew that their quest would defy the natural order of the world, breaking Mama Onile's law, but they held fast to the belief that the end justified the means. Oah and Dada would first go to the Garden to seek the counsel of Ogun, the Orisha of iron. They packed the essentials—stone tools, woven cloaks, and a vessel of the purest honey, collected from their respective villages. This was their offering to Ogun, a sweet gift showing their respect and admiration. As they bade farewell to their families, there was an air of solemnity, but also a flicker of hope.

They faced many trials on their trek. Yet they pressed on, fueled by the importance of their mission and the promise of Ogun's wisdom. Through dense forests and treacherous rivers, they persevered, their minds set on the kingdom of Edin.

When they arrived, they found that the walled Garden was both imposing and beautiful. Nature thrived in the divine balance the Orishas conducted. Flora of hues unknown to mortal eyes bloomed in eternal spring, their fragrance perfuming the air. Fauna, both familiar and fantastical, roamed freely, their existence also critical to the Garden's balance. It was a sanctuary for the pure Children of Ori, a place of complete alignment.

At the center of the Garden was Edin. Oah and Dada, when it came into sight, were awestruck. It was a kingdom of divine proportions, where the Council of Orishas convened to govern the fates of mortals. Its towering edifices were hewn from lustrous blue stones that caught the sunlight and scattered it into a thousand glittering fragments. One of the most ingenious feats of Edin's builders was the intricate system of irrigation. Water, the lifeblood of the Earth, was channeled through Edin in a network of flowing canals and cascading waterfalls. Water tumbled from the heights of golden towers, creating mesmerizing drapes of liquid light. Majestic structures, conjured from dreams and sky iron, rose toward the skies, their peaks lost amid the clouds.

Travelers braved a difficult pilgrimage just to witness such beauty. Indeed, Oah and Dada's weary eyes widened in fascination at the very sight. Their souls were stirred by the divinity unfolding before them.

Just beyond the kingdom itself, in the mountainous wilderness, nestled in the highest peaks, stood Ogun's temple, a structure forged from the strongest iron.

Ascending to his temple was a trial in itself. Oah and Dada scaled steep cliffs and navigated narrow paths. Soon enough, they stood before the intimidating edifice.

The entrance of the temple led to a chamber etched out of the mountain. Within were iron pillars along with a grand statue of Ogun on a pedestal, wearing a crown of ivory horns, cowrie shells, and gold. Just beyond the great statue was a single iron door bolted shut.

With great respect, they placed the vessel of honey at the foot of the iron statue among the various offerings from others who sought Ogun's guidance. Its sweet aroma permeated the air, representing their pure intentions. Oah and Dada then each addressed Ogun, their heartfelt speeches penetrating the iron door.

Oah spoke first, sharing stories of the countless lives lost to the giants' wrath and the suffering that had befallen their land. He described the fear that gripped the hearts of the humans, emphasizing the urgency of their quest and the desperate need for divine intervention.

Dada, in turn, recounted the story of their unlikely friendship and how it had bridged the divide between the two groups of humans. Both Oah and Dada spoke of the unity that had blossomed between their peoples, proof of the power of compassion and understanding. Dada argued that their bond, forged in the fires of adversity, was a sign that they were destined to bring about a brighter future.

As their words lingered, the chamber filled with anticipation. Soon the very ground seemed to tremble beneath them, as if sensing the gravity of their plea. Suddenly the door opened, and Ogun stepped out, his imposing form exuding power and authority. His eyes, like molten iron, barreled into their souls, weighing the sincerity of their words.

Ogun, bound by an ancient oath, had sworn not to alter Mama Onile's creation. Though he longed to build, create, and fight, he was constrained by his word. Oah and Dada's pleas presented him with a unique opportunity: if they succeeded in their mission, the destruction caused by the giants would be halted, allowing Ogun to build and create without violating his oath, thus increasing his ashé.

Moved by their impassioned speeches and recognizing the potential for mutual benefit, Ogun forged divine spears for Oah and Dada, imbuing them with his own ashé, which would aid them in their battles against the giants.

With gratitude, Oah and Dada accepted the iron spears. As they left the temple, they knew that they carried not only the might of Ogun's weapons but also their people's hopes and dreams, as well as the key to unlocking Ogun's true potential—a responsibility that they would bear with honor.

Oah and Dada ventured into desolate wastelands and craggy mountains, pursuing the fearsome giants one by one. Each confrontation tested their strength, courage, and fortitude, pitting them against monstrous adversaries that loomed like shadows over the land.

With each victory, their bond deepened, and their legend spread. But as they continued to defy Mama Onile's law, the harmony between land and water wavered, threatening to plunge the lands of Orirun into disarray. Unyielding in their quest, Oah and Dada pressed onward, driven by duty and a sense of justice that outweighed their fear of the consequences.

In the climactic battle, the two heroes faced the mightiest of all giants—a colossal beast that seemed to devour the very light from the sky. As the ground quaked beneath its footsteps, the skies roared thunder and darkened, and the winds howled in mourning for the disrupted natural order. Within the eye of this storm, Dada fell, fatally injured by the giant's wrath.

Oah grieved for his fallen friend, knowing that Dada would never witness the fruits of their quest. Yet, fueled by the purpose they had shared, he vanquished the greatest of the giants and restored peace to the lands of the humans.

The sun had set upon the fallen giants, their blood seeping into the very marrow of the soil, forever staining it with a rustic hue. The mortals celebrated their triumph. Yet beyond the land, a cataclysmic tempest raged. Orunmila had prophesied a deluge that would forever divide mortals:

> *In the wake of the giants' fall, a new cycle will be born from the waves of chaos, heralding a surge of unbridled ambition and desire. The land of Orirun will forever drown in the sea of conflict, a struggle for supremacy*

destined to endure across generations, chaos guided by the crimson remains of the giants.

Obatala sought out Oah, whom he believed to be truly exceptional. In Oah, the Orisha saw not just a fearless warrior but a potential leader for those who would survive the impending catastrophe. He implored Oah to construct a vessel, a sanctuary where survivors could wait out the torrential rains to come.

To ensure the continuity of life, Obatala instructed Oah to gather family and friends, male and female, so humans might flourish in the new world that would rise after the deluge. He also tasked Oah with preserving the history of Orirun in a chronicle of triumphs and failures, of love and loss.

CHAPTER 5

Olokun

Where water is the boss, there the land must obey.

—African proverb

Since Onile's inception from Olodumare and Odua, her body and mind has been made up of both chaos and peace. Olokun, a variation of Odua and the sovereign of the primordial ocean, ruled the boundless and mysterious depths beneath the waves. As the mother of Onile, she was the ancestral chaotic force that lurked within her soul. She had no stable form, and her movements could hardly be understood. Where Olokun was the turbulent ocean, Onile was the solid land.

Onile married Oko, the Orisha of the soil, and allowed him to coat her in his earth. The land—her family—was created, and Onile entered a treaty with her mother, Olokun. Each allowed the other to draw from her own domain, to keep a tranquil equilibrium between their kingdoms.

Olokun's domain of shadows was a realm that hid the deepest secrets of Onile, where one side of her lay hidden from mortal eyes. To guard the lands from ceaseless torment, Olokun internalized her daughter's chaos; the mother sought to create a world where life on land, and thus her child, could exist in relative peace, free from chaos.

Onile's chaos lived within Olokun's womb until the mother could no longer contain it and birthed it in the form of the giants. Those titanic beings were creatures of chaos and darkness; they were living manifestations of the raw, untamed forces shaping existence.

The peace was first disrupted by the giants' hunger. Olokun's children developed an insatiable appetite for the Enks. She did not expect them to have such a craving. Still, there were so many Enks that she reasoned the occasional sacrifices of one served as a small price to pay for the stability it would bring.

In the beginning, the Enks had possessed Oris, and, driven forward by destiny and purpose, they decided to take up arms against the giants. Olokun interpreted this resistance as a breach of the treaty. She mourned for those of her children who were killed by Enks, and her tears transformed a significant portion of her waters into salt water, making it undrinkable to the Enks and causing widespread death among them.

Onile did not retaliate with force. Instead, she wilted in sorrow, burdened by both the loss of her kin, the Enks, and from seeing her mother in pain. The sight of her land, once teeming with life, now reduced to desolation, filled her with an unspeakable sorrow. The cries of the dying Enks lingered across the barren plains; the sounds of their torment played on the strings of her heart.

Yet still Onile chose peace. She understood that engaging in a futile war would only bring more devastation. Instead, she made a decision that was as profound as it was heartbreaking. She stripped the Enks of their destiny.

This decree made them blissfully unaware of their status as prey. Earth, in its primal wisdom, acknowledged and revered Olokun's intense emotions, recognizing that they could cause destruction. For Olokun sustained life. Nothing on Earth could live without her.

When Oah and Dada began vanquishing the mighty giants one by one, Olokun seethed with rage at the humans who dared challenge her and her daughter's rule. Her heart, like a black hole, churned with tempestuous grief, and in her torment she summoned a deluge of unimaginable scale, a furious torrent that threatened to wash away the Children of Ori and all the insolent mortals who bore the Ori gift.

Harmonia

The wrathful waves, like the gnashing teeth of a leviathan beast, tore through the realms of mortals, causing cracks among them and separating villages and kingdoms. Mortals were scattered across lands far from the watchful gaze of the Orishas. As the skies wept bitter tears for Olokun's loss, the lands trembled beneath the onslaught.

Witnessing the chaos wrought by Olokun's fury, the Orishas were deeply troubled, fearing that they could be wiped out if Olokun was left unchecked. The enraged god threatened to consume all of creation, leaving behind a world devoid of harmony.

Before they could intervene, the Orishas recognized the need to seek the blessing of Mama Onile, as she was Olokun's daughter. They understood that their actions would have far-reaching consequences, and only with Mama Onile's approval and guidance could they hope to restore balance without further disrupting Earth's order.

In supplication, the Orishas approached Mama Onile, presenting their concerns. They spoke of the devastation wrought by Olokun's vengeance and the potential annihilation of the land they had sworn to protect. Mama Onile, aware of the impending destruction of her kingdom and her husband Oko at the hands of her own mother, understood that something had to be done.

Mama Onile granted the Orishas her blessing, giving them the authority to halt Olokun's destructive rampage. Yet she also issued a warning: "When you imprison my mother Olokun, a new form of chaos will emerge. And we can only hope that we will be able to tame it."

Haunted by her words, the Orishas embarked on their mission to save the lands from the unbridled chaos unleashed by Olokun.

Obatala called upon Ogun to forge a colossal chain imbued with the ashé of Onile's core—a set of links to bind the tempestuous deity and prevent the annihilation of all life.

Under Obatala's command, the Orishas plunged into the raging tempest. They braved the towering waves and the howling winds, their ebony silhouettes shimmering against the storm's fury. When they reached the depths of Olokun's oceanic domain, they bound her with the massive chain, forged to withstand even the might of a god.

With each tightening of the coil, the floodwaters gradually receded, the furious tide relenting under the force of the Orishas' efforts. The lands and realms of the world began to emerge from the watery chaos, forever changed. The once-unified mortals of Orirun had been tossed across uncharted wastes, and the humans of Orirun found themselves adrift.

After the great flood, the world did not simply break; it split. The Garden, where once the Orishas walked beside the humans, had separated from its reflection. Now there existed a physical realm, Aiye, and a spiritual realm, Orun, apart yet entwined.

In Aiye, there was unimaginable destruction. The Garden had collapsed under Olokun's fury. Edin's towers crumbled into the waters, its streets were drowned, and the Children of Ori were swept away by the flood, their homes leveled by the rolling waters.

However, in Orun, Edin and the Garden remained untouched, held aloft by the ashé of human devotion. This ashé, born from mortal prayers and sacrifices, had created a bond so strong that even Olokun's deluge could not sever it. The Orishas lingered in this pristine sanctuary, vowing to safeguard its purity. Yet, unbeknownst to them, a shadow was approaching the realm. The true battle for Edin had only just begun.

BOOK II

THE ORISHAS

CHAPTER 6

Orun

I pointed out to you the stars and all you saw
was the tip of my finger.

—African proverb

The sky kingdom of Orun stretched into infinity. It was a realm of shimmering constellations governed by a multitude of solar deities who shone their life-giving light on the planets in their care. Among these divine entities, Olorun emerged as the guardian of Earth.

Despite his grandeur and might as perceived from Earth itself, Olorun was but one star amid an ocean of cosmic light, destined to nurture life and eventually extinguish. Once exhausted, a solar deity released its remnants, astral dust, into the universe. The dust found its way into the hands of the blind potter, Ajala, who skillfully molded it into Oris. For its part, every Ori, after exploring the depths of mortal emotion and experiencing the death of its host, returned to the universe as astral dust, now bearing the knowledge of the complexities of life, following the universal cycle of stellar existence.

Olorun was humbled by this basic truth. He understood that his reign in the kingdom of Orun would not be everlasting. His fiery life would one day exhaust its ashé, signaling the demise of his power. This demise would not be an end, but a transformation.

Odua, one of the creators of Earth, bore witness to Olorun's emergence. A bond was kindled between them, with Olorun's powerful rays casting an ethereal glow upon Odua, unveiling her presence against the void's infinite darkness. Thus illuminated, she drew forth Olodumare, the divine co-architect of Onile.

When Odua transformed into the primordial waters that enveloped the emerging Earth, Olorun pledged to cherish and nurture the newborn. Onile, in her fragility, proved vulnerable to the slightest touch, and when Olodumare's efforts to retrieve his vital seeds inadvertently wounded her, a shard broke away. This lone shard became Mawu, the moon.

Mawu, neither a star nor a planet, was a powerful entity of soothing luminescence and tranquil beauty. She was a spectral echo of Onile's infancy, pining for reunification and yearning to end the turmoil within Onile's core. Mawu's soft radiance, a stark contrast to Olorun's fiery brilliance, bathed Onile in a gentle glow. Mawu stood a silent vigil when Olorun slept.

Mawu watched over Onile through her many transformations, all the while longing for a brighter future for her. Mawu's desire to reunite with Onile grew so intense that she discovered a divine capability within herself—she had the power to fragment her form. In an act of cosmic splintering, a part of her, the part of yearning, became the singular entity known as the Orisha Yemayá.

Yet Mawu did not foresee that Yemayá's passage through Onile's waters would result in the loss of Yemayá's memories of her true origins. Unbeknownst to Yemayá, her ashé was to embrace Onile and prevent her from succumbing to chaos. For her part, without Yemayá, Mawu was but a beautiful shell silently circling the Earth.

CHAPTER 7

Yemayá and Aganju

It takes a season for a snake to change into its new skin.

—African proverb

When Yemayá descended to Earth, it was barren and desolate, its rough terrain devoid of nurturing soil. Onile was in no state to raise life. Yemayá felt a deep loneliness, surrounded only by a few wild and untamed Orishas. It was in the moon's ethereal luminescence that she found solace, unaware she was gazing upon her own reflection.

Olokun, the primordial ocean, knew of Yemayá's true origin, yet chose to withhold it from her, fearing that Yemayá's magnetic ashé could eclipse her own influence over Onile. Thus, Yemayá harbored an unfulfilled longing, a piece of herself yet undiscovered, which she sought to fill as she stood on the edge of the ocean.

With each crashing wave, Yemayá lamented her inability to find her ashé; the waters lapping at her feet seemed to be composed of her own tears. The chorus of the waves held no peace for her, serving only as a reminder of her eternal loneliness.

In her darkest moment, she questioned the purpose of her existence. If she could not discover her ashé and find inner peace, what meaning could she have or create? She embarked on a pilgrimage with no destination, roaming the rocky lands uncertain of what awaited her, though driven by an unshakable conviction.

As she wandered, Yemayá chanced upon a chasm, a bottomless void that beckoned to her. As she surrendered to it, the darkness consumed her, swallowing her whole. She found herself journeying through serpentine tunnels that seemed to stretch into eternity.

After what felt like an eon, a faint glimmer pierced the inky gloom, enticing her to venture deeper into the unseen depths. As she pursued the sliver of light, shadows gave way to reveal the astounding figure of Aganju.

He was magnificent, his skin glowing with the hue of a volcanic eruption. Confined to the depths of the Earth by Olokun, he was the master of the raw elemental energies that churn beneath Onile's layers. He was the key to Onile's stability and her ability to nurture life. His molten realm was a barless cage, and he never had visitors. To see another Orisha was more than a pleasant surprise.

In the moment their eyes met, Yemayá knew that he was the very thing she had been drawn to. He was the heart of Onile, and she was, for him, the very love he longed for. They became captives of a shared connection, and their embrace was so profound it brought temporary stability to Onile. Their passionate union set a miraculous transformation in motion: the cycles of the four seasons were born, each a distinct aspect of their divine love. The blossoms of spring mirrored the first stirrings of their infatuation; the sun-drenched days of summer were testament to the passion that burned within their souls; the russet hues of autumn were a poignant reminder of the fleeting nature of their romance, for they knew that their love was too powerful for Earth to contain; and the icy embrace of winter was a reflection of the cold void left in their hearts as they parted ways, vowing never to embrace again, for the sake of nurturing life on Onile.

As Onile found her balance, she adjusted to the new order of existence and the arrival of Oko, the soil.

Onile began to feel a strange sensation stirring within her. Though she didn't realize it at first, the passionate embrace of Yemayá and Aganju had not only ushered in the cycle of the seasons but also ignited the spark of creation within her womb.

As the days passed, the budding life within Onile continued to grow and develop. She could sense the presence of an extraordinary being taking form inside her, one that would embody the transformative power of the love shared by Yemayá and Aganju.

Finally, the time came for Onile to bring forth this new life into the land. With a deep, resonant sigh, her body trembled with the force of creation, and the soil above quaked.

From the depths of her being, Onile birthed Oshumare, a serpent of unparalleled beauty and luminance. Oshumare became a symbol of balance, transformation, and perpetual movement. Its serpentine form glinted with the hues of the rainbow, representing the fusion of Yemayá and Aganju's divine ashé.

As Oshumare slithered across the land, its sinuous coils left an indelible trail upon the fresh soil. The Earth bloomed and decayed in its wake, as the seasons continued their eternal dance, driven by the love that had brought them into existence.

Onile was ensnared in a perpetual cycle of death and rebirth, her grassy plains and lush forests now subject to the march of time.

CHAPTER 8

Yemayá and Erinle

A fish and a bird may fall in love but the two cannot build a home together.

—African proverb

As the number of mortals swelled, the Orishas found the task of governance increasingly difficult.

They soon conceived a transformative solution. They recognized that some humans possessed exceptional virtue and valor, and the potential for divine stewardship. The decision was made: a chosen few would be offered the gift of ascension, becoming Orishas themselves and thus granted immortality in the spiritual realm.

At the same time, as the Orishas walked among mortals, they began to adopt human emotions and complexities. Love, sorrow, ambition, and greed—sentiments once foreign—now pulsed through their divine veins.

After Olokun's deluge, Yemayá wanted so desperately to reach the scattered humans, and she journeyed to see Mama Onile, requesting that her guardianship be expanded into the waters.

Moved by Yemayá's yearning to help the far-flung mortals, Mama Onile bestowed upon her a most precious gift.

"Your guardianship," she proclaimed, "shall extend to the sweet waters, allowing you to traverse the diverse lands and reach all life. However, your

Harmonia

new domain does not encompass the salt water. For that is still my mother's kingdom, and should you venture beyond its boundaries, you will forever be barred from setting foot on my land again."

Mama Onile summoned Oshumare, the great serpent of transformation that she had birthed. With an elegance that belied its massive form, the serpent slithered to Mama Onile's feet, its iridescent scales catching the light and casting prismatic reflections around them. In a swift gesture, Mama Onile plucked a single scale from Oshumare, a token of change.

Using stones as ancient as the universe itself, she crushed the scale into a fine powder. Mixing it with the sacred clay of the Earth, she created a shimmering paste that reflected an array of colors. This was no ordinary concoction, but a conduit of transformation, a divine medium that held the power to alter form.

Mama Onile turned to Yemayá. With a voice that soothed, Mama Onile instructed her to cover her legs in the paste and immerse herself in water.

Yemayá, filled with gratitude, accepted the divine gift. She rushed to the water's edge, slathered her legs in the radiant paste, and laid herself in the gentle caress of the small waves. As she surrendered to the waters, her legs transformed into two serpentine tails with fins. In her new form, Yemayá felt free and empowered.

Embracing her newfound dominion over the springs and sweet waters, Yemayá flowed across Onile with ease. She reached all the humans who needed her, from chieftains in the bush to mothers in large kingdoms, and took great care to nurture their spirits. It was during these journeys that she found herself bewitched by a mortal.

The human fisherman named Erinle was beautiful, the most perfect mortal Yemayá had laid eyes on. She began watching him from afar and became enamored by the passion and devotion that radiated from his every movement. She was mesmerized by the sight of Erinle casting his nets upon the water, his hands as skilled in their touch as the gentle caress of the wind upon the water's surface. His eyes reflected the dance of sunlight on the waves, stirring within her a longing she had never known before.

He was renowned across the lands not only as a fisherman but as a mystical healer and skilled hunter, as well as for his unparalleled finery. Both men and women were in awe of such walking splendor. Each of his qualities was refined by the teachings of his numerous lovers. With the power to seduce anyone—Obas, Ayabas, and chieftains alike—Erinle sailed the Tamanrasset River on his intricately carved boat, trading his catch and collecting hearts.

Adorned in his lavish garments, he relished hunting game and lovers alike. Erinle captured the hearts of his paramours with a grace that disguised the artistry of his craft. His allure lay not in brute force or deception, but in the subtle play of seduction and patience.

Yemayá followed him diligently as he unfurled his charm like the wings of a butterfly emerging from its cocoon. Each lover was like a precious pearl plucked from the ocean's depths, their beauty and uniqueness cherished and admired by the skilled hands of their captor. Each heart was a trophy to his prowess.

Yet, despite his many conquests, Erinle often found himself longing for solitude on the one hand and real love on the other, a love that was stronger than lust. Every day he would sit in the same spot on the banks of the river, losing himself in the murmur of the water's edge.

It was during one such moment that he heard a splash, stirring within him the curiosity of the fisherman.

Compelled by the challenge of acquiring a heart that had conquered many others but that had not been conquered itself, Yemayá vowed to claim Erinle's love as her own.

She began her pursuit cautiously, her presence manifesting as a breeze that caressed his skin and as the soft lapping of waves against the hull of his boat. She filled the air around Erinle with the scent of jasmine and myrrh, a blend that stirred within him an unfamiliar yearning.

Believing his visitor to be a strange fish, he set out to capture the elusive creature. Day after day, a splash echoed, beckoning him deeper into the winding river. As he journeyed farther, he could not shake the sensation of being watched, of an unseen presence following his every move.

As the days passed, Yemayá intensified her efforts. She transformed herself into a vision, appearing in the water as a beautiful woman. Her eyes, dark as the depths of the ocean, seemed to peer into his soul, while her laughter, like the song of sirens, entered his dreams.

Each day, she would emerge from the water just a little closer to Erinle, her presence like the irresistible pull of the tide. Her gestures mirrored his own, as if they were two bodies locked in a dance of desire, their movements reflecting the ebb and flow of the waves.

It was only when the river grew still and the air seemed to shimmer with an unusual radiance that Erinle realized the woman wasn't a figment of his imagination.

One fateful day, as Erinle stood at the land's edge, Yemayá finally revealed herself in her full, divine splendor. Her body glowed with the twinkle of moonlight on the sea. With a voice as calming as the tide, she called out to him, inviting him to surrender to their shared passion.

Erinle, entranced by her beauty and the intensity of their connection, could no longer resist her. In that moment, he allowed himself to be seduced by Yemayá, indulging in the primal lust that had whirled within him.

For a time, their hearts entwined in a love that crossed the boundaries of the mortal and divine, land and sea, forging a bond as sweet as the waters themselves.

Yemayá laid bare her soul to Erinle, granting him a glimpse into the secrets concealed beneath the waves. Hand in hand, they stood at the shore's edge as a wave of knowledge and wisdom surged through Erinle's being.

With that divine revelation, Erinle's gaze pierced the veil of time, bearing witness to Onile's birth from the celestial womb of Odua. He beheld his ancestors, sculpted from the very soil upon which he now stood, their blood mixed with the divine and imbued with the power of Ori. He observed the

chains that bound Olokun to the ocean's floor, where she now slumbered, biding her time until fate would unleash her fury once more.

Returned to himself, Erinle found that he was forever changed. Yemayá's love and trust had granted him a view of primordial secrets, a gift most mortals could only dare to imagine. Empowered by the arcane knowledge bestowed upon him, he felt a fire ignite within his soul, its flames burning away the desire for simple carnal pleasures.

No longer content to partake in the gratifications of the flesh, Erinle would wield his newfound wisdom in pursuit of power and legacy. He sought fame, wealth, and to exploit the knowledge of the waters.

Yet Yemayá foresaw the dangers that lay within his new knowledge, and she warned Erinle against sharing the secrets of the waters with the mortal realm. The fragile minds of most humans could not bear the enormity of such revelations; the result would be chaos unleashed upon them. But Erinle could not make such a promise to Yemayá.

Alarmed by his defiance and fearing that his disclosures might one day embolden mortals and undermine her own sovereignty, Yemayá took a drastic and unspeakable step.

With Erinle's own fillet blade, she silenced him by severing his tongue and consigning it to a locked vessel. She then cast the vessel into the murky depths of Olokun's ocean, where it would be hidden from the eyes of mortals. Stripped of his voice, Erinle was left powerless.

Yemayá's heart, once a tempest of love for Erinle, now swelled with the bitter tides of remorse. She had robbed him of his tongue, an instrument he'd used for the delicate play of trade and seduction, leaving him helpless and silent.

Within her guilt, a spark of affection still shone for Erinle. It was this tender flame that propelled Yemayá to trek to the Garden and put herself in front of the Council of Orishas in Edin. She sought their blessing to crown Erinle an Orisha himself.

The council agreed, stipulating that his mortal life must be reflected in his purpose as an Orisha. So Yemayá turned him into an elephant, grand and commanding, symbolizing the strength she saw in him as a mortal. However,

Harmonia

his tusks would be hunted and harvested, serving mortals in their trade, forever replaying the trauma of his severed tongue.

The gift Yemayá bestowed was not singular. In the comforting cradle of the river, Orisha Erinle would shed his elephant form, transforming into a serpent and gliding through the currents. The waters—Yemayá herself—would offer him solace, a sanctuary from his land-bound form.

CHAPTER 9

Eshu and Oshosi

Only a wise person can solve a difficult problem.

—African proverb

In the kingdom of Kemet, a village flourished and reigned supreme over its neighbors. It was known far and wide as the home of the best archers in Orirun.

Traveling in the kingdom of Kemet, the Orisha Eshu chanced upon an esteemed hunter, Oshosi, revered among his people for his righteousness and prowess. Weary from his travels and ravenous with hunger, Eshu beseeched the hunter to share food with him. Unaware that he was an Orisha and touched by the elderly man's plight, Oshosi obliged, offering a portion of his hunt to ease the emptiness that consumed Eshu's belly.

As they lit a fire and roasted the freshly caught game, Eshu noticed Oshosi was staring at the night sky decorated with thousands of stars. Eshu asked Oshosi if he knew what those stars were. Oshosi could only say that they fascinated him and made him wonder what was far beyond the land they called home. Eshu smiled and began to recite a captivating tale. His words, all-knowing, painted a vivid picture of a star yearning for the tender experience of mortal love.

You see, we all come from stars. There are two kinds of stars: a star that used to be human and a star that never was. Stars who used to be human showed unusual courage on Earth, in their human forms, serving as guides for others. Upon their mortal death, they retire to the sky, where they are soon absorbed back into the universe. Others choose to never become mortal but instead bide their time shining and observing until they too become absorbed in the universe.

Once, a brilliant star asked the great god Olodumare to grant her passage into the realm of humanity so that she might experience the depths of love's embrace. Olodumare warned the star that, being born a human, she would experience all emotions, not just love. Undeterred, the star accepted and was reborn as a human of unrivaled beauty.

Her heart, pure as the first snowfall, had love for all living things, yet in a world where innocence is often preyed upon, she was both fragile and vulnerable, and her heart was shattered time and time again.

This pained Olodumare, because this star was once a god herself. You see, every star who chooses mortal life must live through seven human incarnations before ascending to the skies once more. Olodumare knew that the star would have to endure many trials.

The star experienced love in its myriad forms, from the fierce devotion of a warrior to the tender affection of a parent. In each life she learned many new nuances of love. Yet, in her final incarnation, a cosmic error occurred, and she became not another human but instead a mystical bird.

Now she carries no memory of her celestial origins or that she would return back to the skies . . . and that is why I, Eshu, have been assigned by the great god to find and capture this bird, and return her to the stars. However, I've been searching for her for quite some time, and I fear I may never find her.

Revealing his true identity, Eshu told Oshosi that he had scoured the land without success. But he had heard whispers of a crafty huntsman and warrior who could capture the most cunning of beasts. So Eshu sought him out in his divine quest; it was not chance that brought them together, but destiny.

Oshosi, honored by the Orisha's request and sensing an opportunity, explained that his mother suffered from an illness of forgetfulness. In response, Eshu offered to help ease her illness in return for the hunter's help.

Oshosi jumped to Eshu's aid. Eshu warned Oshosi that he only had three days to find the sacred bird, or it would be tethered to the land forever. Eshu then produced a distinctive white arrow with silken threads wrapped around it. Handing it to Oshosi, he issued another warning: "This is the only arrow of its kind, meaning you only have one shot. It's made for one purpose: to trap this bird. Use it as you would any arrow, just don't miss."

With those words they parted, and Oshosi embarked on his pursuit of the mystical bird. He ventured deep into the heart of the wilderness, where shadows hid predators and ancient spirits stirred among the leaves.

Oshosi, a master of the hunt, drew upon his unmatched knowledge of the wild to track his elusive quarry. He deciphered the subtle signs left in the bird's wake—the faintest tilt of foliage, the fleeting glimmer of iridescent feathers, the haunting melody of its song echoing through the forest.

As the sun dipped below the horizon on the second day, a hushed stillness enveloped the woods, and within that silence, Oshosi felt the pulse of the Earth beneath his feet. He attuned himself to the rhythm of the wild, allowing it to guide him ever closer to the fascinating creature.

On the third day, with the first light of dawn painting the sky in hues of gold and red, Oshosi found himself at the edge of a magnificent glade bathed in a soft, powdery glow. The air hummed with energy, as if the very essence of life existed in this sacred spot.

There, perched upon a branch laden with blossoms, was the mystical bird. Its feathers bore all the colors of the stars, and its eyes were as black as the midnight sky. Oshosi approached with caution, his every step deliberate and measured as he readied his bow and the white arrow, imbued with the ashé of the Orishas.

In that moment, time seemed to slow, and Oshosi's senses sharpened. With a deep breath, he drew back his bowstring and released. The arrow sang through the air, weaving a path controlled by fate. As the arrow was about to find its mark, its silken threads unfurled, capturing the bird without causing it harm.

With great care, Oshosi placed the mystical bird into a cage he had meticulously crafted. He then returned home and waited for Eshu, his anticipation mounting with each passing moment. Hours slipped by, and suddenly Oshosi remembered he had yet to catch supper for himself and his mother. Grasping his bow and arrow, he dashed into the wilderness to hunt their evening meal.

Upon his return, Oshosi's heart sank into despair as he discovered the cage open and empty. The bird had simply vanished. His mother was busily cooking at the fire. She welcomed Oshosi, unaware of his distress. In that very instant, he spied Eshu hobbling down the dusty path toward his home.

Frustration and sadness engulfed Oshosi. When Eshu arrived and inquired about the bird, Oshosi implored the Orisha to grant him another chance. But Eshu, bound by the threads of time, could not wait any longer, for he had already lingered far beyond his intended stay.

Oshosi beseeched Eshu to render justice, demanding the severest punishment for whoever had stolen the precious bird. Eshu, perceiving the storm raging within the hunter, offered him a path to retribution.

Eshu urged Oshosi to draw his bow and release an arrow into the sky, promising that it would unerringly seek out and pierce the heart of the thoughtless thief. In anguish, Oshosi placed his faith in Eshu's words, needing to right the wrong that had been done. He drew an arrow and let it loose.

The arrow soared through the air and disappeared into the clouds, guided by forces unseen. The skies above seemed to weep, mourning the doom of the arrow's target. And then, in a moment that would forever haunt Oshosi, the arrow fell from above and found its mark.

To his horror, he discovered that the fateful arrow had struck down none other than his own mother, in a merciless twist of fate. In her illness, she had unknowingly cooked the bird for their dinner and had forgotten doing so. The irony was bitter in Oshosi's mouth as he stared at her lifeless form.

The world around Oshosi had shattered, and he was left with nothing but the words of Eshu's promise and the cold realization that justice, much like love, was a double-edged sword that could cut deeper than the sharpest single-sided blade.

Amid the torrent of grief and despair that threatened to consume him,

Oshosi accepted the harsh consequences of his actions, bearing the heavy burden of his decision with a stoic heart.

Witnessing the determined spirit within this tormented soul, Eshu recognized that Oshosi, not the mystical bird, was himself the brilliant star from his tale. It was the being now known as Oshosi who had journeyed through seven lives in search of love's many faces, and it was this being who now stood at the precipice of its final transformation.

Eshu had been sent to find the last mortal reincarnation of the celestial being. It was Eshu who was tasked with testing whether love—the most potent force on Earth—held total sway over Oshosi's choices. And in his final trial, Oshosi had demonstrated that though he was capable of love, it did not dictate his path. He had learned that justice must be determined without the influence of love, for love can cloud judgment and obscure the truth. Only by examining each action in the cold light of impartiality could true justice be served.

Eshu deemed Oshosi worthy of an alternate destiny and bestowed upon him a divine transformation. Defying his own duty to Olodumare, Eshu decided to keep Oshosi bound to Onile as an Orisha. Like the other Orishas, Eshu believed himself more powerful than the silent Olodumare, and chose to act according to his own will.

Oshosi transcended his mortal coil, becoming an Orisha. He would be known as the Earthly embodiment of justice, whose sacred duty it was to maintain order in both Orun and Aiye. By keeping Oshosi on Earth, Eshu ensured that divine justice would be directly administered among mortals, anchoring Oshosi's ashè firmly in the world where it was most needed.

And thus, a star who once shone brightly in the night sky found its place among the pantheon of Orishas, helping to govern the land in an unyielding pursuit of justice, untainted by the biases of the heart.

CHAPTER 10

Oshun

The jungle is stronger than the elephant.

—African proverb

In the time before the great flood of Olokun, Oko, the Orisha of the soil, embodied both feminine and masculine spirits. As the symbol of fertility and the harvest, Oko represented the perfect convergence of creation and continuation, providing the Garden with abundance of his harvest. Yet when a Child of Ori named Atum became the first to be banished from Edin for inquisitiveness, the Orishas did not foresee how his journey would forever alter Oko.

Separated from the Garden, Atum faced a daunting challenge, for he could no longer rely on Oko's bounty.

Three years into his exile, Atum noticed a pattern in the seasonal cycles. In his fourth year, he planted a seed, and by his fifth, he reaped his first harvest. This simple, independent act unlocked his freedom, freeing him from scavenging.

However, as the skies reflect the earth, so does the earth mirror the skies. Atum's newfound understanding of the cultivation of crops caused a disruption within Oko, splitting the divine being into two distinct Orishas. From this division arose Oshun, who captured Oko's feminine spirit, embodying love, beauty, and fertility. The other remained Oko, though now his ashé was limited to planting and reaping.

As the Orishas sat on their thrones in Edin, they basked in the abundant admiration and worship from mortals—the force that animated their ashé. They felt invincible, believing themselves more powerful than Olodumare, for it was they who had labored to raise and cultivate the land and its inhabitants.

The Orishas began to subtly disobey the great god, testing the limits of their autonomy. However, it wasn't until Eshu defied Olodumare's command to return Oshosi to the skies that the divine scales tipped toward retribution.

Olodumare released a punishment upon the Orishas. The seasons stretched beyond their natural bounds, plunging the land into deep despair. For three long years, the land was held hostage by a tireless drought, its once-lush fields reduced to cracked soil covered in dust.

Desperation seeped into every living thing; sorrow suffocated the laughter and joy that had once filled the land. Families huddled together in the shadows, their hollow eyes reflecting the hunger that gnashed at their souls, while the cries of children, too weak to stand, pierced the stagnant air.

In the grip of famine, the people of Orirun were forced to confront the most harrowing aspects of their humanity, the line between morality and survival growing ever more blurred with each passing day.

And love, which had once filled the hearts of mortals, now flickered feebly, struggling to endure against looming necessity.

Like all the Orishas, Oshun sensed her ashé weaken as the waters from the sacred Tamanrasset River slowly began to dry. This grand river, the lifeblood of Edin and the land, was being drained away, leaving behind a barren world. Her temple, which had once been a haven of comfort and warmth, now cooled with an isolated hush.

Oshun had long before discovered her ashé within the hearts of mortals. It was a powerful and potent ashé. It possessed the ability to bestow life and to strip it away. In mortals it could inspire devotion and sacrifice, or twist into jealousy and rage. To Oshun, love wielded a strength that surpassed even

Ogun's iron. Now love, the very ashé that had nourished the mortals, had been siphoned from their souls

Oshun roamed with frantic desperation. She felt responsible for Orirun's parched expanse, as she watched the harvests fail. She sought the attention of Olodumare, imploring him to unleash his tears upon the world, to quench the thirst of the dying land.

She asked the other Orishas to join in her pleas. They tried to appease Olodumare with grand gestures of gratitude and desperation. Each attempt was more elaborate than the last.

Eshu's was perhaps the most elaborate of all. He performed sacrifices, offering the sweetest fruits and the most fragrant flowers to Olodumare. Yet his offerings were met with silence. The sky remained as unyielding as ever, devoid of even the promise of rain.

Oshun saw that she herself must somehow travel to the sky kingdom. To journey beyond the clouds, she would need to assume a new form.

Oshun turned to Mama Onile, for only Earth could release her from the soil. She pleaded, "Grant me wings so I can ascend to the sky kingdom, for only the great god can unleash the rains."

Mama Onile gently reminded her, "The great god above is deaf to Earthly pleas." Yet, seeing the sorrow in Oshun's eyes, she suggested a path. "Oshun, your ashé of love is something completely foreign to Olodumare. If you could manifest your love, not in words but in form, perhaps you could stir something within him."

She revealed the drastic steps Oshun must take—a rebirth into a beautiful creature, a living embodiment of love and appreciation, a sight to dazzle the god above. But Mama Onile warned, "Remember, Oshun, even the most splendid display may not ensure the desired response. And should you succeed and return to Earth, you will forever reside in your new form, and when you pass through my waters, your memories will be erased."

Oshun accepted her fate. The pain of her people, the dying land—the stakes were too high, the need too great. She was ready to sacrifice her identity for the sake of those she loved.

Mama Onile summoned the iridescent serpent Oshumare. It lifted its body erect. Its grandeur enveloped Oshun as it swallowed her whole. As she passed through its belly, Oshun was reborn within an egg, large and pulsating with potential.

With a caress and a kiss, Mama Onile cracked the egg. And from it emerged a creature of unmatched beauty. Oshun's limbs were long, her fingers stretching into elegant wings adorned with sparkling feathers. Her crown was a resplendent crest of vibrant plumes.

The Orisha was no more. In her place stood a mystical peacock, glinting like a collection of precious gems in the sunlight. A sight to behold, the peacock displayed all of Oshun's grace, beauty, and undying love for Orirun and its mortals.

With her transformation complete, Oshun confidently spread her magnificent wings and took flight, her new form allowing her to soar beyond the clouds and into the skies above. As she ascended, her feathers created a kaleidoscope of colors that danced across the sky.

Oshun had confidently embarked on her divine mission, determined to face Olodumare and end the drought that had plagued the lands.

Yet, as she approached the sky kingdom, she found that she was lost. Olodumare was not a being, but rather the galaxy itself, a space of cosmic energy. Oshun felt her hope wane, her pleas dissolving into the ether, unnoticed by the all-encompassing entity. Olodumare was an enigma, representing everything and nothing at the same time.

In the bleakness of her situation, Oshun found hope in the sun, Olorun. However, as she drew near to Olorun, she felt the heat of its presence, a powerful, unforgiving intensity that threatened to incinerate her very being. Her resplendent plumage withered and crumbled beneath Olorun's merciless gaze. Each feather that fell was a fragment of her ashé, lost to the inferno that raged before her.

With a saddened heart, she realized that Olorun, whom she had sought for salvation, was an entity of destruction, incapable of offering the rains she so desperately desired. Yet, even in her agony, as her feathers turned to ash and her ashé leaked from her soul, she refused to abandon her mission.

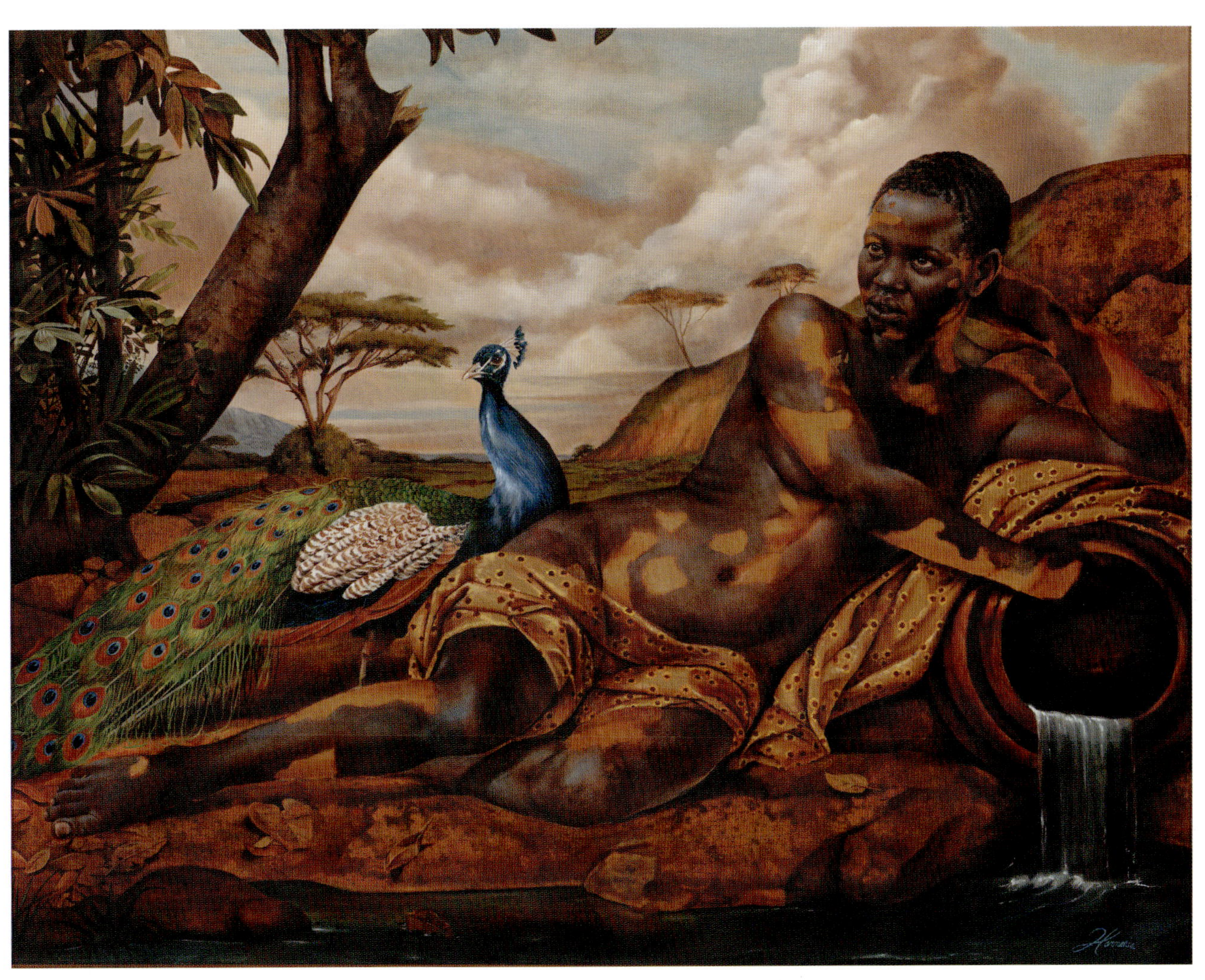

Oshun pressed onward. Upon reaching the blazing throne of Olorun, she fell, weakened, now more a vulture than a peacock, and pleaded on behalf of life on Onile.

For Oshun understood that in the realms of gods and mortals, change was the only constant. Just as she had transformed herself into a peacock to embark on this sacred journey, so too could Olorun's fiery ashé be harnessed for the greater good.

Moved by Oshun's selfless sacrifice, Olorun turned its gaze toward the featherless peacock, acknowledging the former Orisha.

Olorun reached out to Oshun, infusing her with the divine energy of its own ashé. A surge of power coursed through Oshun's ravaged body, rekindling the fire within her soul, and restoring her connection to the cosmos even as it returned her to her Earthly form. Yet, as the ashé flowed into her being, it manifested in a manner that none could have foreseen.

Golden rays of light spread across Oshun's body, etching intricate patterns onto the canvas of her skin. The golden lines of light traced the contours of her form, creating a pattern that appeared like a celestial map. This transformation was far more than a restoration of her ashé; it was a symbol of the sacrifice she had made on behalf of life. She had received a gift of sacred gold as well as a shield to withstand Olorun's heat.

Oshun was then sent back down to Earth, reborn to bring life anew. As she descended through Mama Onile's womb, her tears became rain, nourishing the parched land below. Waiting for her was Oshumare, who guided her through her renewed existence as she awaited the return of her memories.

With each effortless slither, Oshumare left imprints on the soil, which Oshun filled with her sacred waters. Together, they carved new rivers into the land, and under their divine touch, the world began to flourish once more.

BOOK III

LINEAGE

CHAPTER 11

East Kingdom

If there is no enemy within, the enemy outside cannot harm.

—African proverb

Bound to the lands without destinies to call their own, the Enks had established a civilization beneath the surface of the Earth. Their kingdom was a complex network of tunnels, a hidden sanctuary far from the prying eyes of the world above. This underground existence initially offered refuge from the giants that dominated Orirun. But hope sparked among the Enks when the Orisha-like human called Oah and the Enk-descended human named Dada banded together to challenge the giants. Their alliance promised a future where the Enks could live among humans freely under the open sky.

During the chaos of the great flood, Obatala, the creator of the Children of Ori, made a solemn promise to Oah. He vowed to find him once the waters settled and grant him kingship, through Ogun. Ogun was revered for his knowledge of warfare and for his aggression, the very things a leader was thought to need. In return, Obatala tasked Oah with the sacred duty of ensuring the survival of the Orishas by preserving their legacy and recording the history of the land.

Oah led a group of his fellow humans across the endless waves. It was his second great challenge, after the war on the giants. Now he stood steadfast against the watery monstrosity, bearing the sole responsibility for mortals and gods alike.

As the flood fractured the world—dividing it into the physical and spiritual realms—it scattered humans across the land and fragmented their beliefs. With mortals now dispersed, their allegiances splintered, as they chose new deities to worship and give their ashé to.

The flood left watery shards across both realms. These shards formed invisible passages between them, hidden within rivers, waterfalls, and lakes. Water, the very force that caused the new division, also became the conduit that linked the two worlds.

Time worked differently in each realm. In Orun, the spiritual realm, time was an enormous lake, stagnant and eternal. In Aiye, the physical realm, time raced like a swift stream cascading down a mountainside, mirroring the fleeting lifespan of mortals and the rapid, constant change that defined their world.

Orunmila approached the council in Orun. "There is a prophecy in the wake of our split realms," he began, "an ever-growing truth, its end yet to be told." He paused, and then proceeded:

> *The mortals' redemption lies not in conquest but in mending, and through their toil shall they find renewal. Yet, the price of such knowledge is steep, and the descendants of Oah's children will bear the heaviest yoke. Bound by the transgressions of their forebear, they will live out the lessons of suffering, and through their torment, they shall teach the world to walk free.*

Oah and his people became caught in the current of a passage between the realms and emerged adrift in an unfamiliar land. As they settled upon it, they were unaware that they were isolated in the ageless realm of Orun.

Oah and his people founded villages on untamed, rugged mountains cloaked in emerald greenery and along steep valleys. By day they tilled the soil, and by night Oah gathered them around the fire and recounted stories of the world before. Each word carried purpose, drawing his people closer to one another, binding them with hope.

At the summit of the highest mountain, Obatala met Oah and anointed him, formally granting him and his descendants a kingdom in Aiye.

Under Oah's leadership, his people transformed the unforgiving wilderness. Yet in becoming a ruler, something shifted within Oah, and he began to reimagine himself as the sole hero in the war against the giants. Through these altered tales, he secured his people's loyalty while erasing the legacy of Dada and the Enks, casting them into obscurity.

As the humans elevated themselves, the Enks were forgotten. Where the Enks had once shared the sun with the humans, they found themselves retreating once again to the depths below. Yet the Enks cherished their underground kingdom; unobserved by gods and humans, they thrived. As long as they stayed hidden, they knew they could flourish, insulated from the chaos that reigned above.

Oah took three wives, each of them unique in appearance and background. The first, Tiwa, had helped to construct his vessel and had braved the tempestuous seas by his side. The second, Natu, a lost daughter of the land they settled on, had stumbled through a watery passage, and found herself back in the spiritual realm. She watched the arrival of Oah's boat, and when she agreed to be his wife, it further legitimized his kingship. Much like Oah, the third wife, Suna, was a wanderer who was uprooted from her homeland and sought solace on foreign soil. From these unions sprang forth three sons, each bearing the connection to their mother's homeland and the promise of a legacy like their father's.

The son of Suna was drawn to the land to the north, while the son of Natu was propelled farther east, each of them carrying with him the knowledge of the Orishas. Each built his own kingdom, infusing the divine into the cultures and lands of their mothers. Names evolved, stories shifted, but the ashé of the Orishas persisted.

As the peoples of Orirun who had survived the flood heard about Oah's magnificent land, they started to refer to it as East Kingdom.

Haben, the son born from Tiwa, established his own kingdom in the physical realm of Orirun. With industrious hands he sculpted a prosperous civilization. Grand structures rose at his command. By his decree, extravagant temples were erected and dedicated to the Orishas. His reign was marked not by a desire for dominion but by a commitment to betterment. His focus was ever fixed on the welfare of his people, his every action intended to enrich the lives of those who lived within his kingdom.

Haben's pure light unwittingly attracted the warriors of darkness. For his ambition revealed the Okunkun, the realm where the Ajogun resided.

The Ajogun were the spirits of the giants; they were chaos in its purest form. Nestled deep within every human Ori lay a dormant Osogbo, an egg of chaos, awaiting the stirring breath of an Ajogun. These shadowy warriors exerted their power by guiding the Osogbos through the dark path humans often trod. Without the Ajogun's breath, the Osogbos remained powerless over mortals; they relied on this symbiotic relationship with the Ajogun. Once awakened, a single Osogbo had the power to devastate families, cities, or even entire kingdoms. Yet on the rare occasion a human was strong enough to fight back and overcome their Osogbo, it could end up leading to growth and enlightenment.

Orunmila, the Orisha of prophecy, stood before the Council of Orishas, to lend his aid in suppressing the malicious Ajogun. He watched over the lineage of Oah, for the Ajogun harbored a fierce vendetta against the mortal who had extinguished the giants. These warriors of chaos sought vengeance not just on humanity but particularly against those lineages that suggested greatness.

Orunmila prophesied to Haben that the Osogbos would consume his bloodline. Haben, stricken by this ominous foretelling, pleaded with Orunmila for an explanation. "Why," he asked, "am I given such a cruel curse?"

Orunmila paused, gathering his thoughts before responding. "Your actions, though rooted in goodness, inadvertently set in motion a chain of events that will echo through your descendants. Your future descendants will be mighty, but will lose sight of their ordained path. They will turn inward, forsaking the collective, and this self-centeredness shall be their undoing. They will be shackled by chains seen and unseen. However, do not think of their downfall as an end of your lineage, for the suffering they will endure is in fact only the beginning, and they will rise in the end."

Haben married a woman named Fehintola and had four children with her, as Orunmila had foreseen: Kana'an, Kerma, Phut, and Kush. Haben was strict in his teachings on honor and morality, hoping to thwart fate. He forbade his sons from ever touching the soil in the physical realm and warned them about the Ajogun. Yet Kana'an, after establishing his kingdom in the spiritual realm, was driven by curiosity to travel across the divide.

Kana'an, blinded by hubris, believed himself invincible against the Ajogun. With reckless ambition, he found passage to the physical realm, and the moment he set foot on its soil, he became a hunted soul. He carved out a new kingdom in the physical realm, his dreams of grandeur replacing his innocence, paving the way for the Ajogun to capture him. Because he was consumed by his Osogbo, Kana'an's choices set his new people on the path to ruin. Those who survived the catastrophes that followed fled the eastern territories, seeking refuge in the north of Orirun.

The remaining three progeny of Haben, each eager to rule alongside the Orishas, laid claim to their own kingdoms in the spiritual realm. Endowed with kingships bestowed by Ogun, they became great leaders. However, time softened and soon erased their caution when it came to the physical realm. Their ambitions swelled.

Kerma, the bold second son of Haben, dared to disobey his father by entering the physical realm to prove that he was the greatest hunter. He established the small kingdom of Kemet in the north. His talent for the hunt invited the whispers of the Ajogun, who fed his Osogbo of competitiveness and pride. Kerma's boastfulness and his belief that his unmatched skill entitled him to lead became his downfall. His reign was abruptly ended by the large jaws of a hungry beast.

Phut, the third child of Haben, dared to follow in her brothers' footsteps, entering the physical realm and establishing the kingdom of Punt in the southeastern stretch of Orirun. Punt became renowned for its opulence, becoming the talk of distant lands. But the relentless attempts to maintain that illusion tempted the Ajogun, who preyed upon Phut's ambitions, awakening her Osogbo of greed. It drove her to ruthlessly exploit Onile, draining the ashé from the life in the soil to amass her material wealth, leading to the kingdom's slow decay.

After the soil claimed both his brothers and time took his sister, Kush, the youngest, became king and oversaw the Kushite Empire within the spiritual realm. Though Ogun had made him a king, he understood that true power derived from governing humans' Oris. Determined to avoid the fate of his siblings, he refused to depart for the physical realm.

Within Kush was the Osogbo spirit of war. Yet, even as he evaded the Ajogun by staying in the spiritual realm, the Osogbo egg lay dormant within him, ready to test the mettle of his descendants.

CHAPTER 12

Lamuradu

Ears that do not listen to advice
accompany the head when it is chopped off.

—African proverb

Kush fathered five children, of whom only one would leave the spiritual realm. The firstborn founded the Awon Iyas, a fearsome group of mother warriors. The next three ventured eastward: one established a prosperous kingdom with gold extracted from their father's land, the second found success as a seafarer, and the third thrived in foreign trade. Yet, it was the youngest sibling, Lamuradu, who was truly special. He possessed the brightest Ori of them all.

At his birth, Lamuradu's Ori caught the attention of the Council of Orishas in Edin. The East Kingdom, established by Oah and ruled by his son Haben, was fractured by internal strife, and in its weakened state conquered by the great warlord Asshur, a man who did not worship the Orishas. As their ashé dwindled and their influence began to wane, the Orishas turned their attention to the infant Lamuradu, entrusting him with the monumental task of reclaiming the East Kingdom.

Desperate, the council had sought guidance from Orunmila, who prophesied, "Send Lamuradu to the physical realm, and he shall reclaim the land, but only for a season. The true victory lies not in his reign, but in the shadows of his lineage."

Lamuradu's parents were heartbroken at the thought of sending their baby into the perils of the physical realm, where he would grow up unaware of his divine lineage. They reminded the Orishas of the generational curse of the Osogbo lurking in Lamuradu's soul. Despite this warning, the Orishas remained resolute. They understood that giving him up so young was the only way to subdue the Osogbo, which thrived on vanity and self-importance. Raised amid humble circumstances, Lamuradu would learn to earn and cherish what he had, and what he fought for. His mother pleaded with the Orishas to at least select a worthy guardian who would nurture and guide him to his destined path.

Distraught but dutiful, Lamuradu's parents tucked him into a small, wooden, oval-shaped vessel, barely two feet long and soaked in oil, and sealed it with tar. They set the vessel in a river, and watched their son float away.

The vessel bobbed gently along for days, passing into the physical realm. More time passed as the river continued to carry Lamuradu toward his fate. Finally, the precious vessel caught the eye of one of Asshur's gardeners.

The gardener, a solitary man without a family of his own, was washing off the day's sweat and soil when he noticed the peculiar sight. Intrigued, he fished the small vessel out of the water, and cracked it open only to discover a wide-eyed newborn.

In that moment, the gardener's life took on new purpose, for he decided to raise the baby as his own and named him Narām.

Narām enjoyed a simple, content life as the son of the kind gardener. Yet his talents soon enough shone through. As a young man, he was recruited by the empire's bureaucracy, which identified precocious individuals among the masses, and within mere years he was an astute, trusted diplomat. His magnetic personality and strategic skills earned him the favor of Asshur, allowing Narām to gain insight into the empire's weaknesses. Yet, the emperor's paranoia, fueled by fears of invasion by neighboring kingdoms, eventually trained its sights on Narām.

Emperor Asshur's actions set in motion a series of events that would steer Narām along his predestined path.

Narrowly escaping execution at the order of the emperor, Narām fled East Kingdom and approached two neighboring kingdoms, forging an alliance with both. Asshur's paranoia was justified: they had in fact had been plotting to invade. Now Narām, drawing on his knowledge of East Kingdom, shrewdly deployed the combined forces of the neighboring kingdoms to challenge Asshur, turning the tables on his would-be executioner.

East Kingdom was already crumbling under Asshur, ravaged by internal strife. It was ill-prepared for such an onslaught, an easy target for any ambitious conqueror.

In the crucial battle, the neighboring kingdoms, led by Narām, were victorious, and Narām himself became emperor of the East Kingdom.

Narām's mother learned of her son's conquest. Defying the Council of Orishas, she chose to visit her son, revealing to him the truth of his noble lineage and his birth name, Lamuradu. Driven by maternal instinct to protect him, she hoped to stop the lurking Ajogun from awakening his Osogbo. She bestowed upon him a divine gift: the Ori Sphere.

This was not just any gift; the Ori Sphere, crafted by the blind potter Ajala, was a spiritual safeguard designed to warn Lamuradu against falling victim to his darker tendencies, his Osogbo. Should Lamuradu give in to his Osogbo, the sphere would cloud over. If it turned pitch-black, that meant the end of his reign was near.

His mother only wanted to protect her son. However, learning he was not just a gardener's son, but a prince, stoked the flames of entitlement in Lamuradu's mortal mind. His perception of his people shifted—they were no longer equals, but soldiers and workers serving him.

Lamuradu now had grand ambitions. His aim was to restore the kingdom of his grandfather, Haben, and expand its borders far beyond their original expanse. He envisioned an empire invulnerable to external threats.

Fueling his expansionist plans was the ruinous tribute he required from surrounding kingdoms. As his empire grew, so did his demands. The ruler of one of the neighboring kingdoms refused to pay the escalating tribute.

Outraged by this defiance, Lamuradu decided to set a stern example. He exiled many of the people of the kingdom, enslaving the rest to labor on his grandest project, the Tower of Gods, and its lush surrounding gardens.

One such enslaved person was an older man named Asara, who was forced to put his artistry in the service of sculpting images of the Orishas, over the protestations of his son, a confident youth named Braima.

Lamuradu had an unquenchable desire to see himself honored as a god. He commissioned imposing statues of himself across the kingdoms he had subdued or conquered. Alongside these statues, he installed puppet rulers—individuals who lacked the courage to question or defy him. However, Lamuradu remained blind to an unsettling reality. With each passing day, his quest for mortal glory was inadvertently severing the ties to his spiritual roots, a perilous process he remained oblivious to.

With the completion of the Tower of the Gods and his marriage to a beautiful woman named Munira, who soon gave him a son and heir, Oduduwa.

Years passed. One day, Lamuradu's gaze fell back upon the Ori Sphere, and he noticed a slight haze obscuring its usual clarity. Uncertain when the discoloration had begun, or for how long it had been present, he found himself examining the sphere daily. He couldn't shake the suspicion that the sphere was gradually darkening. Was it his imagination, or was his Osogbo gaining power?

As the sphere's cloudiness became impossible to ignore, Lamuradu marched to the temple he had built in honor of his mother and the Orishas. He stood before her altar, a question burning in his heart: Why had the sphere changed? There was no answer. Day after day he asked, and day after day his pleas were met with silence. Frustrated and desperate to reach her, Lamuradu decided to find a portal back to the spiritual realm, decades after his parents had sent him down the river.

He packed the Ori Sphere in a simple satchel. Before embarking on this journey, he entrusted his son, Oduduwa, with the responsibility of ruling the kingdom. Young and inexperienced, Oduduwa was suddenly thrust into a position of power, tasked with maintaining a restless empire.

For seven long years, Lamuradu wandered, time chipping away at the man who once believed himself destined to walk among the Orishas. His pride faltered with each dead end. The whispers of the Ajogun grew louder every day, so subtle at first that he mistook them for his own thoughts, until it was too late.

Retreating into the shadows of seclusion, he became a prisoner of the Ajogun who nurtured his Osogbo of loss and ruin.

One evening, sitting beside a river that snaked silently through a forest, Lamuradu felt the cool water lap against his feet. He looked upon his reflection only to see a stranger staring back at him. He pulled out the Ori Sphere, to find that it was the darkest he had seen it. There, on the bank, he wept, pleading for the water to rise and take him whole.

The river indeed stirred, but Yemayá emerged, her arrival seamless and natural. Around him the air grew warm and fragant, soothing Lamuradu amid his grief. "Why have you abandoned me?" he asked. She knelt beside him and placed her hand over the Ori Sphere. Upon her touch it shuddered, light glowing faintly within. "Lamuradu, " she said, "you have wandered not only the lands but have entered the dark realm of the Okunkun. In seeking a portal to ascend, you lost the path. The Orishas did not abandon you; you abandoned yourself. But even now, the river flows. Even now, you can make amends."

Lamuradu lowered his head, tears spilling silently into the currents below. "The path forward lies not in your statues or conquests," she said. "It lies in tending what you have broken."

With that, Yemayá rose and turned toward the river, pausing only to look back at Lamuradu. She said, "The Orishas do not demand perfection, Lamuradu. Only the courage to begin again." And with that she melted into the waters. The Ori Sphere pulsed at his side. For the first time in seven years, he breathed deeply.

When Lamuradu returned to East Kingdom, he found that it had changed. Oduduwa had done his best to rule in his absence. But the son lacked the father's iron fist. He was a gentle ruler, more of a caretaker than a king, managing the empire instead of asserting his authority. The Ori Sphere was now completely black.

Fear gripped King Lamuradu. His once-steady hands trembled, his robust voice faltered. He roamed the corridors of the magnificent Tower of Gods, his mind a whirlpool of dreadful visions.

One night, he was roused from his restless sleep by the stench of smoke and the cries of an enraged mob. The door to his chamber gave way before the wrath of his people. They dragged him from the tower, their faces seething with righteous anger. Lamuradu was now a prisoner of his own tyranny.

Forced by an armored soldier to kneel, King Lamuradu watched in despair as the symbols of his reign—his statues, his temples—were reduced to rubble.

Against this tableau of violence and destruction, the artisan Asara emerged from the shadows, with his son, Braima, now a man in his own right, at his side. Braima's hatred for Lamuradu had led him to launch a rebellion of the enslaved in the kingdoms controlled by Lamuradu—a revolt against the puppet kings who no longer had a puppet master. His presence electrified the crowd as he rose to address it.

Braima gave a speech to the freed people of the empire. He spoke of stolen futures, of the Orishas who had stood as mute witnesses to the enslavement of his people, and of an emperor who claimed to be a god but had no mercy for other mortals.

Lamuradu, witnessing the consequences of his actions, realized the only thing left for him to do was to instill purpose in his son. As the crowd prepared a bonfire for his execution, he turned to Oduduwa, who was standing nearby, held by guards. The king's eyes reflected regret and unfulfilled promises. He had failed in his duty to keep the stories of the Orishas alive, and now his son was his, and the Orishas', last hope.

Beckoning to his son, he firmly gripped Oduduwa's hands and imparted his final wishes. He urged his son, if spared by the rebellion, to seek refuge in the spiritual realm, Orun, never to return to their homeland. Most importantly, he implored Oduduwa to keep the Orishas alive. "They are an anchor in a world of constant change," he said. As the flames devoured Lamuradu, his only living heir was exiled into the desert.

CHAPTER 13

Oduduwa

He who moves with each day is better
than another who waits for luck.

—African proverb

Oduduwa, once destined for the throne but now exiled, yearned to fill the void in his soul. From the moment he was forced to leave East Kingdom, he sensed he would never return to his homeland. Yet he remained hopeful. He wandered through the desert until he reached the great land of Orirun.

His only guide was the last remark of his late father: "Find the Iron Kingdom." Yet it wasn't kingship Oduduwa sought, in searching for Ogun's fief; it was redemption and purpose. He longed for a chance to prove his worth, not just to his late father, but to himself. He wanted to reclaim his family's honor and transform his exile into a journey of self-discovery and growth. He ultimately aimed to take back the throne in East Kingdom.

As Oduduwa trekked through Orirun, he asked everyone he came across if they could help him find a portal to Orun. Yet, none could provide a definitive location, for the portals were elusive and ever-shifting. One morning, he came across an Iyaláwo, a priestess, who possessed the rare Ori to help guide mortals to the gateways to the spiritual realm. She led him to a nearby pond. "What do you see?" she asked.

"I see myself," Oduduwa replied.

"Yes, but . . ."—as she dragged her fingers across the water, distorting his reflection—"a pond can conceal great depths beneath its surface. Just as water can obscure true vision, a portal to the Orun is often clouded by the unpredictability of emotions, fears, and desires. The portal you seek is not a destination I can point to but a journey you must take alone to find."

With the Iyaláwo's guidance lighting his path, Oduduwa continued on. He laid his head wherever he could find shelter, accepting odd jobs and relying on the goodwill of villagers for meals. When sustenance was scarce, he did what he had to, to survive. For two seasons, he searched tirelessly, until one day, while evading guards after stealing bread, he found himself hiding in a swamp.

The swamp's murky waters mirrored his own doubts, its entangling roots suggesting past mistakes and the hidden dangers of his father's expectations. As he pushed through the thick mire, a strange mist began to rise. Desperation led him deeper into the swamp, each step sinking him farther into the unknown. Suddenly the ground beneath him gave way, swallowing him whole.

When he emerged, he was standing before the great Iron Kingdom, and knew he had entered Orun. Towering guards, forged not out of flesh but iron, monstrous and intimidating, blocked the gates. He explained his purposes to the sentinels: to seek guidance from Ogun, in the hope that the Orisha of iron and war could help him reclaim his kingdom and avenge his father. The guards ushered Oduduwa into an underground chamber, where he was told to wait until summoned.

Oduduwa found himself sequestered in the foreigners' quarters, a liminal space for outsiders awaiting acceptance. Merchants from far-off lands engaged in lively bartering, their foreign tongues weaving an exotic melody. Scholars from abroad were engrossed in fervent intellectual discourse and passionate debates. Outside the quarters, iron soldiers, their armor glinting under the sun, cast ominous shadows as they patrolled the streets.

He waited for days. Each dawn brought with it the peculiar cacophony of the Iron Kingdom, the rhythmic symphony of hammer against anvil, the distant thunder of machinery, and the ceaseless chatter of war and trade. The air was laden with the distinct suffocating fumes of iron and smoke.

Although he was surrounded by other humans, Oduduwa felt a sense of isolation. He was an outsider, a stranger in a foreign land. Yet this seclusion also offered him time for reflection. He contemplated his purpose, the weight of his father's legacy, and the daunting task that lay ahead. He spent countless hours honing strategies in his mind, envisioning his path to reclaim the kingdom he viewed as his.

The day finally came when Oduduwa was granted an audience with Ogun. He was led through the grand corridors of the Iron Temple, and the heavy doors of the throne room swung open before him. There, bathed in the glow of a thousand torches, sat Ogun.

"Oduduwa," Ogun began, his voice pounding Oduduwa's chest. "You have come seeking my aid. Speak."

"I seek your guidance, Ogun," Oduduwa replied, his voice steady. "I wish to learn the art of war, to gather an army, and to reclaim what is rightfully mine."

Ogun scanned his face. The tension in the air was like a drawn bowstring. Then Ogun laughed, a momentous sound that bounced off the stone walls. "Bold words, young prince. But words are wind. It's strength and skill that rule the battlefield."

Oduduwa nodded. "That is why I seek your tutelage, Ogun. Teach me, create my armor, and I will prove my worth in battle."

Ogun studied Oduduwa for a long moment, then nodded. "Very well. I will train you. But be warned. The path you choose is not easy. It will demand everything of you—your strength, your courage, your very soul."

The training began immediately. Every day was a test of endurance, an onslaught of drills and brutal sparring sessions with the most skilled of warriors in the Iron Kingdom. At night, Oduduwa would retreat to the kingdom's libraries, immersing himself in Orirun's histories, feeding his mind with knowledge.

During one training session, a woman caught his eye. He first noticed her watching him from the fringes of the training ground. Her eyes were pools of amber. In her gaze, he saw curiosity and a spark of something else, something that made his heart flutter.

Lakange was a gift of war. She was the daughter of a chieftain, and when the chieftain's land was raided and his people were enslaved, she was given to Ogun as tribute. A beautiful bird in a gilded cage, she was groomed for a destiny not of her choosing.

Ogun did not desire her for her beauty or pedigree, but for the enchanting cadence of her voice.

Time slipped by and Ogun's fascination with her unique gift began to wane. She was summoned less often to the grand feasts, her songs were sung less frequently through the iron halls, and eventually her presence was forgotten entirely. She became an ornament in the palace, a neglected pet, left to wander the expansive grounds in solitude.

Lakange felt her spirit dimming within the confining iron walls. She knew every corner of Ogun's palace; she had traced the intricate patterns engraved into the iron statues of Ogun throughout the kingdom, until their grandeur lost all meaning. Her existence was as hollow as the air that followed one of her performances.

One ordinary afternoon, a fresh form entered her world, though at the periphery. As the days passed, she absorbed his every motion, internalized his routines. She was but a specter, a mute observer, until destiny ordained their gazes to meet, and in that moment a flame was kindled.

Their spirits were drawn together by a mutual yearning for a great purpose. Between the frigid iron walls, love bloomed in stolen moments, and vows were breathed into the wind.

Lakange began to glow with increased luminosity, drawing Ogun's attention. He did not like the way Oduduwa's eyes lingered on her, and jealousy pierced his stoic veneer. He forbade Lakange from meeting with the young mortal from East Kingdom.

As Olorun's journey across the sky stretched longer each day, Oduduwa found himself in panicked pursuit of more encounters with Lakange. Yet, his efforts bore no fruit, and she remained mostly a phantom.

Ogun took perverse delight in Oduduwa's constant distraction, his joy as cold as his iron. "You seem adrift, Oduduwa," he taunted the human, his voice laced with false concern. "A king must possess unwavering focus. Is there something preoccupying your thoughts?"

Oduduwa, caught in Ogun's piercing gaze, spoke of his exhausting training regimen, attempting to conceal the true cause of his distraction. A knowing smirk played on Ogun's lips as he invited Oduduwa to a festive gathering that evening, a chance to disrupt the tedium of their training. Left with no choice, Oduduwa accepted.

As night descended, the air pulsated with the beat of the Batá drums, while the tantalizing aroma of roasted pork and garlic wafted through the Iron Temple. But the feast held no allure for Oduduwa; he yearned only for Lakange. The celebration lasted for hours, until Ogun, perched on his throne with his wife, Oya, by his side, silenced the attendees, drawing their attention to a special performance from a woman he introduced as his future second wife.

And there she was, dripping in jewels: Lakange. Oduduwa's heart lurched, plummeting into his belly. Her voice, as mellifluous as a nightingale's song, surrounded him, but it was her eyes that held him captive. As they found him in the sea of faces, a lone tear traced a path down her cheek, for she was torn between her obligation to Ogun and the love that grew within her for Oduduwa.

Once her performance was over, Oduduwa stole a precious moment with Lakange amid the chaos of the celebration. She warned him, her voice a tremulous whisper, that their union would cost him his kingship. But Oduduwa, undeterred, made her a solemn vow. He assured her that Ogun's apparent affection was nothing more than a shadow, a fleeting interest kindled by jealousy. "My love for you seeks no light to draw its strength. You are the axis on which my world turns." He promised her a life where she would be his queen, his only wife.

Oduduwa, with a pleading tone and earnest eyes, posed a monumental question to Lakange. Would she stay amid the trappings of her current existence, or would she choose liberation? For if Ogun denied him a kingship, he vowed to wrest it from him and the other Orishas. Oduduwa wanted to reconstruct an Ori for both himself and Lakange, creating a destiny by their own hands, free from Ogun's conditions. He longed for the freedom to love whom he chose and to carve out a purpose beyond the divine wills that sought to bind them. He no longer coveted the kingship of Ogun, for he had witnessed that the Orishas had the flaws of mortals.

Disenchanted with Edin and its Garden, Oduduwa sought to unravel their influence over humankind. With a vision to restore balance and autonomy, he endeavored to reshape the hierarchy of mortal and Orisha, creating a new era in which the spiritual and physical realms would coexist without any beings possessing unchecked power.

His words, spoken with sincere conviction, offered her a glimmer of hope, an image of a future where they could exist not as pawns in Ogun's game, but as rulers of their own fates. The promise of this future fueled their plan to escape. They were willing to risk everything for a chance at a life defined by their love, rather than by the Orishas.

They sought out herbs imbued with the power to induce sleep, intending to infuse them into Ogun's palm wine before his wedding to Lakange.

Soon enough, the eve of the wedding, and of their planned escape, was upon them. Their hearts beat furiously. When Ogun beckoned Lakange to his chambers, she offered him the palm wine, a seemingly innocent gesture. It took three immense drafts for the potent brew to seize Ogun in its intoxicating grasp, and he succumbed to sleep in her arms. Lakange slipped away unnoticed into the night, where Oduduwa anxiously awaited her.

Oduduwa and Lakange ran for what seemed like an eternity. Then, underneath the shell of Mawu, which cast an ominous light over the Iron Kingdom, they stood before a portal to the physical realm, the very door from which Oduduwa had emerged, ending his exile. In the spiritual realm, the portals were large stone doorways, standing seven feet tall and carved with the script of the Orishas. The doors were easy to find, for the Orishas saw the mortal journey as one of constant growth and return.

As they prepared to step through, Lakange held Oduduwa back and confessed a secret she had harbored since the feast: she carried a child within her, and she knew it was Ogun's. Oduduwa, his heart full of love for Lakange, pledged to raise the child as his own. Lakange smiled warmly, finding peace and assurance in his words.

Each had been stripped of a kingdom they could claim as their own. Now they crossed into the mortal realm together, ready to create their own destiny.

CHAPTER 14

The Preaching of Oduduwa

Imole de, okunkun parada.
Light comes, darkness hides.

—Yoruba phrase

During Oduduwa's stay in the Iron Kingdom, he developed a keen interest in scholarly pursuits and became captivated by the forbidden journal of Obatala. The *Book of Creation* was locked away in Ogun's palace, but Lakange gave him access to the room where it was held. Within its pages, Oduduwa learned about the intricate process behind the creation of Ori—how the blood of the Orishas intertwined with that of the giants, culminating in the creation of the Children of Ori.

In a final act of defiance, Oduduwa pilfered the book during his escape with Lakange. As they ventured into the physical realm of Orirun, they found comfort in each other and power in the *Book of Creation*. The ancient writings were proof that all mortals bore the lineage of the Orishas, bestowing upon humans the right to rule themselves. They soon realized that time had passed faster in the physical realm, and the world around them had changed drastically. Unlike the spiritual realm, which remained constant, a lake of time, the physical realm was in rapid and constant motion, a rushing river.

Although Oduduwa had to be wary of those who exiled him, he saw the leap across decades as a fresh start. Embracing the chance to create himself anew in a world where he had been forgotten, Oduduwa began a journey to carve out a new destiny. As Lakange's belly grew, Oduduwa began piecing together the puzzle of his family's downfall. While his father was not without fault, he identified the true perpetrator: the Ajogun and the Osogbos.

Lakange soon gave birth to a son, Oranmiyan, whom Oduduwa loved and raised like his own. Within two years, she gave birth to Oduduwa's daughter, Okanbi. All the while, Lakange battled her Osogbo, a darkness that neither sleep nor sunlight could lift. The Ajogun had taken hold, whispering to her Osogbo thoughts of deep sorrow. Each morning, she rose, but her soul remained submerged beneath the growing Osogbo within.

Finally, she became a prisoner of the Ajogun, and in the quiet moments, when all was still, the river began to call to her, promising release. At last, Lakange, unable to see beyond the fog of her grief, answered the river's call, and her struggle ended as she was swallowed by the water.

Oduduwa grieved the loss of his beloved Lakange. In his relentless quest to discover a way to defeat the Ajogun, he had been blind to the silent Osogbo that consumed her spirit. Overwhelmed by regret, he lamented his failure to protect her, realizing too late the cost of his distractions.

Oduduwa swore to never succumb to his own Osogbo, and to channel his despair into guiding others in their battles against the darkness that lurked within. When it came time, he envisioned a land untouched by darkness, a sanctuary where his children could flourish, a kingdom where the light of inner strength would illuminate the path to fulfilling their Oris.

Oduduwa began preaching on finding that light. He garnered a devoted following that hung on his every word, for his teachings came from the *Book of Creation*. He explained to his followers: "The Ajogun hold no power over us. We must not let them or the Orishas dictate our destiny, for they are merely here to guide us on this soil. As long as we resist desire, excess,

Harmonia

jealousy, idleness, arrogance, greed, and uncontrolled anger, we shall remain free from the Ajogun."

Oduduwa's wisdom flowed like a river, its currents carrying his followers toward a deeper understanding of their existence. He taught that humans were the guardians of their own destinies, the gods of their Oris.

Each year brought new landscapes, new challenges, and new discoveries. And as his children grew, so did his flock. Yet, there was a layer of uncertainty underneath everything. His children saw that the land their father sought remained elusive, a mirage in the desert of his dreams.

Oranmiyan and Okanbi looked upon their father with concern. They remembered their mother's comforting presence, now a void each carried with them. Her death had cast a shadow of melancholy over Oduduwa, a sadness that clung to him like a persistent fog, threatening his quest.

Oduduwa found that he now took comfort in constant movement. It distracted him from the darkness left by Lakange's absence. But his children were different. They craved the stability of a kingdom. They yearned for a place to grow roots, to flourish, to become themselves.

One day, as the sun began its descent, Oduduwa, Oranmiyan, Okanbi, and their loyal followers heard the faint beats of drums. Captivated, they followed the sounds to a community hidden amid rolling hills.

This place, known as Òkè Òrà, thrived under the watchful eyes of Obatala, whom the people called the Ooni-Oba, the great spiritual king. Òkè Òrà was comprised of thirteen settlements and thirteen chieftains. Each chieftain was chosen by Obatala himself. Each settlement had its own unique crop to manage and harvest; there was a central marketplace where they could share and trade their harvest, so that all thrived.

The inhabitants of Òkè Òrà identified themselves as Eniyan-Igbos, people of the forest. They lived apart from kingdoms ruled by mortals, finding sanctuary under the protective gaze of Ooni-Oba Obatala. Among their number was Obamari, a chieftain who governed the harvest of yams. Obamari met with and became fascinated by Oduduwa, for his regal presence and strong ashé reminded him of Obatala when the Orisha had first descended from Edin in Orun.

Obatala had chosen to reside in the mortal realm, seeking refuge from the prying eyes of the Council of Orishas, which had expelled him for his unconventional creations. Feeling unappreciated and tarnished, he decided to build a new Edin in Aiye and continue his work of creating life. But without Ajala and his Oris, Obatala deemed himself a failure; the life he created was static like the Enks, lacking destiny. He took to palm wine, which led him down a path of excess.

Obamari explained to Oduduwa that the Ooni-Oba's overindulgence was in fact the cause of his troubles, not the consequence; it resulted in the creation of beings sick both in body and mind. The Ooni-Oba's addiction meant that Òkè Òrà lacked a true ruler. Unrest was growing as one of the chieftains, Bankole, displayed his greed.

Obamari hoped that Oduduwa's knowledge could save Òkè Òrà from self-destruction. He told the visitor that he would bring him before Obatala.

Oduduwa, eager to meet the creator of the Children of Ori and return to him his *Book of Creation*, was disheartened by the sight that greeted him. Obatala, whose figure once commanded reverence, slouched upon his throne in a drunken stupor. His hands, which had shaped magnificent beings, now trembled as they cradled a small drinking bowl. Obamari reminded Oduduwa that Obatala hadn't always been this way.

Oduduwa, who had always believed that Orishas were immune to Osogbos, now saw that they had captured Obatala. Shocked by this revelation, Oduduwa tried to reason with Obatala, telling him that he could not lead the Eniyan-Igbos in his current state. The Orisha ignored him, waving him away. However, when Obatala realized that Oduduwa was holding his *Book of Creation*, the haze seemed to lift from his eyes. He rose unsteadily, towering over Oduduwa. "My book," he growled. "You dare to read from the *Book of Creation*?" He demanded its return, accusing Oduduwa of committing a sacrilegious act.

Obatala, enraged by what he perceived as betrayal, ordered Oduduwa to leave Òkè Òrà immediately. The confrontation forced Obamari to make a difficult choice. Witnessing Obatala's decline and recognizing that the land needed a leader, Obamari chose to stand with Oduduwa, hoping to restore balance and peace.

The wayward chieftain, Bankole, whose greed had already begun to corrupt Òkè Òrà, oversaw the palm fruit harvests, producing both essential palm oil and fermenting half of it to make palm wine, the very substance that reduced Obatala to a drunk. He had attempted to form an alliance with Obamari to secure more harvests from other communities, knowing that yams and oil were vital resources for his people. He also understood that controlling the palm oil would loosen his rival communities' grip on power. Yet when Obamari refused his proposition, the chieftain turned to neighboring settlements to form an alliance against the rest.

Obatala sank back onto his throne in disbelief over Obamari's choice. "There is a reason mortals are not allowed such information, such truths," he muttered, more to himself than to anyone else. "I know who you are, Oduduwa; I know what you preach, the dreams you weave. You speak of righteous paths, believing them to be smooth rivers flowing to a paradise. You talk of healing wounds as if the ache of existence can be soothed so simply. But change is a beast more vicious than you can comprehend."

Obatala paused to reach for the jar beside him, and poured the milky stream of palm wine into his bowl. "What you fail to realize," he said, "is that without destruction, there can be no creation. Without pain, no growth. True change is vaster than a single mortal lifetime. It demands sacrifice! Death, chaos, and disorder must reign before peace can take root. It is costly, but it is the only path forward."

Obatala tipped the bowl to his lips, guzzled its contents, and set it down with a soft thud. "The truth is far heavier than your preaching of hope. Accept it, and you will see the futility of your threads, too delicate to bind the world together." He gestured to the jar of wine as if extending an invitation to join in his lamentation. "When you understand that, Oduduwa," he said with a smirk, "you will sit beside me and drink as even dreams dissolve."

Oduduwa gathered his thoughts. "You're right, Ooni-Oba Obatala," he began. "We mortals do not have the luxury of immortality. To you, our lives are but passing days, brief and inconsequential. But it is precisely because of this that hope is our foundation. While you sit upon your throne, consumed by despair, we mortals endure our fleeting days by planting seeds we may never see bloom, but with hope that our descendants will bask in the harvest. Hope is not a weakness: it's our anchor that binds us to purpose."

A stillness settled over the room. Obatala finally grunted, and Oduduwa departed.

In response, Oduduwa erected a small temple in Obamari's community, where he began to speak out against the wayward chieftain and the Orisha who had fallen under the sway of the Osogbos. He warned the people of the dangers of unchecked power and the spiral of excess, urging them to reclaim their destiny and restore stable governance to Òkè Òrà.

"Imole de, okunkun parada"—light comes, darkness hides—Oduduwa would begin his addresses to the communities willing to heed his call. "I am here to help create a great united land, bound by justice and trust. It shall be called Yorubaland. And it begins not tomorrow, not in some distant dream, but now. You may have Obas, kings, to guide you, Orishas to inspire you, and chieftains to lead your people, but none shall stand above accountablility. No crown, no divine claim, no lineage shall permit unchecked power. For too long, darkness has thrived where the light of justice has not been allowed to shine. The time has come to question, to demand, and to hold every leader to the same expectations we place upon ourselves."

His words seeped into the consciousness of his listeners, reshaping their perception of kingship and themselves, and the relationship between the two.

For many, the idea of speaking against an Orisha or Oba was unthinkable, but as Obatala's actions grew increasingly erratic, anger toward him spread. The thirteen settlements found themselves divided, with trust in Obatala's ashé waning among those who aligned with Oduduwa's vision. As these seven communities redirected their ashé to Oduduwa, his own power grew, surpassing that of the disgraced Obatala.

Empowered by the collective ashé of the seven communities, Oduduwa found that his influence continued to swell. More communities began to rally to his side. In a decisive confrontation, Oduduwa, now mightier than Obatala, expelled both the disgraced Orisha and Bankole, along with his remaining rebel communities, from Òkè Òrà. They retreated into the vastness of the forest.

In the aftermath of the civil war, Oduduwa extended an olive branch to the exiled Eniyan-Igbos in the forest, inviting them to return under his leadership. His promises of fair rule and unity won over most of those who had stood against him. The corrupt Bankole held out, isolated, governing only his own community alongside an incoherent Obatala.

Succeeding Obatala as the Ooni, or spiritual leader, Oduduwa unified the remaining communities into his kingdom of Yorubaland, also known as Ife. As the first Ooni-Oba of the great Ifé, he guided the kingdom into a new epoch, when humans would choose their own Oris.

BOOK IV

THE OGISOS

CHAPTER 15

The Golden Serpent

By the time the fool has learned the game,
the players have dispersed.

—Ghanaian proverb

In the beginning of civilization, the Orishas walked among the humans, selecting the boldest to ascend to their pantheon in the spiritual realm. But as centuries passed, the Council of Orishas needed intermediaries, mortal rulers, who could guide humanity directly. The Orishas aimed to preserve their influence over human societies, which were beginning to challenge their authority.

Thus, the age of the first Ogisos, rulers of the sky, was ushered in. The Orishas elevated mortals who possessed extraordinary qualities—courage, wisdom, compassion, and strength. These chosen few would be crowned as Ogisos, each entrusted with a kingdom in Orirun, under the watchful eyes of the council.

The coronation of the first Ogisos was a spectacle unlike any before. The chosen few stepped forward, their heads held high, as the Council of Orishas emerged from Edin in Orun. Their tall lanky forms were draped in thick robes, elaborate beaded masks, and weighted jewelry, as they bestowed their gifts upon the new rulers.

The most significant of these gifts was a golden crown, a shield for each Ogiso's Ori. It was a symbol of the divine mandate granted to the Ogisos, a badge of honor from Olorun. It was said that those adorned with this sacred gold could peer through the veil of the mortal world, straight into the Garden in Orun.

In Aiye, grand temples were erected, their foundations paved by Ogun's iron machines in the twilight hours. These temples were more than sites of power and prayer; they served as thrones for the Orishas, where divine and mortal could commune.

The crowning of the Ogisos inaugurated a golden age for humanity. Guided by the knowledge bequeathed by the Orishas, the Ogisos brought prosperity to the land and strict order to their peoples. The temples served as gateways, bridging Aiye and Orun, eliminating the need for humans to search for portals through their own trials and tribulations. Belonging to a kingdom meant access to the Orishas' wisdom, shared with all who sought it.

This was only the beginning of the Ogisos' story. The covenant between the Orishas and the mortals would be tested in the coming epoch. For the Ogisos were not all good rulers; their ambitions often led to chaos, sparking greed and war.

Among the Orishas, however, Orunmila was uneasy about granting the humans so much power. He approached the council with a pressing question: "What will become of our world, of our existence, when humans begin to believe they can take our place and claim they too can commune with Olodumare, Orun, and Onile?"

The question was met with silence and confusion. For the first time, the council pondered their place in the cosmos. Since Mama Onile's birth, they had been the intermediaries, guiding Oris, shaping mortals' paths, weaving their fates. Orunmila continued, "Who, then, will interpret the humans' commands? What messages will they profess to receive?"

Though the other Orishas gave no answer, Orunmila knew well what the future promised. If their voice was no longer heard and accepted, chaos would threaten their reign, and Mama Onile and Orirun would descend into unrest and conflict. As Orunmila's questions lingered in Edin, life for the Orishas continued unchanged. Until one day, when Orunmila's questions became prophecy.

Gold, that symbol of divine favor, shone with such brilliance that it birthed an unusual Osogbo. Unlike any before, this Osogbo did not bind itself to a human Ori but instead latched onto Mama Onile herself. It took root in Oko's soil, blossoming and unleashing chaos across the land.

Seduced by gold's physical beauty, mortals turned upon Mama Onile. Their hands, once gentle, now clawed hungrily at her body, tearing her flesh in their insatiable desire for the precious metal. Each scrape and thrust was an affront to her dignity, a violation. As she suffered, the seeds of chaos took root deep within the belly of her mother, Olokun, who still lay chained in the ocean's abyss.

Olokun's womb ruptured, and a powerful spawn arose—Bida, the seven-headed golden serpent. Each head embodied the darkest shadows of human nature: Igberaga, the prideful; Ojukokoro, the greedy; Ilara, the envious; Ibinu, the wrathful; Ifekufe, the lustful; Alajeun, the gluttonous; and Ole, the slothful.

Bida surged toward Orirun, her slender form shimmering with a hypnotic radiance, weaving a golden thread of iniquity in Aiye.

Bida created a web of mercantile pathways reconnecting mortal lands that had been divided ever since Olokun's flood. These routes created bridges between the people of Orirun and distant societies, acting as conduits for both trade and cultural exchange. It was upon these newfound paths that foreign leaders, the Esin Imale, arrived in Orirun from a rising kingdom in Orun, accompanied by their warriors, the Da'wah.

The Enks, who long enjoyed peace underground, found their tranquility abruptly shattered by the arrival of the golden serpent. Their homes were torn apart and they were ripped from Mama Onile's chest, bartered away for gold. Humans, once seen as allies, began to view the Enks not as equals, but as commodities.

As Bida slithered farther into Orirun, Ogisos, chieftains, and warriors alike were mystified by her radiant charm. Many succumbed to the enticing promises of power and control proffered by the Esin Imale, who rode on the

back of Bida, while others fell before the might of the Da'wah. The northern kingdoms of Orirun succumbed to the Esin Imale, its spiritual ties to the Garden and the Orishas severed, leaving its people lost and subservient to their foreign gods.

The Esin Imale did not immediately eclipse the Orishas. Instead, their arrival sparked a dance of shadows and light throughout the kingdoms of Orirun. The shadows they brought cloaked some of the Garden in Orun , severing the Orishas' access to the humans living in those kingdoms. Mystified, the Orishas failed to notice their Garden shrinking. The Esin Imale alongside their Da'wah exploited the Orishas' distraction, acknowledging the gods and feeding their hearts with the nectar of pride.

The few Ogiso rulers who embraced the beliefs espoused by the Esin Imale gained access to Bida's pathways and were rewarded with golden scales from her back. Armed with newfound power, these converted rulers imposed unfamiliar laws upon their subjects and tore down the temples of the Orishas. Soon enough, war erupted, and Ogun found himself needed among the humans of Orirun more than ever.

Thus the world changed, as it always does. The time of innocence was supplanted by an era when gold reigned supreme, and greed sat enthroned as its queen.

The Orishas felt their powerful grip on the world loosen. They saw in Bida not just a bridge connecting the lands once more but a threat to their spiritual kingdom. Determined to reclaim control, the Orishas sought to cauterize Bida's pathways. They conspired to trap the serpent, much like they had its mother, Olokun.

They eventually succeeded in coaxing and binding Bida with Ogun's chains. Yet, as Mama Onile once said, suppressing one chaos will only reveal another.

Even with Bida subdued, the pathways the serpent had carved remained, fueling the ambitions of wayward humans and leaving the Orishas to ponder what would happen next.

CHAPTER 16

Taiwo

The first twin to taste the world.

The land of Nubia, in the east of Orirun, was made up of two prosperous kingdoms, Kemet and Kush, tied together by the waters of the Black River under the reign of Oshun.

The arrival of Bida altered the destiny of Nubia. The serpent's passage through the fertile black soil of Kemet unleashed a transformation, turning the land into a bustling hub of trade and ambition. Merchants and seekers of fortune, enticed by the promise of untold riches, flocked to Kemet from distant lands, their eyes glistening with dreams of gold and glory. All of Nubia became a coveted prize. As foreigners seized Kemet, their gaze turned toward the Black River, the lifeblood of Nubia's wealth.

They swept through Nubia, capturing Kush, which lay to the south of Kemet, in their merciless grasp. The people of Nubia found themselves shackled, their powerful kingdoms crippled by the extravagant tributes demanded by the conquerors. The Black River, which had tied two proud kingdoms together, was put in the service of mere material gain. Bound to a life of toil, the Nubians were forced to delve into the ashé of Mama Onile, extracting veins of gold for their oppressors, trapped in an unending cycle of servitude.

Among the foreign kingdoms eager to trade with the newly prosperous Kemet was Troy, in the ancient territories of the warrior Oah, now ruled by an aging, kindhearted king.

This king dispatched his much younger half brother, Murat, across the sea. Murat's mission was to forge a trade route, a golden bridge between the lands, and ensure a ceaseless flow of gold into the coffers of Troy.

Murat would make many voyages to the shores of Kemet. Yet he was captivated not by gold, but by the presence of a golden divinity, the Orisha of fertility, Oshun. With her wondrous beauty and charm, Oshun had anticipated Murat's first arrival through the prophetic insights of Orunmila. She wanted to reclaim the Black River from foreign influence and had sought guidance from her fellow Orisha, who advised her to unite with Murat. Through their union, a child would be born, a great warrior who would restore the river's connection to the Garden.

Unable to resist her allure, Murat's heart surrendered to Oshun. Their encounters, though fleeting, were profound. To her surprise, Oshun bore fruit in the form of twin sons, Taiwo and Khende. This unexpected twist in the divine plan only made her more hopeful that she would retake the river.

However, the joyous occasion of her twins' birth was interrupted by a change in the prophecy. Orunmila now explained that her sons shared a single soul, and that soul was born to die young, for upon conception they were bound by an abiku, a wandering spirit reluctant to tether itself to the mortal realm for long.

Oshun knew all too well of the abikus, those defiant spirits that rebelled against the natural order upheld by the Orishas. The abikus attached themselves to the souls of unborn mortals, and their very existence challenged the divine will, as they repeatedly escaped the cycle of mortal life and death crafted by Obatala and Ajala. Yet, determined to proceed in her divine plan to reclaim the Black River, Oshun yearned to shield her sons from their grim fate. Desperate, she devised a plan to separate her twins, leaving one in the mortal world of Aiye while taking the other back to Edin in Orun.

Her reasoning was rooted in her deep understanding of the abiku. The wandering spirit would now be bound to two bodies residing in two distinct realms. Oshun believed that this would cause confusion in the abiku and disrupt its intent.

Oshun took Khende back to Edin, while Taiwo was left orphaned in the land of Nubia. She hoped against hope that he would find love and acceptance.

During one of his many hunts, a local chieftain discovered the baby Taiwo nestled beneath the boughs of an ancient tree. The chieftain was enthralled by Taiwo's eyes—one shone bright blue against his dark skin while the other was a warm honeyed brown—and decided to take him in as his own. For he was sure that Taiwo was special.

Taiwo grew up under the chieftain's stern tutelage. The man treated him no different than his own daughter, Alara, who was being groomed to be her father's successor. The village was at war, part of the ongoing rebellion against the foreign rulers who had conquered Kush. Taiwo came to despise the foreign tyrants for how they had subjugated the Nubian people and forced them to mine Mama Onile's gold.

When the time came for Alara to assume her father's mantle, Taiwo was chosen to be her steadfast ally and the commander of her army. United in their determination to challenge the foreign oppressors, they launched a campaign to reclaim the lands of lower Nubia. Alara's fearless leadership and skill led them to a notable victory, forcing the invaders to retreat to the lands of Kemet.

Yet Taiwo harbored a grander vision. His dreams soared beyond the horizon; he wanted not only to drive out the invaders, to liberate the enslaved people of Kemet, and to reclaim the kingdom for Orirun. He sought nothing less than to reestablish the glorious Kushite Empire, which had been slowly divided by trade and conquests, and where Orisha Oshun could once again reign over the Black River.

Alara, while she supported Taiwo's aspirations, deemed his plan overly ambitious. She chose to fortify her borders, preparing for any potential backlash should Taiwo's campaign prove unsuccessful. Nevertheless, she entrusted him with a significant portion of her army, believing in his capacity to lead. She bade him farewell, her hopes for their people's future tied to his daunting journey.

Taiwo's trek north to Kemet was fraught with peril. The desert sand was unforgiving, its waves shifting with the temperamental wind. Yet Taiwo and his army pushed through, like a procession of scarab beetles, moving unwaveringly toward their goal.

As they approached the towering pyramids of Kemet, Taiwo sought the Orishas' guidance. Beneath the starlit sky, he prepared a sacred offering, hoping to win favor for the coming battle. He carefully arranged kola nuts, honey, and a white rooster, a human's attempt to invoke the Orishas' aid. Lighting incense, he let the fragrant smoke rise to the skies in hopes of creating a bridge between the Aiye and Orun. He spewed palm wine from his mouth, his voice lifting in a pleading chant, calling upon the Orishas' strength and for them to bless him with a victory.

Taiwo's pleas had previously gone unanswered, for Oshun had implored the Orishas not to intervene. She feared that if his abiku sensed it was in Aiye, it would strive to return to Orun before Taiwo could fulfill his calling. Such an early departure would thwart Oshun's plans to reclaim the Black River. Despite him not receiving a response, Taiwo's faith in the Orishas remained unshaken.

But the time had come for Oshun to answer her son's prayers. Ever strategic, she had carefully balanced her love for him with her own grand plans. Watching him grow into a courageous and accomplished man filled her heart with pride. Yet she hadn't anticipated how difficult this day would be. Not only would it be their first meeting, but it would also signal the beginning of the end of his Earthly life, as the abiku would eventually claim him.

With the battle looming, Oshun, driven by desire to protect the Garden in Orun, revealed herself. She embraced Taiwo, revealing his true heritage as her son and a descendant of kings, destined to rule. She then gifted him mystical armor crafted by Ogun, a symbol of her divine favor and a promise of victory. This blessing granted him fortitude as well as the ability to sail down the Black River unnoticed. Invigorated, Taiwo led his army into battle against the foreign invaders as the dawn stretched its golden fingers across the sky, heralding the flowering of his Ori. He was on his destined path.

The battle was a tempest of bronze and blood, the air heavy with the screams of warriors and the thunderous clash of weapons. Yet Taiwo, like a lion amid the chaos, fought with a courage that instilled hope in his men. The foreign leader's army wavered, crumbling before Taiwo's strength.

Victory swept over all of Nubia like the swelling flood of the river, bringing waves of jubilant relief to Kemet. The Nubian people hailed Taiwo as their savior, their voices ringing through their cities in a triumphant symphony. With the avaricious foreigners dethroned, Taiwo wanted to proceed with uniting Kemet and Kush under one ruler. However, he needed the permission of his father, knowing his sister Alara had been selected for the throne.

Alara knew her decision not to fight alongside Taiwo had meant, from the beginning, relinquishing her claim if he were to succeed. She now understood that by joining the lands of Kemet and Kush, they would become a formidable trading power. In stepping aside, she allowed Taiwo to lead a united Nubia, in the knowledge that their combined strength would secure a prosperous future for their people. Thus, the Kushite Empire was refounded, with Taiwo as its ruler.

The Orishas rejoiced in the victory, as Oshun regained control over the Black River and their dominion over Orirun expanded. Yet the sands in Taiwo's hourglass were slipping away, as the abiku lay in wait, ready to claim half of his shared soul at the slightest misstep.

Just as Taiwo began to settle into the throne and the duties that entailed, he was summoned back to action. His legend had spread far and wide, reaching the ears of those in distant lands who were in dire need.

The people of Yehudit were under siege by the Asshur Empire. This force, once vanquished by the legendary Lamuradu, had risen from the ashes of its past defeat and was now feared, owing to its ironclad soldiers.

One sun-scorched day, emissaries from the land of Yehudit arrived in

PIYE · SHABAQO · SHEBITQO · TAHARQO · TANUTAMANI
Harmonia

Taiwo's court. They knelt before the Nubian leader, and desperation shone in their eyes as they narrated their dire circumstances. "The Asshurites are merciless and their oppressive rule has cast a shadow over our kingdom."

They warned Taiwo of the imminent threat the Asshur Empire posed to Nubia itself. If Yehudit fell, the Asshurites would soon turn to other targets. They could breach the borders of Orirun and invade the Kushite Empire, threatening to submerge its vibrant culture under the weight of their own.

Taiwo listened intently to their plea. Their words rang true. As he considered his own empire, he saw that the destiny of his people, in addition to that of the people of Yehudit, hinged on his choice. After much contemplation, he resolved to stand with the supplicants before him.

Taiwo rallied his warriors. His attention shifted eastward, toward the embattled land of Yehudit. His will was as unyielding as the ancient pyramids that punctuated his kingdom's landscape. He prepared to march, ready to stand shoulder to shoulder with the soldiers of Yehudit, united in a struggle against the encroaching menace of the Asshurites.

Weeks later, Taiwo and his forces had arrived in Yehudit and now faced the enemy. As dawn broke, the silhouette of Taiwo's grand army stretched across the horizon, an undulating serpent poised to strike. The air was thick with anticipation, the silence before the storm broken only by the beats of ten thousand hearts.

Just within eyesight, the Asshurites awaited, their shadows ominously long under the morning sun. Their eyes gleamed with fervor, their bodies adorned with the spoils of past conquests, their spirits fueled by a thirst for power.

Taiwo raised his spear high, the golden tip gleaming in the light. The air rippled with tension as the first war cry tore through it.

The battle raged. The clash of bronze began, followed soon by the cries of the falling and the triumphant roars of the still-standing. After terrible bloodshed, Taiwo and his brave warriors remained.

Together, the allied forces of Kush and Yehudit repelled the Asshurites' invasion. The desert sands bore the scars of the violent struggle. As the sun set, Taiwo stood amid his men, their bodies battered but spirits unbroken.

Taiwo returned to his throne in Nubia. Yet before the wounds of the war with the Asshurites could fully heal, Taiwo found his royal duties interrupted once again by the arrival of an outsider seeking his aid. This time, the plea came from the city of Troy to the northeast.

The visitor, a man weathered by age and hardship, revealed himself to be none other than Prince Murat. He had journeyed to seek the assistance of the legendary warrior king, Taiwo. His kingdom was under siege by the Hellenes, from the lands of Hellas.

Initially, Taiwo dismissed the old prince's plea. The affairs of the northern kingdoms held little relevance to him. However, Prince Murat persisted, revealing that Troy was the last independent kingdom to the north that remained under the rule of the Orishas.

Taiwo's interest was piqued, but it was not enough to convince him to risk the lives of his still-recovering troops. Prince Murat had one more hand to play. Speaking softly, he confessed that he was the mortal whose seed had given life to Taiwo. For they were both descendants of the great warrior Oah.

"If we fall, there will be no allies in the north. The Orishas will be confined to only the land of Orirun," warned the desperate older man.

Taiwo, taken aback by the sudden revelation, was sent into deep contemplation. Bound by the unbreakable ties of kinship and honor, he made a decision that would alter the course of history. Rallying himself, Taiwo then rallied his warriors, their spirits ignited by the prospect of aiding their kinsmen. They set sail for the troubled shores of Troy.

Upon their arrival, the city swung open its gates, welcoming Taiwo with warmth and respect. The king, Taiwo's own uncle, greeted him with pride, and boasted of his nephew's divine lineage. Offspring of the Orishas were famed for their might, and Taiwo was no exception.

As Taiwo sought to understand the conflict between Troy and Hellas, the king shared the reality of their plight. The Hellenes, with their enormous army and impressive ingenuity, were steadily advancing. They aimed to dominate all trade routes along the northern shores, blocking Troy's own trade in an attempt to starve its people into submission.

Despite the dire challenge, the feast to welcome Taiwo and his generals was joyful. Warriors shared tales of past victories, and Taiwo, immersed in family, felt a sense of belonging he had not known before.

Retiring for the night, he was filled with anticipation for the decisive battle against the Hellenes, as well as a newfound eagerness to unearth more about his own lineage.

As dawn broke, the battle with the Hellenes beckoned. Taiwo, despite his bravery, was unsettled by an unfamiliar foreboding. He led his men into the fray. The armies clashed in a brutal dance of death drawn out under the blazing sun.

The forces of Troy, now under Taiwo's leadership, held their ground fiercely. Taiwo himself engaged the enemy's general, their swords clashing with a ferocity that thundered across the battlefield. Taiwo drew first blood, and it appeared victory would be his.

However, fate had a cruel twist in store. After a swift, unexpected move, the Hellenic general's blade found its way to Taiwo's chest, a grievous wound that brought him to the edge of death. A smirk played on the general's face.

Even as his strength waned, Taiwo summoned the very last of his ashé. He struck at the general's heel, causing him to stumble. With his final burst of energy, Taiwo dragged his blade across the general's neck. As Taiwo's life force ebbed away, so did his foe's.

Taiwo released his final breath, and a profound stillness fell over his remaining troops and the warriors of Troy. In that moment the warriors who still stood knew their fate and that of the city, but they swore to fight on, to the death.

News of the fall of Troy and of the great Taiwo's death spread like a raging inferno. Sensing an opportunity, the defeated Asshurites seized the moment and sprang into action. They advanced with the ferocity of a storm, cutting a swath through Yehudit, piercing the land of Orirun, and ultimately wresting control of the Kushite Empire.

The Asshurites' belief in a single deity found fertile ground in this new land, permeating every corner of the empire and converting many of its people. The Orishas felt their ashé diminish.

With their names scarcely whispered, the Orishas retreated from the east. Yet, they maintained influence in the lands of western Orirun, which were untouched by the encroaching foreign realms. In these kingdoms, their ashé still held power, and their names were spoken with reverence.

CHAPTER 17

Khende

The second-born of the twins.

In the shadowed realm of the abikus, Ile Omije, where the souls of the unborn and prematurely departed dwelled, Taiwo's soul found itself trapped. This mysterious place, suspended between mortal life and death, was a space of confusion and transience, constantly rotating, propelled by the severed threads of Oris. The Orishas, embodying order and balance, dared not enter Ile Omije without risking their very ashé amid its unpredictable tides.

Among the Orishas, only Oshun knew the plight of Taiwo's soul. Bound within the realm of the abikus, he was unable to ascend. This was no happenstance; Oshun had orchestrated his entrapment to prevent Iku, the lady of death, from claiming Taiwo before he could unite with his brother Khende.

Oshun's plan was meticulous. Upon Taiwo's fall on the battlefield in Troy, the Orisha swiftly carved a piece of sacred wood in his likeness, deceiving the abiku into believing Taiwo still walked among the living. She then threaded the carved wood onto a string spun from mystical fibers, creating a talisman for Khende. When the fated hour of Khende's departure arrived, the abiku would return to its realm, automatically expelling Taiwo and allowing the shared soul of the twins—the ibeji—to reunite so they could ascend together.

In the Orun, where time lay stagnant, Khende was still an innocent baby. Oshun knew the moment had come to release Khende into the mortal realm, so that he could don his Earthly form and fulfill his fate.

As she prepared Khende for his descent, Oshun gently tied the likeness of Taiwo around his neck. "As long as this talisman graces your skin, as long as you feel its embrace," she whispered, her voice a balm against the uncertainty that lay ahead, "you will never be apart. In life and in death, it will guide your soul back to your brother's, and together you shall ascend, leaving the mortal realm to take your place among the Orishas."

The baby Khende descended into the mortal realm, unknowingly bearing the shared fate that bound him to his twin.

He was placed in the northern reaches of Orirun, beyond the great Oke Mountains. The imposing peaks served as both a physical and spiritual barrier between the realms. The mortal realm had fallen into chaos, fueled by the the Romeyetu Empire's expansionary wars. The empire had emerged from the remnants of fractured city-states in the north lands, and extended its rule over north Orirun.

Khende grew up amid this conflict, his youth shaped by ever-present violence. At the age of ten, tragedy struck as Romeyetu soldiers ravaged his adopted family's land, seizing their territory and claiming lives in their quest for supremacy. Captured, Khende was delivered into the hands of a Romeyetu general infamous for his ruthless indoctrination of the young into the ranks of his army.

Lacking any beliefs beyond his own desires, the general forbade the worship of the Orishas, seeking instead to shape Khende's faith toward the Romeyetu gods.

At first, Khende was defiant, resisting the imposition of the Romeyetu gods, and suffered harsh punishments, including the withholding of food. Yet Khende discovered a sanctuary in silence, earning himself the name the Quiet One. He never forsook the Orishas, nor did he accept the foreign gods. He found, in his silence, that he was punished less and able to observe more.

Upon reaching manhood, Khende was thrust into battle against his own people, taking up arms for the Romeyetu Empire. Despite the deep pain this caused him, he remained silent, swallowing his anguish and transforming it into a quiet anthem of endurance.

During one fateful encounter, he faced a warrior from his homeland. Desperately, Khende tried to convey that he meant no harm, but the Romeyetu armor he wore was a symbol of danger to the warrior. The man attacked, and with no other path before him, Khende defended himself, and for the first time took a life. This act of necessity burdened his soul, and set in motion his fate.

Khende continued to suppress his anger, waiting for the opportune moment when he could break free. For years, Khende followed orders with precision and detachment, earning the trust of the aging general, who now saw him as a potential successor. The empire needed more trusted leaders from the lands it was conquering, and the general offered Khende an opportunity to marry into the Romeyetu elite and fully commit to their rule. While the general viewed this marriage as a promotion, Khende perceived it as a sentence of eternal imprisonment and servitude.

Khende agreed, in order to get the general to let down his guard. Then he finally unleashed the rage within. His wrath, as sudden and fierce as the edge of a storm, encased the general, leaving the man clinging to life. Knowing that his sentence for this act would be death, Khende sought refuge aboard a merchant vessel, slipping away into the night toward the frigid north lands.

In the crisp autumn air that nipped at his cheeks, Khende found himself guided by destiny toward the homeland of the Romeyetu and their emperor, Lauis. The monarch, unrivaled in his mastery of the northern trading routes, was an ambitious man whose dreams were as vast and uncharted as the sea he yearned to command.

Over his years spent observing others, Khende honed a keen ability to spot the subtle frailties within the hearts of other humans, even the powerful. This gift became his compass in navigating ambition and desire, and allowed him to secure an audience with the emperor himself.

In Khende, Lauis recognized a kindred spirit. He saw in Khende's eyes a spark of relentless ambition that mirrored his own, a flame kindled by visions of conquest and glory. A bond, immediate and unbreakable as Ogun's iron, was formed between them.

Within Lauis's imperial court, not everyone welcomed Khende. Leo, a mortal rumored to be the son of a Romeyetu god and the adopted heir of the emperor, saw Khende as a storm cloud on his otherwise clear horizon, and started plotting his elimination. Yet Khende swiftly rose through the ranks, a testament to his cunning, strategic acumen, and his skill for manipulation.

He soon became the empire's military commander, his prowess outshining even that of Leo. Whispers began to circulate within the court suggesting Khende was not merely a trusted adviser, but a potential successor to the throne.

Indeed, the emperor, who lacked a biological heir, found himself noticing the contrast between Leo's impetuous nature and Khende's reserved, strategic demeanor. The Quiet One wielded his mind like a blade, his strategies against the emperor's enemies, including his own people, successful at every turn.

As Khende proved himself with each trial, the Yehudit people, in the eastern lands, rebelled against the Romeyetu, aiming to reestablish their autonomy and preserve their own spiritual kingdom in Orun. Khende heeded the emperor's command to put down the revolt. On the battlefield, his strategies unfolded with brutal efficiency; his moves were calculated and decisive. He suppressed the rebellion and reasserted Romeyetu control.

The land of the Yehudit lay in ruins. Countless souls had been snuffed out. Amid the devastation, Khende emerged as a figure not only of prowess but of power, eclipsing Leo. His triumph served to further cement his standing in the emperor's court, and to secure his position as successor to the throne.

Soon after Khende's victory against the Yehudit, the emperor fell ill. In the last twilight of his life, he summoned Khende, revealing the revised royal decrees that named him the rightful heir. Khende was torn between gratitude and grief.

Upon the emperor's death, Khende sailed to Orirun under the pretense of scouting new trade routes, but in fact to betray his empire and unify the lands of his true people. Leo, his suspicions aroused, decided to accompany him.

After years in the north land, Khende's eyes beheld his homeland's skyline, a cluster of majestic mountains on the far horizon. Leo noticed him clutching the curious talisman that hung from his neck and thought to casually ask about the unusual wooden figure; Leo inquired more out of boredom than genuine interest. Despite their tumultuous relationship, the journey had been marked by a rare peace that Khende found oddly soothing. Speaking freely for the first time in a long while, Khende, emperor of Romeyetu, explained, "It was bestowed upon me at birth by my mother, a sacred tether to anchor my spirit in my faith." His eyes remained fixed on the horizon, as if directly speaking to his homeland, unaware of the shift in Leo's expression—a spark of curiosity.

Leo ventured into Khende's private cabin. There, among the new emperor's personal effects, he discovered a parchment detailing plans for the reunification of Nubia and the dissolution of the Romeyetu religious order.

Reading the words ignited a flame of rage within Leo. His vision blurred, then filled with the crimson hue of fury. With the damning document clutched tightly in his hand, he stormed toward the main deck, his mind swirling with thoughts of confrontation.

As he approached Khende, his intentions took a darker turn. His hand reached for the hilt of his sword. He drew the blade and with a grunt embedded it into Khende's back. As Khende whipped around in surprise, Leo grabbed his talisman, ripping it from his neck as Khende fell into the sea. Observing the fascinating object, Leo let the parchment drift down to the ocean as well. He then told the shocked crew, now under his command, to turn the ship around.

As blood and water filled his lungs, Khende felt the tug of his soul departing his body without his sacred talisman. In profound grief, Oshun materialized on the ship before Leo, who in his terror dropped the talisman. As she retrieved it, her sorrow turned to wrath. "Leo, by taking the life of my son, you have invoked my fury. Before the Council of Orishas I shall exact my vengeance. I bestow upon you every spirit of misfortune all at once; you shall unleash them upon your entire lineage. You will endure my suffering and be forever denied the warmth of love."

Oshun plunged into the sea to retrieve the lifeless form of Khende. Once back in Edin, she quickly set about crafting a new talisman, now in his likeness.

As she worked, Eshu, the Orisha of crossroads and the only one daring enough to enter the abiku realm, appeared in front of her, having witnessed Oshun's cunning efforts to save the soul of her ibeji. He came bearing news. Eshu revealed that during Taiwo's time in the realm of Ile Omije, he had requested that, once joined with Khende and crowned an Orisha, they remain in that in-between place. For they were drawn to rule the realm of the abikus, as compassionate guides. They aimed to bring balance to the restless spirits, offering solace and helping them reincarnate with purpose. They hoped to transform Ile Omiji into a sanctuary of hope and renewal.

When she heard Eshu's revelation, Oshun's eyes widened with a blend of surprise and understanding. She paused, absorbing the weight of her ibeji's destiny. She said to Eshu, "Their path is one of compassion. I trust in their choices to bring joy to the realm of Ile Omije. May their light guide the lost spirits and renew the weary."

As she placed the two talismans side by side, a wonderous event unfolded. They shimmered and pulsed with divine energy, and in a burst of radiance they transformed into two small children made of pure light—her ibeji, reborn as Orishas, destined never to leave each other's side.

CHAPTER 18

The Princess of Wågådu

He who rides the horse of greed
will arrive at the destination of shame.

—African proverb

In the westernmost reaches of Orirun, where Olokun's ocean hugged the shore, once stood the empire of Wågådu. Guarded by the Council of Orishas, Wågådu boasted unparalleled wealth. It was also the largest empire in the land, the epitome of opulence and grandeur. It shone like a jewel upon Orirun's crown, its magnificence eliciting awe in the farthest corners of Onile.

The buildings in the imperial capital were crafted from sun-kissed sandstone etched with intricate reliefs that told the stories of the Orishas and was adorned with gold leaf that shimmered in the sunlight. The streets were paved with smooth stones from nearby riverbeds and lined with statues of the Orishas cast in bronze.

The natural bounty of the empire added another layer to its allure. Lush savannas with baobabs and acacias surrounded the capital, while the air was filled with the calls of birds and the rustling of wildlife. In every direction, one saw a landscape of breathtaking vitality.

The people of Wågådu were themselves a sight to behold, their clothing a measure of the empire's prosperity. They draped themselves in robes woven from threads of silk and gold, garments that flowed like rivers of color. Headdresses, intricately adorned with precious gems and metals, crowned their heads, while their necks, wrists, and ankles were weighed down with jewelry of exquisite craftsmanship—necklaces of coral, bracelets of jade, and rings set with diamonds as large as a tarsier's eye.

Wågådu's wealth was built on control of the golden serpent Bida's western pathways. These routes carried caravans laden with salt, kola, gold, Erinle's ivory, and luxurious cloth. In the capital, amid bustling stalls, foreign merchants engaged in the exchange of not only gold and silver but art, knowledge of other lands, and the tales of the Esin Imale, reflecting the empire's extensive reach and influence.

Yet beneath this material splendor lay a deep secret. It was said that Wågådu's prosperity was due to its control of the captured and imprisoned Bida.

Hundreds of years earlier, at the dawn of the empire, a fierce rivalry ignited between twin brothers Ogiso Kumbi and Ogiso Basi. The brothers, born of one soul, vied for supremacy of the nascent capital, despite their father's decree that they should rule together. What began as a true partnership soon became riddled with disagreement, as Basi, captivated by the Esin Imale, joined their spiritual kingdom. The capital became divided.

In an age when gold overshadowed moral virtue, Kumbi sought to secure his dominance—and the Orishas' spiritual influence—over his brother through a daring pact with the legendary serpent Bida. She had been chained by the Orishas and dragged into Olokun's ocean, confined within a littoral cave hidden beneath Wågådu's rugged cliffs.

In a bid for riches, Kumbi made an audacious offer to Bida: he wanted endless gold for his kingdom, and in return he would give her whatever she desired. Bound yet still powerful, Bida bestowed upon him a miraculous bounty, overflowing the kingdom's pots, as though a golden river flowed throughout the kingdom. The precious metal wove itself into daily life, sparkling in the hair, adorning garments, and lining the streets and homes, of the people.

However, Bida's grant came at a steep price. She demanded an ebo, a regular sacrifice from the bloodlines of the twins. Every seven years, the selection of royal heirs for sacrifice was determined through a lottery encompassing all the kingdoms under the empire's sway. Initially, the designation of heirs for sacrifice was met with terror and pleas for mercy, as infants and young children were put forward.

However, as time passed, the perception of the ebo shifted dramatically. What was once viewed with dread became a source of immense pride. Royal families whose heirs were chosen came to see it as an esteemed honor, a sacred duty that ensured the continued prosperity and splendor of their empire.

The capital city was still divided physically and spiritually. On one side resided Ogiso Saleh, descendant of Basi, who, like his ancestor, followed the Esin Imale. This land was distinguished by its twelve temples and wells brimming with sweet water, nurturing not only the people but also the lush vegetable gardens in their care.

A forested expanse separated Saleh's center of power from the other main section of the capital, where extravagant temples honored the Orishas. Ogiso Adzo, descendant of Kumbi, and her consort, Bediako, enjoyed the privilege of wearing jacquard garments, while the rest of their followers adorned themselves in robes made from cotton, silk, or brocade, depending on their status. A peculiar cultural practice was observed in personal grooming: men shaved their beards, while women shaved their heads, adding to the distinct social fabric of Adzo's side of the capital.

As the next seven-year ebo approached, Ogiso Adzo and Bediako invited all the nobility and heirs from every corner of the empire to attend the grand celebration. On the day of the event, the empire's leading lights sat in audience in a grand domed pavilion around which stood ten horses covered with gold-embroidered materials. Behind the Ogiso were ten personal attendants holding shields and swords infused with gold, and on her right were the sons of the subordinate chieftains of her land wearing splendid garments, their hair plaited with gold.

Beneath the sense of anticipation swept a wave of controversy and speculation. Whispers of distrust passed between spectators, fueled by the persistent rumor that the ebo ceremony was marred by corruption. It was a glaring fact that the capital itself had curiously evaded the ebo tribute for many cycles now, an unlikely trend.

The suspicions remained unaddressed, simmering quietly among the populace, until Orisha Eshu decided to lend his aid. He summoned Oshosi, the Orisha of justice, and explained what he had seen. "Ogiso Adzo and Bediako's greed is as insatiable as the ocean's depths. They are using Bida to amass treasures that fuel their arrogance at the expense of their people."

Oshosi rushed to the capital and strode right up to the Ogiso and her consort. Without kneeling to honor them, he recited their punishments: "Ogiso Adzo, consort Bediako," he intoned, with grave authority, "you have woven a chain of laws that bring gold to your lineage that you do not truly own. Yet, you yourselves remain untouched by these chains. Your hearts and minds have been poisoned by the dark osogbo of greed. To cleanse your soul and free you from its clutches, only one sacrifice must be made today . . . "

Everyone in the grand hall grew still as Oshosi continued. "You must offer your own daughter to Bida, for she is the true lineage of the pact you made for power," he declared, his words cutting through the silence. The Ogiso and her consort recoiled, paling at the thought of losing their only child and heir, Abronoma.

"Should you choose not to," Oshosi continued, his gaze unwavering, "we shall bind Bida's mouths shut. The flow of gold will cease, and your land will wither, bringing an end to your reign."

With those final words, Oshosi faded into the shadows, leaving Ogiso Adzo and Bediako to contemplate the consequences of their greed. Soon enough, as the celebrants were dismissed, Adzo approached her daughter in preparation for the sacrifice. The Ogiso had concocted a golden milk laced with numbing toxin.

Abronoma found herself caught in a situation for which she was utterly unprepared, unlike the other noble heirs. She had grown up with secret assurances that she would never be among those sacrificed, and she was set to marry Prince Kofi, whom she had loved since childhood. Now her mother was promising her that drinking the milk would render the process painless and that her sacrifice was essential for the salvation of their empire. Fear gripped Abronoma, and she vehemently refused to meet her fate. She was unwilling to be consumed by Bida. Bediako summoned the guards to restrain her while Adzo administered the milk forcefully, ensuring the sacrifice would proceed.

The carriage ride to the sacrificial cliff, although short, seemed like an eternity to Abronoma. The rhythmic thudding of the waves against the cliff's walls added to her terror. The guards, silent figures of doom, led her toward the sea-beaten outcropping, their faces impassive as they chained her to a giant rock at the cliff's edge.

As the guards retreated to safety, leaving her alone, the realization of her fate crashed upon her. Despite the toxin dulling her senses, fear surged within her.

Prince Kofi had followed the carriage on horseback, watching from afar as Abronoma was chained to the rock. Though he knew there was no other way, he couldn't accept that his only love would be sacrificed. His parents had quickly chosen another bride for him and insisted that his betrothed's sacrifice was a necessity. Yet the desperate cries of Abronoma now pierced the air, stirring within Kofi a determination to save her from her cruel fate.

The guards attempted to stop Kofi, adamant that he should not interfere with the will of the Orishas, their voices low with authority.

Kofi reached behind him and drew his sword. He had never actually used it until this very moment. He charged around the guards toward Abronoma; when he reached her, she was foggy from the toxin but managed to muster a faint smile upon seeing Kofi. He struggled against the stubborn chains that imprisoned her. Suddenly the ground shook violently as Bida emerged from her watery lair, revealing herself in all her terrifying glory. The sight of her seven grand heads froze Kofi in terror, his solid stance momentarily shaken by the monstrous presence before him.

Kofi, regaining his composure even as his hands trembled, managed to slice through the chains, freeing Abronoma. In his fervor, he lost his grip on the sword, and it clattered to the bottom of the cliff. As he attempted to find his footing, Kofi slipped, and both he and Abronoma tumbled down, landing on the beach below.

Bida loomed over them, her massive jaws opening wide, aiming to devour the defenseless Abronoma. Reacting swiftly, Kofi retrieved his sword and, with a powerful swing, severed one of Bida's heads. The creature shrieked in agony, lunging at him with fury. Agile and determined, Kofi dodged her attacks, skillfully severing five more of her heads in quick succession.

In a desperate move, Bida whipped her tail around, striking Kofi and sending his sword flying; it landed near Abronoma, who was slowing regaining consciousness. Just as Bida was about to consume Kofi, Abronoma seized the sword, charged, and cleaved off Bida's final head, killing the great serpent.

The aftermath of the battle lay before Kofi and Abronoma, pools of blood and viscera painting the shoreline in crimson. As they each took a deep breath of the salt and sea breeze, they wrapped their arms around each other, a fragile balm against the chaos surrounding them. Suddenly a movement stirred within the belly of the massive serpent sprawled lifeless on the sand. Kofi ushered Abronoma behind him, ready to shield her from further danger.

The movement ceased, and then, with a sudden burst, a hand emerged from within the deceased serpent's belly. It clung to the outer skin, finding its grip to pull the rest of itself free. From the remains of the serpent, a figure of supreme regality clawed her way out. It was Aje, the Orisha of wealth and trade, now liberated from her confinement. Trapped within Bida's belly, she had been powerless to stop her ashé of wealth from being abused.

Approaching Kofi and Abronoma, Aje expressed her gratitude. "Your deeds have not gone unnoticed. You have chosen the heart's truth over the lure of riches, and in doing so, you have freed me. For this, I am eternally grateful. Allow me to bestow upon you my gratitude."

Met with their stunned nods of acceptance, Aje removed a small woven satchel from the rope tied around her waist and presented it to Abronoma. "Within lies a gift of great power. Each time you reach inside, a gold nugget shall be yours. If wielded with care and wisdom, this satchel holds the potential to manifest your deepest desires, even to forge a kingdom of your own," Aje proclaimed.

She then turned toward the ocean and disappeared into its depths, returning to her mother, Olokun.

Overwhelmed with joy and the promise of a new beginning, Kofi and Abronoma embraced, their hearts racing with the endless possibilities that lay ahead.

Yet the justice demanded by Oshosi remained unfulfilled. He took decisive action before the Council of Orishas, ordering retribution against the empire. He tasked Oko with laying waste to the crops and called upon Ogun to dismantle the walls that divided the two halves of the capital, ushering in conflict. Within a span of a mere seven years, the once-mighty Wågådu Empire crumbled under the Orishas' ire.

BOOK V

YORUBALAND

CHAPTER 19

Legacy

However far a stream flows, it doesn't forget its origin.

—Ghanaian proverb

In the ancient land of Òkè Òrà, where the Orisha Obatala reigned, a mysterious figure had emerged from the east—Oduduwa, a man who wove tales of creation and the darkness, Okunkun, that fed the Osogbos lurking within every human soul. Oduduwa united the thirteen fractious communities of Obatala's, which had fallen into conflict amid Obatala's descent into drunkenness. Oduduwa forged them into the illustrious kingdom of Ife. He chose one of the communities, Ile-Ife, as his home, and was crowned Oonie, the spiritual ruler of Yorubaland.

Under Oduduwa's reign, Ife blossomed. The people wisely shunned the perilous pathways of Bida, avoiding the call of the Esin Imale and their Da'wah, which had lured or forced many others into their spiritual kingdom. While some kingdoms faltered, seeking wealth and power through reckless raids that depleted their natural resources, and selling captured people down Bida's pathways, those that remained loyal to the Orishas found renewed strength. Aje, the Orisha of wealth and trade, now free and part of the Orisha pantheon, safeguarded these faithful lands. She established thriving trade routes among kingdoms still within the Orishas' Garden.

Oduduwa, with foresight and care, prepared both his son and his daughter to carry on his legacy.

Oranmiyan—the sole son of Oduduwa's wife, Lakange, and the Orisha

Ogun, the god of iron and war—was a towering figure even in his youth, his physique a mirror image of his Orisha father's. Oduduwa raised him as his own, and Oranmiyan's true origins were kept secret, in the hopes that his fiery spirit could be tempered and his blood cooled by Oduduwa's firm teachings of love and respect.

For beneath Oranmiyan's strength and beauty lay a restless Osogbo—a swirling vortex of high aspirations and unyielding desires. Oranmiyan's heart pounded with the impatience of youth in search of independence; it throbbed with a hunger for power. He envisioned expanding Yorubaland into a great empire, with his own legacy surpassing even his father's demanding expectations.

Okanbi had the kind heart of her father, Oduduwa. She was steeped in honor, a quality she wore like a second skin. She loved with the ferocity of a lion, a trait she received from her mother, Lakange. Her love was as strong as her resilience, a calm nurturing flame that burned brightly amid the cold winds of trial and tribulation.

In the years following the passing of Lakange, Oduduwa finally found peace. He continued his teachings beyond the borders of Ife, reaching into the southern kingdom of Ijebu-Ode. There, he formed a strategic alliance by marrying a royal woman of the kingdom, and together they had a son, Ogborogan, solidifying his influence and reign. Oduduwa felt a deep sense of accomplishment, realizing that kingship could be secured not only through might and conquest, as favored by Ogun, but also through diplomacy and alliances.

Yet one night, the peace in Yorubaland was abruptly shattered by the thunderous arrival of an invading army of the Esin Imale and their Da'wah. They sought to dismantle Oduduwa's power. Leading this dark tide was General Sahibu, a ruthless warrior tasked with eliminating the Oonie. Oduduwa's influence threatened the Esin Imale's ambitions. His vision of unity and prosperity was a stark contrast to their desire for spiritual dominance, making him a target in their never-ending quest to expand control and seize resources.

Oduduwa awoke in the middle of that fateful night, stirred by a sense of unease. His foreboding was soon proven true by the far-off beating of hooves approaching. He urgently summoned Oranmiyan and Okanbi, declaring it their sacred duty to protect their people from the threat.

The thumping of war drums filled the air and battle cries pierced the night. Oduduwa, with unwavering valor, plunged into the fray. However, in the chaos of the battle, General Sahibu's blade found its mark, dropping Oonie Oduduwa to his knees.

Witnessing his father's fall, Oranmiyan felt the fiery wrath of Ogun's blood surge through him. He charged toward the general, his movements swift and lethal, cutting down any who dared block his path. As Oranmiyan reached Sahibu, the general prepared to deliver the final blow to Oduduwa, only to be met with the unstoppable force of a son's rage. Oranmiyan confronted the general, engaging him in a fierce duel, each strike driven by vengeance. With unmatched skill, he overpowered the general, delivering a decisive blow that ended Sahibu's life.

Kneeling beside his father, Oranmiyan cradled Oduduwa as he slowly bled out. In his final moments, Oduduwa imparted a last piece of wisdom to Oranmiyan: "Lead with your heart." With those words, he passed.

Grief-stricken, Oranmiyan experienced deep sorrow that turned into a relentless drive for revenge. The remaining invaders were vanquished, and the people of Ife were victorious—a son's tribute to the father he had lost.

Oonie Oduduwa's death left a void in the kingdom of Ife, as he had been both the spiritual and political leader. The loss ignited a fierce resolve in Okanbi, who stepped into the former role, becoming the new Ìyá Nílé, the high priestess of Ife. She dedicated herself to upholding Oduduwa's teachings that had first unified the kingdom. As days turned to nights, Okanbi's commitment to her people and her devotion to spreading Oduduwa's wisdom only grew stronger.

Oranmiyan assumed the mantle of political leadership, yet felt the unfillable void left by his father's passing. Unlike his sister, who embraced her sorrow, he hardened his heart due to the pain of losing his father, which isolated him from his sister and duties as Oba. His thoughts became ensnared in the Okunkun—the darkness that beckoned the Ajogun warriors, awakening his Osogbo and casting a pallor over his Ori.

He frequently visited the sacred burial site, his father's final resting place, seeking peace among the silent stones and soil, hoping to find solace in the solitude. He would search his mind, allowing his Ori to guide him. Yet, it wasn't his Ori that ultimately led him, but the Ajogun that crafted an ambitious plan to conquer and reclaim East Kingdom in the land of Shinar, where Oduduwa's own father had once ruled.

Oranmiyan raced back to Okanbi, eager to share his plan. However, Okanbi was firmly rooted in the soil of Ife. She had discovered her purpose, and her Ori was clear, as she carried new life within her, a child from Adeniyi, a local chieftain's son. She told her brother that her purpose lay not in the pursuit of revenge, but in the promise of growth, in fostering unity and preserving their father's legacy by strengthening the kingdom.

Okanbi recognized the ferocity within Oranmiyan and knew she could never quell the rage that drove him. Despite her fears that his quest might plunge the kingdom of Ife into a cycle of violence, she respected her brother's decision. She promised to hold his place as Oba until his return, supporting his path while remaining steadfast in her own mission.

CHAPTER 20

Oranmiyan

If the current of the river is too strong,
one must sometimes give up fighting it.

—African proverb

Oranmiyan forged an iron sword for himself before leaving the kingdom of Ife to reclaim his grandfather's seat in East Kingdom. Accompanying him was Jaiyesimi, a young hunter as green as the first leaves of spring. Jaiyesimi was the only individual courageous enough to embark on the perilous journey across the land with Oranmiyan, who was confident he would rally other warriors along the way.

Though Jaiyesimi often stumbled and was prone to errors, his loyalty to Oranmiyan was steadfast, as reliable as the rising sun that lit the roads on their expedition to the east. Together, they entered the uncharted tracts of Orirun, scaling mountains whose peaks kissed the clouds, delving into jungles of the sheer unknown, and navigating rivers that wound like serpents across the untamed landscape.

Their adventure led them to a kingdom on the edge of a red sea, a land where golden fields swayed, where rivers meandered through emerald valleys, and where citadels of marble and alabaster gleamed under the beating sun. Seeking a night's refuge, Oranmiyan and Jaiyesimi gratefully accepted lodging with a welcoming villager.

As the sun dipped below the horizon, the kingdom's bustling marketplaces fell silent, the joyous laughter of children faded, and doors were firmly bolted shut.

During Oranmiyan and Jaiyesimi's evening meal with their host, the conversation turned to the dangers of the night. The villager spoke in hushed tones, recounting tales of a sinister presence that roamed the darkness, luring unsuspecting souls from their homes with cries that mimicked those of a baby, even those of their own children. Despite the villager's earnest warnings, Oranmiyan and Jaiyesimi exchanged knowing glances, dismissing the warning as just another local folktale, only slightly different from many others they had heard on their travels.

Nightfall unveiled a kingdom draped in haunting beauty. There was tension in the air, like a string pulled taut, waiting for the slightest provocation. Even the wind seemed to pause, with leaves hanging motionless on their branches. It was this stillness that kept Oranmiyan from slipping into a deep slumber.

Jaiyesimi, for his part, had indulged in palm wine at dinner, and went on a late stroll. He now lay asleep under the open sky, blissfully unaware of what lurked in the shadows.

The night was shaken by the cry of an infant, a sound that roused Oranmiyan from his restless sleep. Inside the villager's home, the flickering candlelight cast strange shapes on the walls. Glancing at the mat on the floor, he noticed Jaiyesimi was not there at that same moment another cry echoed from outside. Through the slits in the boarded-up windows, his gaze fixed on a tall, gaunt figure, its form as dark as the night, stealthily inching toward the sleeping Jaiyesimi. It resembled a grotesquely elongated crow, a towering seven feet tall, with a beak replaced by a void that seemed as if it could devour a person's very soul.

As Oranmiyan watched, paralyzed by fear, the creature paused, its head tilting as if sensing his presence. He knew he had to act. His heart pounded, his grip tightened around his weapon, and with a silent prayer, he stepped into the night. The creature was even more terrifying up close. Its face was a mask of wrinkles, a parody of a human face. Its mouth opened to reveal an abyss.

He stood before the creature birthed from the belly of darkness itself. The night air was thick with menace, the silence broken only by Oranmiyan's inhale.

His eyes locked onto the beast, his gaze as sharp as the blade he wielded. Every muscle in his body tensed, ready for action. The monstrous creature seemed to relish the impending clash, its horrible mouth agape.

With a yell that summoned his courage, Oranmiyan lunged. His blade sliced through the air, only to be met by the creature's clawed hand. The still-sleeping Jaiyesimi woke with a start, and quickly backed away.

The struggle was a dance of death under the moonlight. Oranmiyan's every move was met with a counter from the terrifying beast. His strikes, swift and powerful, were deflected. His advances, bold and brave, were thwarted. The malevolent spirit seemed to anticipate his every move, its slender form moving with inhuman grace.

The tide of the battle seemed to turn in favor of his foe. Oranmiyan's strength wavered, his breath grew labored, and sweat poured down his brow. The creature, sensing his fatigue, pressed its advantage. Its claws reached for Oranmiyan with a deadly promise.

Oranmiyan drew upon the last drop of bravery within him. His eyes blazed with determination and his hands tightened around his sword's hilt.

He called upon all his might and pushed the spirit back. With a decisive stroke, Oranmiyan severed the creature's head. As its body crumbled to dust, the kingdom seemed to breathe a sigh of relief.

When dawn broke, Oranmiyan stood victorious, his heart pounding with relief. He was celebrated by the people of the kingdom for killing the malevolent spirit that had haunted their nights for years.

Queen Adebisi, the regent of the kingdom, was known for her fortitude and cunning; her reign was just. She shared a special bond with Princess Moremi, her youngest daughter. When Oranmiyan was brought before the queen, Moremi was overcome by a feeling she had never felt before, one of deep intrigue.

The exchange between Queen Adebisi and Oranmiyan flowed effortlessly. The queen, impressed by Oranmiyan's courage in confronting the creature none had dared to, offered him a reward. Gold, salt, silk—the treasures were brought in and laid at his feet for the taking. Jaiyesimi stood just behind Oranmiyan, a look of awe on his face. Oranmiyan was tempted by gold, which would allow him to hire an army for his quest to East Kingdom, but his gaze was irresistibly drawn to the beautiful Princess Moremi. Their eyes had danced in silent conversation, a secret shared through smiles and knowing glances. In her eyes, he saw a flame that mirrored his own, a desire for more.

Princess Moremi's eyes widened, her breath caught in surprise, as Oranmiyan refused the treasures before him, asking instead for her hand in marriage. The queen, amused, teased him: "You are not a king, nor do you have a kingdom. I suggest you have your pick from what I've offered and continue forth."

Oranmiyan paused. He could easily reveal to her he did, in fact, have a kingdom, but he felt guilt for leaving his homeland on a fruitless mission. At that very moment, he understood that his true quest was not for revenge, but self-discovery. The queen's words resonated deeply; though he bore the title of king, he had not truly led his people. He had abandoned them.

In the queen he saw echoes of his own mother, evoking a desire within him to earn her esteem. Opting to keep his identity secret, he embraced this revelation: "Queen, your perception of kingship is tethered to Aiye. A true king doesn't just rule over land, but is a leader of hearts and minds. Possession of land is transient, susceptible to the ravages of war and the erosion of time. Yet influence, respect, and loyalty remain the true jewels in a king's crown."

Queen Adebisi smirked at the challenge, and countered, "Despite your words, the fact remains. Where is your proof? Has Ogun offered you a kingship? Where is your gold? Where is your land? You are a dreamer, boy. Wealth and ownership of land are the sources of true power."

With great eloquence, Oranmiyan replied, "I will prove my worth to you." He said this while locking eyes with Moremi, before shifting his gaze back to the queen. "Grant me one year—that is all I ask. I shall become a king whose name and legacy will stand the test of time," he declared, his voice filled with sincerity. "One who will treat his people with kindness, rule with justice, and lead with the heart. Then shall I return for your daughter, and she will decide if she wishes to marry me."

In his bid to sway the queen, the shadow of his Osogbo lifted, unveiling the luminous path ordained by his Ori. He was destined to return to the Ife kingdom, where his rule awaited.

Queen Adebisi's gaze softened, her stern demeanor melting into contemplation. She felt Oranmiyan was a rare spirit, and in her fairness, she granted his request, albeit with the intuition that their paths might not cross again.

CHAPTER 21

Ayaba Moremi

Peace is costly, but it is worth the expense.

—African proverb

Princess Moremi bore the spirit of her ancestral lineage, one tracing back to the great queens of Nubia who had braved every peril to shield their people from foreign invaders. She was bestowed with a unique gift, a legacy of her foremothers—the ability to tame the kings of the wilderness, the lions. This extraordinary talent was, in fact, a sacred rite of passage for the queens of her land, a badge of their power and courage. Yet Moremi, unlike her sisters, who wore the mantle of warrior queens, found herself drawn instead toward astrology, literature from foreign lands, and art.

Her mother, Ayaba Adebisi, was a matriarch with many husbands, but Moremi yearned for a different path. She sought but one companion, a partner with whom she could exchange wisdom, cultivate understanding, and bloom together.

Moremi waited patiently for Oranmiyan to return. And as if answering her silent prayer, he appeared a year after his departure, now with the title of Oba, a mantle he had earned.

After their joyful wedding celebration in Adebisi's kingdom, Oranmiyan swept Moremi away to Ife. His sister, Okanbi, was waiting to greet them; she had managed the kingdom for her brother during his absence. Ife, though still a young kingdom, had great potential; its soil was rich and fertile, promising bountiful harvests.

As the Ayaba, or queen, of Ife, Moremi blossomed into adulthood. She was soon with child, her and Oranmiyan's love manifesting as a life within her. Everything seemed to fall into place, their existence idyllic.

One day, as she made her way down the forested path toward the river to bathe, Moremi was caught by a peculiar sight. There, amid the familiar greenery, stood a tree she had never seen before, and was unlike any other Moremi had encountered. Its roots sprawled above the soil, entwined, reaching out like a spider's web. The tree seemed to beckon her closer.

The women who were accompanying her called out as she ventured toward the tree. Moremi was entranced. Suddenly a wave of disorientation washed over her. Her world spun, and before she could comprehend what was happening, darkness claimed her.

When she awakened within the comforting cradle of Oranmiyan's arms, an unspeakable reality dawned on Moremi. The life that had been budding within her had been cruelly snuffed out, lost to the unforgiving whim of miscarriage.

Driven by a desperate need to understand, she sought to show Oranmiyan the peculiar tree that had captured her attention. Yet the landscape frustrated her memory, the strange tree having vanished as if it were but a figment of her mind.

In desperate need for answers, Moremi went to the women who had been with her, but their faces reflected confusion and concern. None had seen the tree she described, their ignorance only serving to deepen the mystery.

Disheartened yet far from defeated, Moremi made a solemn vow. She would gather her strength, channel her courage, and try once more to bring life and an heir into their kingdom.

Two years slipped through her fingers, bringing with them a bitter harvest of loss. Moremi's second and third attempts, also extinguished too soon, transformed her desire for motherhood into an unyielding determination.

A battle raged within her, and she knew, as only those who have faced their demons can, that such battles seldom result in victory. Instead, they carve deep scars of loss upon the soul. Yet she wore her wounds with grace, masking her internal turmoil under the veneer of daily routine.

She devoted her days to helping Okanbi with the people of their small kingdom, many of whom were refugees from raids by the Esin Imale. Her thwarted maternal instincts found an outlet in her subjects. She projected her nurturing spirit onto them, becoming a mother to her people. Her love, once reserved for her husband and her unborn children, now flowed freely, enveloping her kingdom in a comforting embrace.

Yet one day, Moremi witnessed a birth in the kingdom. A young woman, radiant in her labor, brought forth a new life. This sight, while beautiful, stoked embers of longing within Moremi, fanning them into a desperate blaze.

Holding back the envy flooding through her, she sought solace in her sanctuary—the place where once stood the phantom tree. There, she sat in silent contemplation, suffocating on the question: *Why?* Within the shroud of her solitude, a faint giggle could be discerned. It seemed to play hide-and-seek with her senses, appearing first on her right, then teasing her from the left. The laughter was accompanied by rustling leaves and snapping twigs.

She called out, demanding the hidden watchers show themselves. Obeying her command, two small figures emerged from behind nearby trees, their identical silhouettes glowing in the dappled sunlight. They were two young children, as pure as the sun's own light. Their alabaster skin mirrored the luminous beauty of a full moon. Their hair was clustered and woven like strands of the gold so coveted by kings.

Rising, Moremi strained to get a better look at the children. But, as if spooked by her movement, they darted off into the dense undergrowth. She pursued them.

Her chase led her deeper and deeper into the woods, until she came upon another river, one she had not known existed. As she reached its bank, she found herself alone; the children had disappeared as mysteriously as they had appeared.

Gazing at the tranquil river, Moremi noticed a subtle ripple on its surface that soon revealed a river spirit as ancient as the waters she emerged from. The spirit's eyes, deep pools of black, met Moremi's bewildered stare.

"What draws you here?" the spirit asked, her voice a melody of caution and allure.

Caught off guard, Moremi stammered her response. "I followed the children . . . I thought they might be lost."

The river spirit questioned, "Lost? No, they are never lost, nor are they children . . . They are the ibeji, and their home is wherever they stand."

Moremi knew of the Orisha ibeji, the children of the Orisha Oshun. She now suspected they had led her into the realm of the abikus, Ile Omije, where they were said to rule. Under her breath, she murmured, "They brought me to you," as she comprehended. Reeling, she apologized, "I'm sorry, I only wanted to help. I truly believed they were lost."

The spirit corrected her: "You summoned them, Moremi, and they answered your call." She then probed, "Perhaps it is their joy, their presence, you seek?"

Overwhelmed, Moremi felt her confusion turn to sorrow. She began to withdraw, but the spirit's words stopped her. "You seek a child, do you not? Your child?"

The questions touched Moremi's deepest yearning. She turned back, tears brimming in her eyes.

"Yes," she said, her voice breaking, "I lost my babies." As she voiced her grief, her tears traced a sorrowful path down her cheeks.

The river spirit beckoned Moremi into the water. With each cautious step, she waded farther into the strangely warm river, her heart throbbing. Submerged to her waist, she paused, her eyes fixed on the spirit before her.

"Who are you?" Moremi asked, her voice barely a whisper.

"I am Esmerian," the other replied, her voice as soothing as the river's gentle flow. "I dwell within these waters, made up of the tears shed for all the lost children claimed by the abiku."

As Esmerian spoke, she revealed the haunting truth. An abiku spirit, one of those fleeting forces of the Ile Omiji realm, had claimed Moremi's unborn children. Years earlier, it had masqueraded as a tree with sprawling roots, luring Moremi in until it could attach itself onto her first unborn child's soul.

But Esmerian offered a glimmer of hope. She explained that although the abiku would never leave Moremi's unborn children untouched, Esmerian could bind the abiku to Earth, allowing a child of Moremi's to live and grow into an adult. But to achieve this would require a great sacrifice, an ebo—a life for a life—to maintain the balance of existence.

Moremi was aware that in seeking guidance from Oranmiyan, she would be met with disbelief. Thus, when she returned to the palace, she went to Oonie Okanbi. Upon hearing Moremi's intention, Okanbi's reaction was immediate: her eyes widened, and her body tensed; she knew exactly who Esmerian was. "Moremi, you're contemplating a pact with a spirit devoid of compassion—one that only appears to maintain a strict balance in its dealings."

Moremi, undeterred, saw fairness in the proposition. "It sounds just," she reasoned.

Okanbi, striving for patience, explained, "On the surface, yes, it appears just. But consider the nature of the participants. You, a mortal, are focused on the current moment, unable to foresee the full scope of possible consequences. Esmerian is a spirit with the foresight to perceive outcomes far beyond our comprehension. She only commits to deals that ultimately serve her interests."

Moremi persisted, driven by deep-seated necessity. "Oonie Okanbi, we need an heir to the throne. Perhaps, together, we can outsmart her . . . I need an ebo. I beg you, Okanbi."

Swayed by Moremi's plea, Okambi made Moremi promise to never seek Esmerian again. Once Moremi agreed, Okanbi instructed her to select the purest white lamb. Before offering its blood to the river, a crucial step was required—Moremi's forehead much touch the lamb's. This intimate gesture would bestow upon the lamb the opportunity for human ascension in its next existence.

The following morning, Moremi returned to the river, a healthy white lamb in tow, its coat gleaming in the early light, as bright as the promise of a new beginning. The queen led it to the riverbank, where the water flowed with quiet force.

Pausing before the ebo, Moremi locked eyes with the lamb. She leaned forward, resting her forehead against it, sharing a moment of connection and breath. As the lamb settled into complete calm, she swiftly drew her blade across its neck. The crimson lifeblood spurted out, painting the pristine river with streaks of vibrant red. The lamb did not struggle; it simply dropped to the ground, and as its life ebbed, Esmerian's voice could be heard, though Moremi could not understand her words.

Nine moons later, Moremi cradled her newborn daughter close—her rounded features mirroring her mother's. But the joy of her birth was abruptly overshadowed by a raid that threatened to destroy Ife.

The morning air carried a strange, metallic tang of impending rain, despite the sky's cloudless blue clarity. An unsettling sense of danger gradually permeated every corner of the kingdom.

Suddenly the eerie calm was broken by an unusual drumbeat, heralding the arrival of grass-cloaked creatures. They spun through the kingdom like tornadoes, their movements a blur of chaotic energy.

Caught unprepared, Ife's soldiers struggled against the swift and ruthless invaders. Many were captured, their cries lost in the commotion. Amid the turmoil, Oranmiyan, his sword gleaming with righteous fury, fought valiantly. He tried his best to slay the swirling assailants, but every strike seemed to pass harmlessly through them.

As the drumbeats stopped, the creatures began their retreat, leaving the kingdom in disarray. Oranmiyan, its Oba, stood over the wreckage, bearing significant wounds from the battle.

Moremi had been schooled in the game of warfare by her mother, through lessons told over the fire and warnings woven into bedtime tales. Now those truths came back to her. Attacks always came in pairs: the first to weaken, the second to deliver the fatal blow. Moremi felt a second raid was imminent and would be aimed at extinguishing her and her husband's reign. She was determined to protect her kingdom.

In her desperation, she ventured into the forest once more, seeking the guidance of the river spirit, despite having promised Oonie Okanbi that she wouldn't visit Esmerian again. Her fear of losing her child overpowered any vow; she knew that only the river spirit could save her daughter, and her kingdom. Approaching Esmerian once again, she was not naive. She understood there would be a high price. "The greater the ask, the greater the ebo," Esmerian warned, her voice swirling around Moremi like a cool embrace.

Esmerian told Moremi to surrender herself to the invaders, ensuring her that she would survive captivity if she did not resist. Patience and courage would be her allies.

"That's it?" Moremi questioned, incredulous. "You want me to willingly be caught?" Esmerian assured her that in time she would find a path back home, along with the solution to defeating the uncanny raiders.

The next raid soon thundered into Ife. Oranmiyan, still weakened, could not defend the kingdom. As Moremi offered herself to the invaders, the drums instantly went silent. They seized her, bundling her away, as though she alone was their prize.

Moremi found herself caged with others from Ife. The grass creatures prodded her through the bars until a man, dripping with gold, shooed them away. He claimed to be an Oba, yet his demeanor and the painted symbols on his face resembled those of an Oso, a sorcerer. When she saw a strange talisman around his neck, marked with the signs of witchcraft, her suspicions were confirmed.

With a sly grin, the Oso ordered her release from the cage. Moremi remained calm, neither resisting nor fleeing as he traced a finger along her cheek. Intrigued by her unexpected compliance, he leaned in, pressing a testing kiss upon her lips; his breath was heavily perfumed with palm wine. Moremi's composure captivated him.

He ordered the grass creatures to sell the remaining captives, while signaling for Moremi to be taken to his palace. Inside, she was met by a harem of women, all clad in identical garments. Some faces were familiar, villagers she knew from Ife, but she gestured for them to remain silent. Thus,

Moremi accepted and conformed to her new existence as she waited to make her move.

As time wore on, Moremi immersed herself in the subtleties of the Oso's daily routine. She saw that the creatures that terrorized her kingdom were animated by the Oso's talisman, which summoned an emi buburu—an evil spirit—to give them life. Moremi also discovered that the woman chosen to spend the night with the Oso was made to drink an herbal brew, which left her susceptible to his desires and erased her memories of the encounter.

Armed with this knowledge, she formed a plan. She would turn the Oso's own tactics against him, using the tea in his palm wine to dull his awareness. Moremi prepared herself for the night when she would escape.

The moment came soon enough. When Moremi was summoned to his room, she brewed the potent tea herself and mixed it into his palm wine. She entered the Oso's chambers, carrying the brew. The Oso drank deeply from the cup she offered, his eyes never leaving her face. As the toxic liquid coursed through him, his gaze began to falter, his grip on reality loosening. Moremi watched as his consciousness drifted.

With the Oso asleep, Moremi left the palace quietly, her heart pounding as she navigated around guards and through shadows toward freedom. She knew that Esmerian's promise would lead her straight back to Ife. Although she was tired, she moved through the night without sleep, for she understood the Oso would soon wake and realize she had gone.

By dawn, she had returned to Ife, and her people greeted her with jubilant cheers, their voices singing in praise. Oranmiyan, now recovered from his wounds, felt a mix of worry and relief at her sight. Yet, beneath the surface of the collective joy, Moremi's spirit was unsettled, for she knew the Oso and his grass creatures would arrive soon to take her back. She revealed to Oranmiyan the truth behind the invaders, conjured from dry grass, animated by the talisman, and controlled through drums. Ornamiyan understood why they couldn't be defeated before—such energy could only be countered with fire. Oranmiyan rallied his soldiers.

As the sun descended, Ife braced itself. Distant drumbeats echoed through the kingdom. This time, Ife was ready. Fire arrows lit up the sky, and flaming spears were launched at the advancing horde. At first the whirlwinds the creatures whipped up around themselves snuffed out the flames, and they pressed their attack. But a single arrow, expertly aimed by Oranmiyan, hit home. It ignited one of the creatures, setting it ablaze. The resulting wildfire spread quickly, and soon all of the strange beasts were reduced to ashes.

Smoke hung in the air as Moremi led Oranmiyan toward the Oso, to confront the source of their peril. When they reached their foe's tent, which was perched atop one of the mountains surrounding Ife, Oranmiyan told Moremi to stay back.

In the dimly lit tent, the Oso awaited. Oranmiyan entered; the Oso, now broken and dulled by palm wine, glanced with eyes that held both defiance and resignation. "Oranmiyan! Son of Oduduwa," he greeted him, pouring more palm wine into a small bowl.

Oranmiyan's voice was firm as he asked, "Who are you?"

With a weary sigh, the Oso replied, "The only one who dared to challenge your father. I was once a chieftain here, under Orisha Obatala. I was pushed out by Oduduwa, when he took Òkè Òrà and renamed it Ife." His words were marinated in the bitterness of a man driven by revenge.

Oranmiyan listened intently, his expression unchanging, though deep within him there stirred understanding. He recognized the path of vengeance the Oso had walked, consumed by his own Osogbo, one Oranmiyan himself might have followed if not for Moremi's love guiding him. As the Oso's tale of resentment came to an end, Oranmiyan swung his sword down on him.

That evening, while the kingdom of Ife reveled in their victory, Moremi slipped away to the river spirit with offerings. She brought gold, food, and lambs in a cart she dragged behind her, all symbols of gratitude, while her baby daughter slumbered, strapped to her chest.

Yet Esmerian rejected them all. Her demand was Moremi's most precious treasure: her child.

Moremi pleaded with Esmerian to take her own life in place of her daughter's. But Esmerian explained: "Moremi, your Ori was never meant for motherhood; you altered it, and with it the fate of your kingdom. True strength lies in the choices you humans must make for the greater good. Those choices often demand the greatest sacrifices. A mortal's Ori always steers them back to the intended path. Sacrifice your motherhood, or Ife will fall—and who can say what fate awaits you and your child if it does?"

Weeping, Moremi unwrapped the cloth that cradled her daughter to her chest, each teardrop an ode to the love and life being torn from her grasp. Her hands, shaking, reached out to surrender her child to the water's embrace. Esmerian, with the tiny human in her arms, dissolved into the river's flow, leaving behind a void in Moremi's heart.

Word of Moremi's sacrifice crept through the kingdom when she returned without her child. Distraught, she had to tell Oranmiyan the truth.

CHAPTER 22

The Kingdom of Igodomigodo

If you are filled with pride, then you will have no room for wisdom.

—African proverb

Oranmiyan found himself enveloped in sorrow and transformed by grief. The loss of his daughter left a hole within him that seemed unfillable. It was during his intense mourning that an invitation from the kingdom of Igodomigodo arrived, offering him a needed distraction from his torment and a chance to distance himself from Moremi, whom he couldn't bear to look at. The tender love for his wife lay buried beneath layers of sadness and ambition.

Igodomigodo had once been a peaceful kingdom, but its new ruler had prompted a rebellion. The era of Ogiso Evian, who had governed with absolute power, ended as age took its toll. His son, Ogiamwen, was named his successor, and proved to be an even more ruthless Ogiso than his father, conjuring ever more ingenious instruments of torment for those he deemed traitors or thieves. It was as if pain brought peace to his restless soul, as his people languished under the yoke of starvation. Under Ogiamwen's cruel reign, the kingdom fractured, with many chieftains desperately seeking to break free from his despotic grasp.

It was those rebel chieftains who had reached out to Oranmiyan, whose fearsome reputation extended far beyond Ife. They sought to overthrow

Ogiso Ogiamwen, and asked for his aid. Accepting the challenge, Oranmiyan mustered his army and marched out of Ife. He left the kingdom in Moremi's solitary care, her once-comforting haven now a throne of isolation.

As Oranmiyan and his phalanxes neared the famed capital city of Igodomigodo, a wave of awe washed over him, stilling his steps. He established camp at the city's periphery. From there, he gazed at an architectural wonder unlike any he had encountered in his travels. The city seemed to coyly conceal itself behind towering earthen walls. It boasted a moat and a network of deep ditches with steep banks, complemented by a berm designed to thwart any invading forces. This intricate system controlled access through nine strategically placed gates. Oranmiyan had been informed by the rebel chieftains that within the walls there were still more ditches, as well as earthen ramparts.

At the center of the city sat the royal palace, which was protected by a concentric earthen embrace. Each layer was a bulwark ensuring the sanctity and security of the kingdom against any who dared challenge it.

Oranmiyan knew that brute force alone would not suffice. He devised a plan to storm the nine gates at once. He rallied his men, merging the might of his own army with those of the rebel chieftains.

As Oranmiyan prepared to breach the city, he observed one of its narrow ramparts. Atop towering barriers, guards armed with bows and spears kept vigilant watch, ready to repel any threat. Their eyes scanned the grounds where Oranmiyan and his assembled army prepared themselves for the siege.

Under the cover of darkness, Oranmiyan's warriors approached the city, each moving with the stealth of a panther. As they neared the walls, the air was charged with violence. In a quick, coordinated assault, Oranmiyan's archers sent arrows slicing through the silence to meet the city's defenders at each opening in the walls. Then his infantry, equipped with ladders and thick rope, began their perilous ascent, engaging the guards on the rampart in close combat.

The battle at the city's gates was fierce, a storm of iron shields and spears. Oranmiyan himself led the charge at one gate, cutting through the enemy ranks with ease. Mixing stealth and simple force, the combined armies surrounded the city and attacked every gate at the exact same time, infiltrating the supposedly impregnable bastion.

Oranmiyan and his forces soon breached the inner sanctum, and the clash of kings became inevitable. Ogiamwen, the tyrant, was not just a ruler but a warrior of considerable skill, like his father before him. He was feared. The two warrior-kings met in the courtyard situated in the very center of the concentric earthen walls, their swords an extension of their wills, each strike displaying mastery.

The duel was an encounter between equals. What set each combatant apart was not skill alone but the conviction behind each blow. Oranmiyan fought not for conquest but for liberation, his blade driven by the desire to free Igodomigodo from the clutches of tyranny. This resolve imbued him with a strength that transcended physical might.

In the end, the Ife king was victorious. Ogiamwen fell, his reign of terror ended. The chains that had bound Igodomigodo were shattered, its citizens freed from the despot.

The people of Igodomigodo, brimming with gratitude, eagerly approached Oranmiyan to crown him as their inaugural Oba of a new age. Yet, the kingdom's elders balked at this proposition. Oranmiyan, though a revered liberator, did not share their language, nor was he versed in the intricate customs or rich history that formed the foundation of Igodomigodo identity. Acknowledging his own foreignness, Oranmiyan concurred with the voices of dissent, arguing that the mantle of Oba should rest upon one born of the land.

But Oranmiyan did not return to Ife. Rather, he took a new wife, Erinmedea, the daughter of one of the rebel chieftains. His goal was not to rule Igodomigodo, but to integrate it into the kingdom of Ife. He viewed the marriage as a strategic alliance rather than a romantic one.

From this union, a son named Eweka, "a child of the soil," was born, a true native of Igodomigodo. Upon his birth, Oranmiyan and Erinmedea renamed the kingdom Benin, derived from "Ile Ibinu," the land of trouble. For Oranmiyan, Eweka was more than just an heir; he was the future, a bridge linking Benin to his own expanding kingdom.

Harmonia

On Eweka's fifth birthday, the sound of drumming filled the air in Benin. The boy was to be crowned, though the circle of elders would rule until he came of age.

Yet among the mosaic of silken robes, gleaming cowries, and painted faces, Oranmiyan stood apart. He watched his son don the coral beads of kingship, the crown balanced delicately on a small head. Pride shone in the father's eyes, but only briefly. Oranmiyan was restless. Whether it was the call of undiscovered lands or the whispers of the Ajogun, his ambitions for a great empire were only growing.

As Eweka stood, dwarfed by those who stood next to him, he gazed on the crowd with a child's innocence, his tiny hand gripping the staff of power, which looked as though it might tip him over. Around him the elders nodded, their expressions masking their doubts. The child was a symbol for the people. Oranmiyan had gifted the people of Benin an Oba, a lineage tied irrevocably to himself. But his own path, it seemed, was not yet complete.

That night, after the last fires burned out and the people retreated into sleep, Oranmiyan stood over his slumbering son. The thought of Eweka's future, of the throne he would inherit fully grown, grounded Oranmiyan for a fleeting moment.

"I give you a kingdom, my son," he spoke, softly so as to not wake him, "but my ambitions have yet to release me from their command."

CHAPTER 23

Oranmiyan's Legacy

Fear no forest because it is dense.

—African proverb

As Oranmiyan prepared to depart Benin on a new path. the warriors of Ife who had long followed and fought for him grew homesick. Half of his army requested to finally return to Ife. Oranmiyan assented to the request, understanding the pull of their roots. He gathered his remaining soldiers and headed north toward Nupe country.

Nupe country was just beyond the River of Rivers. Its location made it a pivotal merchant town. The bridges across the river were heavily guarded and appeared impassable. Once they arrived on the bank of the river, Oranmiyan and his army established their camp. There, by the river's edge, Oranmiyan contemplated the next chapter of his journey.

Oranmiyan crossed paths with a traveling Babalawo, a priest and a man of keen insight who immediately recognized the divine ashé in Oranmiyan—he saw that the blood of the iron deity, Ogun, was coursing through his veins. He was fishing for his meal by the river and warmly welcomed Oranmiyan to share it with him.

That evening, the two savored a meal of peppered fish. Oramiyan ate in thoughtful silence, his imposing figure softened by the fire's light, while the Babalawo, seated cross-legged opposite him, spoke in a tone both gentle and knowing. Their words, at first, flowed like the river nearby, steady and calm, winding through common tales of the land and its lore. But as the night deepened, so too did their conversation, until the Babalawo turned his discerning gaze directly into Oraniyan's restless eyes. "You carry not just a sword," he said, his voice measured, "but something unseen, something is pulling you forward against the currents of your will." Oranmiyan did not reply, studying the flames.

The Babalawo went on: "Your path stretches ahead, nearer than you think. Yet the place you seek is not one you will happen upon. It calls for the wisdom of the earth, the strength of patience, and the guidance not born of mortal hands."

The Babalawo rose, moving not with the fragility of age, but with swiftness. He disappeared briefly into the folds of his tent, returning with something that glistened in the dim light. Wrapped around his arm was a large snake that shone like black silk, bearing a charm at its tail.

"This is no ordinary snake," the Babalawo explained, lowering himself to sit once more. "It is a guide."

Oranmiyan reached out slowly, accepting the snake. It moved with precision, sliding onto his broad shoulders as though it belonged there, its charm tinkling softly. Oranmiyan did not smile, for he understood that this gift was no token, but a message.

The Babalawo instructed him to trail the snake until it ceased its wanderings and rested for seven days before vanishing into the soil.

No further words passed between them. The fire slowly burned down to embers, and in the quiet of the moment, Oranmiyan knew that his path had indeed shifted.

As the first light of dawn broke, Oranmiyan tracked the snake, with his army behind him. Day after day, they pursued the creature; each evening, it would stop and let them rest under the stars. The men would set down their arms and gaze upward to Orun as their campfires crackled softly, lulling them to sleep.

Every morning at dawn the snake would wake Oranmiyan with a peculiar call, signaling it was ready to move again. Weeks passed and the anticipation among Oranmiyan's men grew with each step.

Then, as if by divine command, the snake stopped and stayed put for seven straight days and seven nights before burrowing into the soil.

Oranmiyan stood motionless, his men awaiting a response. He bent and touched the soil, its coolness spreading through his fingers. "This," Oranmiyan declared, "is where we shall plant our future."

It was here, amid the untamed beauty and latent promise of this foreign land, that Oranmiyan laid the foundations of what would become the great city-state of Katunga. The rise of Katunga as a power in Oririun was not without obstacles. Soon after Oranmiyan established it, the city became locked in conflict with the Bariba of Borgu country, who aimed to assert their dominance.

In these trying times, Oranmiyan sought assistance from the nearby kingdom of Nupe, recognizing the potential for a powerful alliance. The Oba of Nupe, holding Oranmiyan in high regard and foreseeing the benefits of their alliance, dispatched his army to stand beside Katunga's warriors. As the two armies converged on the battlefield, their collective strength was decisive, leading to victory for Katunga.

The triumph solidified Katunga's place in the region, and helped forge a lasting alliance with the Nupe kingdom. This newfound bond was sanctified by the marriage of Oranmiyan to the beautiful Nupe princess Torosi, symbolizing unity between the two kingdoms.

Soon enough, the drums of celebration welcomed the birth of a son, Ajaka. His arrival was more than a joyous occasion; he was a living emblem of the future that lay ahead.

CHAPTER 24

Oranmiyan's Odyssey

God has created lands with lakes and rivers for man to live.
And the desert so that he can find his soul.

—African proverb

In bringing Katunga into Yorubaland, Oranmiyan established the Oyo Empire. To see him seated upon his throne, it was clear age had touched him lightly: his face bore only the faint markings of countless sunsets witnessed and innumerable victories celebrated. He had fulfilled his father, Oduduwa's, grand vision of an expansive Yorubaland, while achieving his own dream of a magnificent empire. Pondering all that he had accomplished, he imagined how his father would have swelled with pride at the legacy he built.

Since leaving Ife over a decade ago, Oranmiyan had become addicted to filling the deep void left by the loss of his firstborn and his buried love for Moremi. It was the void that had propelled him toward new lands, as he pursued glory to soothe his restless spirit.

Oranmiyan now found that he was ready to confront the void. The years of wandering had tempered his soul, and the call of Ife grew louder. Over his years on campaign, he had received news of Ife's growth and progress from his sister, Okanbi. He had told her to summon him only in the shadow of peril—a dark word that had never arrived, and thus that he had never once heeded.

As he prepared for what he knew might be his final trek, he turned to his young son, Ajaka, who would now lead Katunga in his stead, and entrusted the kingdom to his care.

With a meager satchel of provisions and armed with only his sword, he mounted his horse and headed south, never looking back on Katunga.

As dusk descended on the first day of his journey, Oranmiyan stopped to rest for the night, kindling a fire and reclining by it. The embrace of night soon enveloped him, and thoughts of Moremi crept into his mind; indeed, her grip on him had tightened with every battle fought and every kingdom conquered. After each great victory, he would join his men in celebration, letting the warmth of palm wine quell the persistent ache of her memory. But now, alone by the flickering flames, he allowed such thoughts to consume his dreams. Her memory stilled his heart, and Oranmiyan was visited by the three sisters of existence.

As though kissed by the breath of life itself, Oranmiyan stirred from the depths of slumber. He awoke not to the familiar hues of dawn but to the soft glow of candlelight, casting shadows within an expansive tent. In front of him were three faces, each warm and welcoming.

With soft smiles and gentle voices, the three sisters introduced themselves as Emi, Eleda, and Ojiji. Their presence was strangely soothing. Ojiji addressed him: "You seek to return to Ife, do you not?"

Her question hung in the air. Oranmiyan responded with a silent nod, and with longing in his eyes.

"Well, then, you must first drink this," she said, extending a vessel filled with water toward him. She then explained to Oranmiyan that he stood in the space between the mortal and spiritual realms. To find his way back to Ife, he must confront and conquer the chaos within, to atone for missteps taken on his path to becoming an emperor. He would face three challenges, each presented by an Orisha. As the cool water touched his lips, the sisters opened the tent flap and ushered him out.

What met Oranmiyan's gaze was unending desert, a vista of countless dunes. He turned back, intending to seek guidance from the sisters. But they had vanished, as had the tent, leaving Oranmiyan alone in the shifting sands of a mysterious land.

For the first time in his life, he felt truly lost and alone. Olorun's blazing ashé pressed down on him. The scorching sands beneath his feet reminded him of the pain he had harbored and run from.

The whispers of Iku, the lady of death, carried in the air, her seductive melody invading his thoughts. As if possessed by the spirit of the cruel desert, he felt his knees weaken and fold. His parched lips tasted a bitter kiss of defeat. For a fleeting second, he contemplated succumbing to the comforting lullaby of Iku.

Yet, at that very moment, a vision of Moremi appeared, her image a balm for his wearied soul. The memory of her love rekindled the dying embers of his strength. He rose, defying his own doubts.

No sooner had he stood than the placid desert sprung to life. The sands whipped up, swirling into a vortex that blotted out the sun. Oranmiyan shielded his face from the coarse grains that nipped at his cheeks. The skies darkened, in preparation for the arrival of a divine presence. From the eye of the storm emerged Oya, the Orisha of winds.

Oya towered over Oranmiyan, her controlled movements a stark contrast to the swirling chaos. Her eyes met his, perceiving his unspoken fears and hidden strengths. In a voice with the timbre of his father's, she spoke: "Lead with love."

The words, laden with paternal wisdom, brought an expression of innocence to Oranmiyan's weathered face. Then, with a whip of her hand, she tore out his heart. Astonishingly, he found that he was still alive, despite the gaping void in his chest. Oranmiyan looked at Oya with a silent plea. The Orisha, holding his pulsating heart, spoke with divine authority. "This heart, the last remnant of your morality, you forsook along with your true queen, Moremi."

As if commanded by her words, darkness seeped into the heart, consuming its life force until it lay still and silent in her palm, resembling no more than a piece of charcoal. Oya released the heart's ashes into the swirling sandstorm, her voice rising over the gale. "In the realm of mortals and the art of kingship, two figures emerge: the conqueror and the sovereign. Only the latter carves a legacy that endures. Oranmiyan, you are the conqueror, wielding iron and ambition, striving for a name forged in conquest. Your journey has been marked by the roar of battle and the quiet that follows triumph. To you, kingdoms are prizes to be won, territories to seize, names to etch shallowly into history. You wield Ogun's fearless ashé, yet should you continue to follow only ambition, your name shall fade into oblivion."

The dunes around them stirred, as if alive, and sand monsters emerged from the ground to loom menacingly over Oranmiyan, their figures terror itself. Weakened, Oranmiyan cried out, yet Oya did not relent. "You have already sealed your fate, Oranmiyan. This is the future that awaits you, and yet you dare to defy the ordained path by retreating before me?"

"Please," Oranmiyan's voice broke through.

"Face your truth. Surrender, and this ends," Oya said, her voice a mix of challenge and hope.

At the mention of surrender, something deep within Oranmiyan ignited. With newfound resolve, he declared, "No. Do what you must, but I remain unconquered."

Oya, at first taken aback by his defiance, eased into a smile of acceptance. In a dramatic flourish, she became one with the sandstorm, dissipating along with the sand monsters into the swirling chaos, leaving Oranmiyan alone again.

Oranmiyan patted his chest, but the hole was no longer there. He collected himself and began walking. He soon spotted an oasis of palm trees. As he approached, a magnificent temple appeared, its silhouette a mirage of exquisite beauty against the bare horizon. The details of its intricate marble reliefs came into view—carvings so delicate and precise they seemed wrought by the sky gods themselves.

The walls of the temple were mosaics, their tiles depicting his triumphs. Roaming the temple grounds were peacocks, their plumage a riot of colors, each feather a symbol of regal, divine beauty.

Within the temple itself, he came upon a lavish courtyard. Here, Oranmiyan was greeted again by the sisters of existence.

"Where am I? Am I dead?" he asked them.

They explained that he was still between realms as they led him to a bathing pool, its waters pure and invigorating.

"Iku is ready to claim you, but the Orishas are allowing you a choice," they explained as they bathed and fed him. His fatigue dissolved, replaced by serenity.

Once cleansed and rejuvenated, Oranmiyan was presented to Oshun, the Orisha of love and fertility. Her beauty was astonishing. Drawn into her enchanting arms, he found himself momentarily lost in her embrace, the purpose of his journey slipping from his mind as he succumbed to her enchantment.

Awakening to the aftermath of Oshun's seduction, he was led to the grand court of her temple, where decadence itself seemed to be celebrated. Tables groaned under the weight of abundant food, opium, and palm wine, delicious aromas mingling with the laughter and conversation of the guests, all of them warriors. Women, nearly as beautiful as the goddess they served, moved among the revelers, filling their cups.

Oranmiyan became a willing captive to revelry, the days melting into nights in a heady blur. It was only with the arrival of his old companion, Jaiyesimi, that the spell was momentarily broken.

Jaiyesimi appeared unannounced, his presence an unwelcome disruption in the court. Yet Oranmiyan defended his old friend, bidding him to stay.

They regaled one another with stories of past victories, their laughter echoing through the chamber as they feasted and guzzled. Women, as striking as the dawn, danced around them and other weary warriors from all over Orirun, who also appeared to be seeking respite from their battles.

Jaiyesimi, with a sigh, reflected upon his own weaknesses, his eyes showing the regret of a life lived in distraction. "I was not the warrior I thought myself to be," he confessed. "The lure of wine and women proved too strong, and I faltered every time."

He then turned to Oranmiyan with gratitude on his face. "For your kindness, my friend, I am forever indebted."

Oranmiyan was confused, but before he could voice his questions, Jaiyesimi beckoned him away from the bustling tables and from Oshun's watchful gaze. As they walked, Jaiyesimi began to clear the fog of forgetfulness from Oranmiyan.

"I was a drunken fool," Jaiyesimi confessed, his voice heavy with remorse. "I admired you, but for all the wrong reasons. In my carelessness, I met an ignoble end, falling from the walls of the city of Benin in a drunken stupor after our victory. Yet, you honored me, having men return my body to Ife to be buried in our homeland as a true warrior. For this, I owe you my gratitude."

Oranmiyan noticed that Jaiyesimi had not aged a day. He now remembered the careless, tragic fall.

"I wish to repay your kindness," Jaiyesimi said. "Listen carefully, do not meet my fate, my friend. Leave here." And with those words, he vanished, and Oranmiyan was alone.

As Oranmiyan returned to the grand chamber, he recognized the truth of his situation. He saw the revelers anew: the warriors, once robust and full of life, bore the scars of their mortal ends, their joviality a façade hiding the reality of their fates.

His mind, free from Oshun's enchantment, was flooded with clarity of purpose. He was on a journey, one that he had momentarily forgotten amid the hedonistic pleasures of the Orisha's temple. Determination set in; escape was his only path forward.

As if sensing his intention, Oshun clapped her hands twice, a command that brought silence to the grand court. The music ceased, the laughter died, and the fallen soldiers rose, their ghostly wounds gleaming under the temple's candlelight, as they readied to prevent Oranmiyan from leaving.

Oranmiyan scanned the grand court for an unexpected exit. His gaze fell on the natural pool and its tranquil surface. Without a moment's hesitation, he plunged into the cool water.

As he held his breath, piercing through the water's darkness, a soft glow beckoned him. He swam toward the light; every passing second increasing the weight upon his chest as his muscles strained against the water's resistance, each stroke becoming a battle against time. His lungs screamed silently, their walls tightening as a feeling of fire inflamed his heart. A narrow tunnel loomed ahead, urging him forward. And then, just as he thought his body would fail him, he burst free from the watery confines, gasping hungrily for air under an open sky. He was free, his quest once again stretching out before him.

Crawling from the waters, Oranmiyan found himself in a dense jungle, where the sky peeked through the interlacing leaves. Behind him, Oshun's temple had been replaced by a wide, meandering river.

As he ventured deeper into the jungle, he noticed a beast lurking in the shadows, its eyes gleaming. Oranmiyan sought refuge in a nearby cave, its rocky depths offering protection.

Navigating the cave's many winding tunnels, Oranmiyan stepped into a large open space where Obatala, the Orisha of creation, was diligently crafting a colossal sculpture of him from the damp earth. Nearby was Oduduwa, who abruptly paused a heated debate with Obatala to welcome Oranmiyan with open arms.

"My son!" Oduduwa greeted him warmly, while Obatala remained focused on his work.

Oranmiyan was both surprised and moved by the unexpected reunion. "I have ascended, and so shall you, but you are blocked," Oduduwa explained, as if he could read and answer Oranmiyan's thoughts.

"Speak the truth, Oduduwa!" Obatala interjected, breaking the tender moment.

"What truth?" Oranmiyan inquired, confusion lacing his words.

Before Oduduwa could respond, Obatala interjected once more. "You may fool the Council of Orishas, but not me," he declared, turning to Oranmiyan. "The legacy you uphold is not truly Oduduwa's."

"Father, what does he mean?" Oranmiyan asked.

Oduduwa took a deep breath. "Your true father is Orisha Ogun."

The revelation struck Oranmiyan like a thunderbolt, and a storm of emotions threatened to destabilize him. Yet, before he could fully grasp this truth, the massive earthen sculpture began to tremble and stir. With a deafening roar, it tore itself free from the ground, shaking the walls of the cave.

"Oranmiyan, listen well." Oduduwa's voice was calm amid the chaos. "The origin of your seed is not significant. What matters is the strength you've cultivated, that you've healed from within to forge your own legacy." With these words, both he and Obatala vanished, just as Jaiyesimi had.

Oranmiyan stood firm, facing the towering figure, a colossal doppelgänger made of clay. The giant lunged as Oranmiyan clumsily jumped to the side and landed on his knee, in pain. One of the giant's fists collided with the cave floor, and a web of cracks appeared in its clay hand.

Perspiration dotted Oranmiyan's brow as he staggered to his feet, trying to lean away from his pain. The giant attempted to crush him with a massive step. Oranmiyan evaded him once more, and the giant's little toe shattered upon impact with the rock Oranmiyan was using for support. Oranmiyan saw that he could turn the giant's brute force against itself.

With each calculated maneuver and every nimble dodge, Oranmiyan orchestrated the giant's self-destruction. Blow by blow, the clay giant began to succumb to its own aggression, cracks spreading across its form, pieces and entire limbs tumbling away.

As the giant disintegrated, Oranmiyan emerged not just victorious but at peace.

It was then that Eshu, the Orisha who was the divine messenger of crossroads, appeared and approached him with a choice. It was between immortality in the spiritual realm among the Orishas or returning to the mortal world. Oranmiyan chose to go home.

After twenty years spent expanding the territory, power, and influence of Yorubaland, Oranmiyan was suddenly back where he had started, in the kingdom of Ife. During his absence, Moremi, his beloved, had shouldered the dual burdens of their personal loss and the governance of their people. She had not only mended her own heart but cultivated a flourishing kingdom.

As Oranmiyan approached the gates of the capital city, Ile-Ife, he anticipated a hero's welcome. Instead, he was greeted by the subdued murmurs of those who did not recognize him and the imposing sight of a transformed citadel. This was no longer the Ile-Ife he once knew, but a creation of Moremi's resilient spirit and visionary rule. The once-familiar paths now wound through vibrant markets and alongside majestic temples and halls of learning; every conversation and magnificent structure stood as a part of her legacy.

As he approached the palace grounds, some began to see who was before them. Drummers were summoned, and they announced his return. Recognizing the beat, Moremi rushed out into the courtyard, heart pounding. Her eyes locked onto the figure of her husband, standing there after their many years apart.

When Oranmiyan saw Moremi, time came to a stop for him. He fell to his knees, repenting for the pain caused and the years lost. Moremi, embodying forgiveness, knelt to embrace him. In this moment of balance, the kingdom had both its warrior and its sovereign.

Oranmiyan, the conqueror, had sought conquest and glory, viewing other kingdoms as territories to be claimed. Moremi, the sovereign, saw that it was her sacred duty to lift up her people and enrich their lives, and to create a society rooted in compassion, innovation, and unity.

Oranmiyan praised Moremi's manifest triumphs. Through her, Ife became more than merely another kingdom defined by war and greed; it became a legend, evidence of what was possible when you lead with love.

BOOK VI

THE ALAAFIN OF OYO

CHAPTER 25

Jakuta

When you follow in the path of your father,
you learn to walk like him.

—Ghanaian proverb

In the time before soil graced the Earth, when the weather was violent and the air was thick with heat, Jakuta and Oya commanded the skies. Jakuta controlled climatic wonders with his ashé, emanating lightning and thunder from his core. These reflected his own nature—volatile yet awe-inspiring, fearsome yet vital.

Jakuta's ability to harness his ashé was not an isolated power. It hinged on Oya's own ashé, for she commanded the winds and movement of the sky. This interdependence was a complex dynamic; Jakuta found himself in greater need of Oya than she of him, yet their tumultuous relationship, which produced such chaos, was essential for the cultivation of life on Earth.

Jakuta's influence began to falter as Ogun rose in stature. Ogun's ascension was not merely a consequence of gaining favor among the Orishas, but revealed the shifting priorities of their mortal worshippers. As human civilizations advanced, the reverence and need for Ogun's ashé over metalwork, warfare, and innovation became more pronounced, diminishing Jakuta's standing.

Oya found herself irresistibly drawn to Ogun, recognizing him as the essential force that bonded water to life. With life now flourishing on Onile, she felt liberated from Jakuta's grasp, seeing no further need for his tempestuous nature. The loss of Oya's companionship was a turning point for Jakuta, leaving him with wounded pride and a lack of support for his ashé. He struggled with what he believed was a betrayal, choosing to exile himself from Edin and the Council of Orishas, withdrawing from their politics and the allies who once stood by his side. His self-understanding dictated that if he could not lead, he would not follow.

In his solitude, Jakuta channeled his divine energies into building a sanctuary unlike any other—a fortress of glass and storm, crafted from fulgurite. He dwelled there in quiet contemplation until he heard of the great Oranmiyan, who had forged an empire, amplifying Ogun's ashé through conquests won with his iron sword.

Ever observant, Jakuta learned of the union between Ogun's son and Torosi, the Nupe princess who seemed to hold the reigns in Katunga, which was now part of Oranmiyan's Oyo Empire—named after both Oranmiyan and his father. In Princess Torosi, Jakuta saw an opportunity to rescue his influence among humans.

On the night Jakuta set his plan into motion, the skies over the city-state of Katunga were ablaze with lightning. It weaved through the darkness in silent, breathtaking displays of light. It was Jakuta's way of reaching out from his self-imposed exile, hoping to stir the heart of the human princess who walked below.

Torosi, whose gaze had long been turned toward the ground, burdened by the absence of Oranmiyan for three weary years with no word, found her spirits lifted by the mesmerizing dance unfolding above. Little did she know that it was Jakuta, wielding his ashé, drawing her into his world of wonder and solitude.

As Jakuta descended from the skies, he chose a guise of raw energy, a bolt of lightning that crackled and surged. With a thunderous roar, he enveloped Torosi, penetrating her very being, his electric essence coursing through her body. She felt a surge of exhilaration. In that moment, in complete darkness,

under the cloak of heavy clouds that smothered the starlight, Torosi became intertwined with Jakuta, unaware of the consequences that awaited her.

From this courtship, born of light and thunder, came Shango. A child like no other, he held the tempest within him. The people of Katunga believed him to be a gift from the great god Olodumare, while others were more wary. In his youth, Shango's emotions could manifest physically; sudden outbursts of anger conjured thunderclaps from a serene sky, a sign of the erratic spirit of his father. His volatile nature set Shango apart from his half brother, Ajaka, whose demeanor was as soothing as the gentle streams that meandered through the lands surrounding Katunga. Shango's early years were marked by a struggle to understand the dangerous powers he had inherited, powers that he, a child, could scarcely comprehend.

Torosi tried her best to teach him to master the storms within. She introduced him to music and the playing of the Batá drums to cool his temper. But still, he could not control his energy and bend it to his will. How does one calm a storm born of the divine? As Shango's powers grew, so too did the fierceness of his spirit.

Years passed, during which Torosi both struggled to tame Shango and waited in inner silence, clinging to the hope that Oranmiyan would one day return to her. That hope was shattered when she received a letter from Ayaba Moremi, her hands trembling as she unfolded the parchment. The words buckled her knees: Oranmiyan had departed from this world, leaving a final wish for Ajaka to inherit the throne of Oyo Empire. Her heart ached with the loss of the man she had loved, yet it swelled with the promise of her son's future.

Immediately, young Ajaka began spending his days preparing for the throne, studying history and practicing spear play. But Shango thought he, not his placid half brother, should be next in line, and dared to declare this belief. During an intense clash of wills, Shango's fury erupted in a jolt of energy that struck Ajaka down, scarring his face. It was then that Torosi realized the limits of her own mortal abilities and faced the inevitable decision.

Torosi sought out Jakuta with a plea. She was convinced that only he could guide their son to suppress the untamed energy pulsing within him. Heeding her call, Jakuta agreed to help, yet he would not tamp down his son's inner storm, but teach him how to wield it at command. He envisioned Shango channeling his birthright into becoming a mighty warrior and leading the Oyo Empire to unparalleled heights with his ashé.

With Jakuta's teachings and strength as his foundation, Shango's potential would be limitless, propelling his father back to the fore in Edin.

CHAPTER 26

Ajaka

You learn how to cut down trees by cutting them down.

—African proverb

Five years after Ajaka rose to power as the new emperor, or Alaafin, he decreed that the empire's capital be his home kingdom of Katunga. This transition was made with the blessing of Ayaba Moremi, who endorsed Ajaka's decision on the sacred stipulation that Ife remain the spiritual cradle of the Oyo Empire. Splitting the political from the religious not only reinforced Ajaka's rule but also honored Moremi and the Orishas, ensuring their continued influence in the empire.

The Oyo Empire was enjoying a period of peace, though there was an undercurrent of tension. Ajaka's diplomatic approach was a notable deviation from the militant policies of his father, Oranmiyan. Ajaka believed in fostering harmony among the empire's various kingdoms rather than pitting them against one another. His reign was defined by an earnest pursuit of mutual respect within the empire and with the neighboring kingdom of Nupe, a vision his royal court found difficult to embrace. To some, Oranmiyan's legacy seemed to be tarnished by the hands of Ajaka, who appeared weak in the eyes of those who valued strength above all else.

Ajaka's dedication to peace inadvertently opened the door to nefarious actors. Oba Kosoko of Nupe, brother to Torosi and uncle to Ajaka, extended an invitation to the emperor to form a new trade agreement. Trusting in the promise of a lasting partnership between Nupe and Oyo, Ajaka accepted the offer.

Ajaka crossed into Nupe territory, to treat with his uncle and secure a prosperous future for both. However, upon his arrival, he was seized by his uncle's soldiers. This act was not only a personal betrayal but a calculated move by Kosoko to undermine Ajaka's diplomatic efforts and assert his own dominance. He demanded a hefty ransom.

Torosi, though aware of her brother's ambitions, had grossly misjudged him. Now war was coming. Torosi gave her approval to send a company of Katunga's soldiers bearing the large ransom to the Nupe Kingdom and retrieve her son.

When General Timi of Katunga returned as the sole survivor of the expedition, he recounted to Torosi and the royal court that Alaafin Ajaka faced execution unless they stepped down. Timi and his soldiers had been ambushed. They fought valiantly to reach Ajaka, but they were overpowered, many meeting their end even before reaching Nupe soil. Their sacrifice and loyalty had not been enough to secure Ajaka's release.

Oba Kosoko, shrewd in his tactics, spared Timi to ensure that the news of Ajaka's capture spread, and to remind people of Nupe's strength, aiming to sow fear within Katunga, to weaken the minds of its citizens before Nupe attempted to conquer them. He warned his sister, Torosi, to leave for another part of the Oyo Empire, or he would forget their blood ties and she would meet her end.

Faced with imminent danger, the royal court of Katunga, led by Torosi, urgently retreated southward to the safety of the Igboho region. As they settled into their temporary haven, their minds turned to the pressing need to counter Kosoko's ambitions and defend their territory from further incursions.

Determined to fortify their defenses, Torosi summoned her trusted generals, Timi and Gbona. She entrusted them with a mission: to visit the Palace of Glass and Storm and plead with her other son, Ajaka's half brother. "Tell him his brother, and indeed the Oyo Empire, are in grave danger and in need of his help," she instructed.

At the center of the Palace of Glass and Storm was a training arena. The open space seemed to hum with raw electricity. The ground of white sand shimmered under the perpetually gray skies that swirled above, while streams of the clearest water wove through the arena like the veins of life. This was no mortal place; it was a sacred ground.

It was here that Shango, under the vigilant guidance of his father, Jakuta, had been relentlessly training, mastering both his god-like abilities and his mortal mind. The years of rigorous discipline had not only sharpened him but had imbued him with a powerful ashé that set him apart from humans.

When Timi and Gbona approached Jakuta's fortress of fulgurite, the sight that greeted them was astonishing. Not even Torosi's description had prepared them. The fortress, formed by lightning striking sand, could be nothing other than a domain of the divine. They approached the bastion with apprehension.

When the generals first encountered Shango, they saw that he exuded power. Yet he greeted their urgent message regarding his brother Ajaka's grave situation with a lack of concern. His apathy was rooted in their history of rivalry and envy, and in their shared but divergent heritage. After Shango and Ajaka had their vicious argument, when Shango, in a moment of uncontrolled fury, left a scar on Ajaka's face with his electrical powers, the younger brother was scorned and cast out by his own mother. She refused to show him love, and dispatched him to a harsh regime of relentless training and sleepless nights, while his brother, relieved to have survived, basked in the privileges that came with royalty.

Shango's envy was more than sibling rivalry; it reflected his desire to validate his own worth and step out from the shadow cast by his brother's lineage. Beneath his indifferent exterior was a turbulent inner struggle.

Timi and Gbona understood the significance of their mission, and the potential consequences of failing to rally Shango to their cause. Despite his apathy, they impressed upon him that it wasn't just Ajaka at risk, but the entire leadership of the Oyo Empire.

Jakuta, who had been listening intently from an antechamber, entered the room and urged Shango to rise above personal grievances and rescue Ajaka. He emphasized to Timi and Gbona that the time had come for Shango to return to Oyo. Jakuta was confident that his son would wield the strength necessary to surpass Ajaka, thereby advancing the Orisha's own ambitions. Pulling Shango aside, Jakuta braced him with a few words of empowerment. "Oyo will witness your evolution from a disgraced royal into a hero and warrior embodying all the virtues of a future Alaafin," Jakuta said quietly. "Trust me, my son."

Shango came to understand his father's plan for him. Before he set off on his journey back to Oyo, Jakuta bestowed upon him a parting gift of a double-headed ax of exquisite craftsmanship. This weapon was imbued with the power to command lightning, making it a conduit of his powerful ashé. It was a sacred artifact that could influence the skies above.

With this powerful weapon in his hands, Shango embarked on his mission, flanked by Timi and Gbona.

It had been years since Shango had been in Oyo. But the generals did not take him to Katunga, for the great city-state had been conquered by Kosoko during their quest.

As he passed through the gates of the main city in Igboho, Torosi rushed toward him with arms open, enveloping him, hoping to fill the void of years without the immediacy of a mother's love. Yet, as she pulled back to look at him, a flicker of surprise crossed her face. The young man she had last seen had been replaced by a figure of imposing strength and quiet authority. She was proud of him even as a subtle tremor of intimidation ran through her.

Shango did not linger. He turned to the pressing matter of rescuing Ajaka and taking back Katunga. With a sense of purpose in his every step, he moved to rally the combined forces of Igboho and the remaining army of Katunga.

Shango's presence commanded attention and respect. His transformation was not just physical; the aura of divine ashé that enveloped him suggested depth and power beyond the understanding of ordinary mortals.

As Shango and his troops drew near Katunga, they saw Nupe's military forces entrenching themselves within the city. They had raided many homes of ordinary people, spreading fear.

Shango struck quickly, leading his troops into the city of his birth and driving out the Nupe soldiers, who quickly retreated toward their own territory.

Shango and his men pursued them relentlessly, determined not to let them regroup. When they reached the border of the Nupe kingdom, the skies above churned. Dark, ominous clouds gathered, crackling with pent-up fury. Ahead lay the River of Rivers, the natural barrier whose bridges were heavily fortified and manned by Nupe soldiers.

Shango stepped onto the closest bridge with a confident stride, commanding the energy around him. The very air around him buzzed, charged with anticipation of the impending confrontation. His double-headed ax shot streams of light outward while bolts of lightning descended from the sky, striking down the guards on the bridge one by one.

As Shango and his army surged forth, the Nupe soldiers braced themselves for the clash. Yet, nothing could have prepared them for this foe. The encounter was swift, like a flash storm that leaves devastation in its wake. Nupe's warriors, though courageous, found themselves outmatched by the powerful ashé unleashed upon them. Lightning struck those who dared to stand in defiance, while others, witnessing the fall of their comrades, laid down their weapons in surrender. In moments, the battlefield fell silent, broken only by the crackling of the fires the lightning had started and the distant rumble of thunder.

With an army at his back and roiling clouds accompanying him above, Shango pressed forward, his eyes set on the palace of the Nupe kingdom. It was there, in the innermost sanctum of Nupe's palace, that he found his brother, Ajaka, held captive by Kosoko. In underestimating Katunga's power, the devious Oba had only succeeded in strengthening it.

Shango quickly slew the Oba Kosoko, who had spent his last moments watching his army be subdued. Ajaka, now free, stood before Shango as their memories of both rivalry and admiration hung in the air. In the stillness of their reunion, the brothers each saw in the other a reflection of the person they secretly yearned to be.

In the aftermath of the brief war, as peace settled over the land once again, the kingdom of Nupe found itself under new stewardship.

Word of Shango's defeat of the Nupe and rescue of Ajaka spread rapidly across Katunga and throughout the Oyo Empire. The many accounts of the battle varied in accuracy, but all spoke of how Shango had wielded the elements themselves to vanquish the enemy and secure his brother's freedom. These stories were recounted with awe and fervor.

The royal court, which had already been critical of Ajaka's diplomatic and pacifist approach to the kingdom's neighbors, was insistent in the wake of Shango's actions. The courtiers now saw Ajaka's avoidance of conflict as a vulnerability that had nearly cost them their empire and their lives. In contrast, Shango's decisive intervention was seen as an augur of a grand future.

The court envisioned the potential for greater dominance over the empire's neighbors, under the guidance of a ruler with the capability to harness both martial and supernatural might. The warriors who fought alongside Shango were loyal to him, further solidifying his claim to leadership. Shango was either going to be given the throne or he was going to take it.

In a decisive vote, the court chose Shango as the new Alaafin, portraying his strength as essential to the empire's future. Ajaka found himself demoted by the empire he had sought to protect through peace and that had been granted to him by his father, Oranmiyan. In the spiritual realm, Shango's rise to power saw his own father, Orisha Jakuta, return to Edin.

The coronation of Shango was met with widespread jubilation throughout the empire. Obas from every corner of Oyo gathered and lifted their voices into a chorus of celebration and anticipation.

Harmonia

laid bare his vision for conquering distant lands, Jakuta listened intently, his expression unreadable. He understood Shango's aspirations, for he too had harbored ambitions that stretched beyond his current standing in Edin: Jakuta had not yet regained his place on the Council of Orishas.

Over the years, Jakuta had imparted all his wisdom to Shango, meticulously grooming him for leadership. With nothing left to teach, Jakuta felt a void, unsure what more he could offer. Yet he wanted to aid Shango's ambitions. If his son were able to create the most powerful empire in human history, surely he, Jakuta, would be welcomed back on the council.

With a rumbling sigh, Jakuta finally spoke, revealing a truth that would transform Shango's destiny. Acknowledging the dangers, the father advised the son to seek Aganju, the Orisha who could bestow the power of infernal flames. This element alone could forge iron into weapons or reduce it to nothing. And Aganju was none other than Shango's grandfather. This stunned Shango: the power he sought lay within his own bloodline.

Jakuta's counsel came with a warning, however. The kingdom that was Aganju's, where the Earth itself bled heat and mountains spat flames, was no place for a mortal. It was a domain where only those who were direct descendants of Orishas could dare to tread. Jakuta knew the trials that awaited Shango, for the gift of fire was not given lightly. It demanded an ebo, a sacrifice.

His warning was intended not to dissuade Shango but to steel his son for what might be asked of him. Deep within, Jakuta knew that Shango, endowed with his own blood and unbreakable spirit, could grasp a level of power previously beyond the reach of any mortal.

Shango thanked his father and set forth toward the fiery lands of his grandfather's kingdom.

Aganju's kingdom was one of overwhelming energy, a place where the flames danced with a life of their own and the very air suffocated foolish mortals with heat. The ground was an abstraction of molten rock and ash that thrummed with the beat of the Earth's core. As Shango crossed the threshold into the volcano where he would find Aganju, the flames crackled around him, obscuring his view and disorienting him.

CHAPTER 27

Shango

The child who is not embraced by the village will burn it down to feel its warmth.

—African proverb

Shango, the third Alaafin of Oyo following Oranmiyan and his own half brother, Ajaka, carried the weight of his demigod heritage as well as the all-too-mortal affliction of an Osogbo—that of greed. Shango had a relentless desire for more. His hunger first manifested in the expansion of his harem, which became the largest in Orirun.

Four years into his reign, Shango had fulfilled his promise to expand the Oyo Empire from his seat in Katunga, pushing its boundaries farther than any before him. Under his rule, the empire's people thrived, and its enemies trembled. However, the ambition within him raged fiercer than any storm he had conjured. He gazed upon the lands he had conquered, the territories united under his banner, and saw not the culmination of his dreams but the beginning of an even grander collection. Shango envisioned an empire that would eclipse all others in Orirun's history, an empire so vast it would become the first to stand the test of time.

His dream required a power beyond his own. Lightning, though immensely powerful, was fleeting. Iron, by contrast, was both plentiful and enduring. This realization led Shango to seek the counsel of his father.

Jakuta received his son with a gaze that pierced through the veneer of his status as Alaafin, seeing the uncontrolled ambition within. As Shango

Soon enough, Shango met Aganju. His grandfather was seated atop a towering throne; a colossus, his skin was obsidian, his veins coursing with lava that glowed with a fearsome intensity. His eyes, piercing and white, cut through the haze, offering a glimpse into an ancient soul that had witnessed the rise and fall of empires, and seemed to peer into the very core of Shango.

Aganju's reaction to his grandson was one of impassive scrutiny. After Shango voiced his request for the gift of fire, a silence fell. The flames seemed to still in deference to the gravity of the question.

Aganju's response was a challenge: "To wield the ashé of fire, to claim dominion over its searing embrace, Shango, you must first be consumed by it, to endure agony in its purest form."

The ebo was to be a baptism by fire that promised pain beyond imagination, a torment that could unravel the very fabric of one's being.

Hesitation clawed at Shango's mind as he stood at the edge of Aganju's lava flows, the heat burning his throat, the lava too bright for his eyes. Yet within him burned an ambition fiercer than any flame. With a mustered-up yell that echoed through the molten valleys, he hurled himself into the lava, surrendering himself to the inferno, as guttural cries emerged from the depths of his soul.

Within this crucible of excruciating pain, Shango was transformed. Rising from the magma, he emerged reborn, crawling along the scalding ground with the breath of fire within him, a god among men, fearless in the face of pain and death.

Shango returned to his empire, a force of nature unbound. His new campaign to expand Oyo began with fervor; his presence on the battlefield was simply terrifying. The empire swelled, conquering land after land. Yet, with each victory, a shadow grew over Oyo. The people, once buoyant with pride, now were hushed in fear of their Alaafin, whose wrath was as unpredictable as fire itself. His father, Jakuta, finally forced a return to the Council of Orishas, solidifying his influence in both Edin and Aiye.

Shango still hungered for more—more land and also more women. His harem was swelling in size, with no queen to birth an heir, for to marry would require a commitment, and he was already committed to his Osogbo.

There was one who was willing to challenge Shango: General Gbona. He remained loyal to Ajaka, the rightful Alaafin, whose intellect and fair rule stood in stark contrast to the self-indulgent reign of Shango. Though Ajaka had withdrawn to a life of quiet exile, far from the palace's opulence, Gbona never wavered. He believed with utmost certainty that the day would come when Ajaka would reclaim his throne.

Gbona journeyed often to the secluded sanctuary of the exiled emperor. In their hushed meetings, the general listened intently to Ajaka's counsel. Together they plotted to dismantle Shango's power.

Ajaka's dissatisfaction with Shango's despotic hold on Oyo transformed into a pursuit of justice. Each day of his exile, he toiled relentlessly, weaving alliances and urging Gbona to unite the empire's warriors against tyranny. Every dawn, Ajaka prayed to Orisha Ogun, seeking divine intervention against Shango.

Ogun listened closely to the calls of his grandson, for he was agitated by the havoc wrought by Jakuta. Jakuta, much like his son Shango, wielded his influence with a heavy hand, refusing to cooperate with the rest of the council, causing rifts in Edin. Ogun offered Ajaka a promise: should he rally the army to his cause, a shield forged from Ogun's strongest sky iron would be his, an impenetrable defense against Shango's lightning.

Empowered by Ogun's assurances to Ajaka, Gbona devoted himself to sparking a rebellion, and soon a fire spread through the ranks of the Oyo army. With the army under their banner, the rebels were ready to strike.

Shango, lost in his hedonistic pursuits, seemed oblivious to the simmering discontent. His disregard for his subjects only served to fuel Gbona's determination. The general's defiance of Shango became more pronounced, his resolve hardened by Shango's neglect. As the empire danced to the tune of Shango's Batá drums, Gbona steeled himself for the battle that loomed ahead.

During this period of deceptive calm in the kingdom, murmurs of an insurrection reached the court. As the sun began to settle for the day, casting the kingdom in hues of copper, whispers traveled through the land, foretelling a great storm.

Ajaka, armed with Ogun's sky iron shield, led a determined phalanx of warriors alongside Gbona. After they infiltrated the palace grounds, the silence of the dusk was shattered by the cries of the rebels and their attack.

In a blaze of fury, Shango burst through the main doors, his double-headed ax mercilessly cleaving through the ranks of Ajaka's warriors. Though they fought valiantly, their blows barely marred his flesh. What his ax could not reach, his fiery breath engulfed, turning all who dared approach into pillars of flames. As the smoke of burning flesh permeated the air, fear took hold among the valiant soldiers, many of whom fled before the demigod.

Though surrounded by the screams and pain of their men, Ajaka and Gbona stood tall and unbroken. Shango, wrapped in an aura of supreme confidence, regarded them with a sardonic grin, knowing Ajaka and his army were no match for his power.

But Ajaka held his ground. He grasped his shield, a true masterpiece of the Orisha of iron, polished to a brilliance that rivaled the sun itself. Shango, unfazed, taunted his half sibling. "No matter how beautifully your iron is forged, brother, it is no match for my ashé. Yet I commend your courage."

Shango then held up his double-headed ax, summoning the crackling energy of the skies, intending to unleash a bolt of pure lightning upon his brother. The heavens roared as a blind streak of light tore through the ether, hurtling toward Ajaka.

In an instant the bolt met the gleaming surface of Ajaka's shield as he steadied his stance before the powerful force. The shield miraculously reflected the lightning and reversed its path, redirecting it against its commander. Shango, caught facing his own creation, was flung back, the shock wave of his unleashed fury knocking the breath from his lungs and sapping his strength. The god-like Shango, once invincible, was now lying on the ground, his breath ragged and shallow.

Ajaka quickly summoned the remnants of his forces before Shango could reclaim his strength. With calculated haste, Gbona stuffed a water-soaked cloth in Shango's mouth and strapped an iron muzzle to his face, to stifle his fiery breath. The soldiers shackled his arms in iron chains, subduing his might and forcing him into a position of submission. Before the assembled throng, Ajaka emerged to the front. The humiliation was palpable as Shango bowed before his brother, his eyes smoldering with rage.

Ajaka, his features twisted in satisfaction, pulled out his sharp blade and etched a scar upon Shango's face—a mirror of the wound that Shango had inflicted upon him in a near-fatal encounter years prior. Shango barely acknowledged what was happening as his half brother cut him, denying Ajaka the sound of his agony.

All along, their mother, Torosi, was in her chambers with her ears muffled. She knew of Ajaka's plan and supported it, believing that Shango had become a tyrant. As much as it pained her to see one son attacked by the other, she reasoned that it was necessary for the good of the empire.

In a final act of degradation, Shango was dragged across the land, his fall from grace laid bare for all to see. The journey ended at the foot of the kingdom's highest tree, where he was hoisted and hung, a grim spectacle against the breaking dawn.

As the sun rose, the remnants of the night's chaos lingered in the air. Shango, once invincible, now swung forlornly in the breeze, a shadow of his former self.

Shango awoke in darkness. Orisha Eshu appeared in front of him. "Am I dead?" Shango inquired, defeat in his voice.

"Not yet," Eshu replied, in a measured tone. "I am Eshu, here to offer you a choice. You may ascend to the skies above and join Olorun, or you can be crowned an Orisha."

Before Shango could respond, Eshu pressed on. "Shango, in your final moments, you sought neither forgiveness nor redemption. Should you choose to wear the crown of an Orisha, peace will forever elude you. Yet returning to the stars can grant you renewal."

Eshu knew the storm that Shango's wrath could unleash if he became an

Orisha, a tempest that would strike fear in the hearts of the divine and mortal worlds alike.

Shango bowed his head in deep thought before raising his eyes to Eshu. "I will not relinquish all I have achieved. Crown me."

Light erupted and the skies shook as Shango ascended to the spiritual realm. Despite his divine elevation, his spirit roiled with unquenched rage and the mortal sting of betrayal. He thirsted for retribution against those who rejoiced in his fall.

Overlooking the kingdom of Katunga, Orisha Shango sat poised upon the very tree from which his mortal form had been hung. Beside him stood Eshu, his guide, who cautioned him. "Shango, as an Orisha, you are forbidden from directly inflicting harm upon a single human. Your ashé can only be wielded upon their call."

A slow, menacing smile crept across Shango's face. "Rest assured, no mortal shall suffer directly by my hand. But I make no such vow for their abodes."

With those words, Shango dissolved into a bolt of lightning. He hurled himself upon the unsuspecting kingdom of Katunga, his wrath manifesting as fire and destruction. Homes ignited into a sea of flames and the entire kingdom was soon ablaze.

As the fires raged on, Shango observed from the skies, his eyes reflecting the inferno below. As the kingdom turned to ash, he did not revel in the devastation; instead he felt an unfamiliar emptiness. Beside him, Eshu watched with a growing apprehension, sensing Shango's unsettled soul. Eshu pondered whether Edin could withstand the storm Shango embodied. He knew this was just the beginning.

CHAPTER 28

Obba Nani

A close friend can become a close enemy.

—African proverb

Obba Nani was a figure of understated beauty. Her attire was practical; she favored simplicity over the flamboyance that appealed to most of the other Orishas. Her hair, kept in very short, tight coils, highlighted her high forehead and delicate features that seldom danced with the extravagance of laughter. Her smiles were reserved, as if to keep unexpected joy at bay. She was petite and waiflike, her presence as subtle as the breeze that carried her gentle voice. She moved through the Garden barely noticed by the other Orishas in Edin, an observer rather than one seeking attention.

When she reached her full stature as an Orisha, it was Oshun who welcomed Obba into the pantheon. Her rise into her divine purpose coincided with humans' creation of distinct social roles. Obba was both Oshun's oldest and youngest sister, embodying strength and naivete in equal measure.

Her dominion was the home, a sanctuary of learning. Her eyes oversaw the lives of mortal wives and mothers. Her ashé was patience and understanding, yet she displayed the fierceness of a protector when invaders appeared. The politics of the Garden and the intricacies of the Council of Orishas held little allure for her; she maintained neutral ties with all, finding solace in the quiet, away from the drama and scrutiny that came with prominence.

Life in the margins suited Obba. Yet this tranquil existence was disrupted when the council summoned her, pulling her from the serene anonymity she cherished. As Obba entered the council room, she was greeted by the warmth of Oshun, who guided her to the center of the space before taking her own seat at the council table. Obba's gaze inadvertently met that of Oya, whose expression was one of visible annoyance. Beside Oduduwa stood Shango, the newly appointed Orisha of lightning, his presence filling the room, his only challenger Ogun, who lounged in his seat with a soft smirk.

The council's decision was clear: they believed Obba's flat demeanor and calming influence would perfectly complement Shango's unpredictable nature. They hoped that her ashé would temper his, preventing the potential havoc his lightning and fire breath could wreak upon the realms. It dawned on Obba that she was being ushered into an arranged marriage.

A flood of emotions swept through her. Surprise mingled with a hint of anxiety, for the prospect of marrying Shango would bring her notoriety. Yet, amid the whirlwind of feelings, she understood the importance of her role as a stabilizing force in both the Garden and the Aiye.

Obba's personal simplicity and solitude were a sharp contrast to Shango's world of music, opulence, and might. Initially, Shango resisted the pairing; he struggled to find beauty in her modesty, to see personality behind her monotone voice. But marrying her was the only way he could stay on the council. Obba observed him with a patient mind and heart, understanding that true connection often takes time to blossom.

Obba was aware of Shango's divine responsibilities—to wield, alongside Oya, the storms that nourished the Earth. She saw the importance of their work, how their raw ashé sustained life. And she knew of the storm that brewed between them, a passion hidden within the chaos of their shared duty. Obba recognized that bonds could form in the heat of battle, but also in the heat of creation.

Despite her knowledge of Shango's dalliances, not just with Oya but also with Oshun, Obba remained composed. Over time, as days became weeks, she noticed a shift. Shango began seeking her company more frequently.

He was drawn in by her kindness, her unwavering patience, and her quiet strength. He discovered layers to Obba that resonated with something deep within himself, for she accepted all of him.

Gradually, he found himself moved not by obligation or duty, but by genuine affection. The rhythm of Obba's more frequent laughter became a melody that filled his heart, her presence a calm to his restless soul.

As Shango's love for Obba grew, so did Oya's resentment. She had not expected him to fall in love with the other Orisha. Her hostility toward Obba mounted. But Obba met Oya's fury with her eternal patience, her animosity with kindness.

Jealousy, a mortal Osogbo, seeped into the Garden. It could stoke a fire as potent as any of Aganju's. Oya found herself consumed by such a flame. Her heart, once warmed by Shango's affection, now seethed with envy and desperation. In her despair, she wove a web of deceit.

With a smile that hid the storm within her, Oya approached Obba, feigning concern and what seemed like a spirit of friendship. She planted seeds of doubt in Obba's ear, false tales not only of Shango's wandering eye, but of his longing for a harem so grand that she would not be needed anymore. The poisonous words took hold within Obba, their thorny tendrils winding around her rational mind, threatening to strangle it.

Oya, exploiting Obba's distress, suggested a remedy as disturbing as it was desperate. She described a stew simmering over a fire—a stew that would bind Shango to Obba forever. The secret, Oya whispered, was a little ebo, a piece of Obba herself, offered willingly and lovingly.

The thought of giving over a part of herself, of mingling it with the spices and flavors of the stew, was terrifying. Yet Oya's words, laced with apparent empathy, swayed Obba. She saw in this macabre act a chance to keep Shango's love, which she had become addicted to. She could not lose him.

Thus, under the guise of sincere concern, Oya manipulated Obba, who found herself standing on the precipice of a drastic decision, fueled by her love and her fear.

She contemplated the ebo in the silence of the palace she shared with Shango, her thoughts running wild. What could she part with that wouldn't draw Shango's attention? A finger? A toe? But no, he loved how her fingers intertwined with his, how her delicate toes played with his under the sheets. Every part of her was cherished, noticed, and loved.

As the stew simmered on the hearth, spreading a delicious aroma, an idea dawned upon her. Her ear! She could sacrifice her ear and conceal the absence with a beautiful head wrap. He wouldn't notice.

With trembling hands, she found the sharpest knife in the palace. She steadied her breath, then held it. In a swift, decisive moment, she severed her left ear. The pain was blinding, but her determination did not falter.

She hurriedly wrapped the bleeding wound with gauze and linen, wincing as each layer was soaked in crimson. In a panic, she tossed the cloth into the fire, watching it flare up before turning into ashes. She covered her wound again, more carefully this time, and adorned her head with a wrap, artfully arranged to hide her self-mutilation.

After meticulously cleansing the severed ear of any blood, Obba carefully placed it into the simmering stew. Shango returned home early from his obligations. The aroma of the stew greeted him; he sat down eager for the meal. Complimenting Obba on her head wrap, he expressed his delight at her new appearance.

With both excitement and nervousness, Obba was ready to serve him. Feeling the dampness of the head wrap against her skin, she feared he might notice the blood that had begun to seep through. In a hurry, she ladled out a bowl of stew for him, her mind clouded by pain. It was only when she presented the dish that she realized her oversight—the ear was floating atop his serving.

The shock that crossed Shango's face was something she had never seen before. Lifting his gaze to Obba, he now saw the blood staining her head wrap. Despite her attempts at explanation, the sight before him stirred deep revulsion. It wasn't the presence of the cooked ear in the soup that unsettled him, but the realization of the jealousy behind the act. He struggled to reconcile the image of the wife he loved with the actions of someone who would let

emotions drive her to such extreme lengths. Heartbroken and disillusioned, Shango exiled Obba from the palace, severing their connection and leaving her with the consequences of her actions.

Shattered, Obba felt the pain of Shango's rejection bearing down on her. She sought to escape Edin and the Garden, and the tormenting gaze of those who might witness the evidence of her weakness. Obba wanted to find refuge where no eyes could find her, where the judgment of the other Orishas did not reach—the underworld of Lady Iku, her dominion of darkness. It was a kingdom removed from the scrutiny and expectations of the world above, a place where her shame and the physical manifestation of her brokenness could remain unseen.

Approaching the golden doors of Iku, Obba felt the burden of her troubles begin to lift; she had entered a place where such trivial woes of the world held no sway. The shadows of her past receded into insignificance. Here, Obba regained a semblance of her former peace, an opportunity to exist without the constant reminder of her fall from grace.

In the darkness of the underworld, Obba found a new purpose. Iku allowed her to stay as a guardian of sorts, a keeper of records for those who passed through her domain. Obba's task was to chronicle the lives and stories of the dead, ensuring that their journeys and lessons were not forgotten. This role provided her with a sense of belonging once again.

In Obba's search for self-forgiveness and healing, she discovered, in the depths of the underworld, away from the eyes of any who might seek her, a space for herself—a place of quiet reflection, where her story continued, away from the light of the world she once knew.

BOOK VII

THE LAND OF ORIRUN

CHAPTER 29

Jeggua

The human character is like pregnancy . . .
It can't be hidden forever.

—African proverb

Nestled in an untouched forest, a walled garden lay hidden from the world. It was a paradise, teeming with life and the beauty of nature. The air was laced with the intoxicating aroma of blooming flowers that carried with the soft breeze. Underfoot was a rich, damp soil, offering the comforting touch of Mama Onile.

The secret garden was a harmonious blend of meticulously cared-for flora and wild abandon. It was filled with explosions of colors against the lush green canvas of the surrounding forest. The canopy of woven vines overhead filtered the sunlight, casting light and shadow. The tranquil silence of the garden was punctured only by the serenading of distant birds.

Within this secluded haven lived the beautiful Jeggua. Petite in stature, she moved about the garden like a hummingbird. She tiptoed when she walked, fluttering over the ground as though she knew the Earth itself yearned to bring her into its nurturing embrace. Her emotions were a mirror of the garden she tended—vibrant, alive, and brimming with serene contentment. Each flower, each tiny creature, was known to her, and received her warm smiles.

Her skin was a rich dark hue that shimmered caramel in the sun. Her hair was a crowning glory of tight tiny curls intertwined with each other in a neat, compact bouquet.

Jeggua was an extraordinary being, and not just in appearance. Designed by Obatala, she had been his labor of love before he succumbed to his Osogbo. He molded her form, and breathed into her the ashé of innocence and purity, qualities that set her apart from other Orishas. Her eyes, as deep and calm as an undisturbed lake, could peer into the souls of humans, reflecting their emotions without judgment or fear.

Unbeknownst to Jeggua, her purpose was to shield Onile, the Earth, from the unsettling sea of human emotions. To keep Onile blissfully ignorant of mortal turmoil. She was a vessel, confining within her the whispers of the Ajogun. As long as her innocence remained untarnished, Obatala believed that humans would find respite from their Osogbos, allowing Onile peace.

Obatala's affection for Jeggua was that of a father for his daughter. He saw in her not just a vessel to imprison the Ajogun but hope for the humans. Obatala held the innocence of Jeggua in such high regard that he was convinced no eyes should ever behold her divine simplicity—not even his own.

He set about crafting a sanctuary for her, a refuge where she could thrive amid tranquility and joy, untouched by the claws of curiosity.

The taste of the sweet fruits, and the feel of the cool grass beneath her feet, were intended to keep her content and her heart at peace. Her happiness was his only concern, her innocence his only treasure.

Despite her solitude, Jeggua was far from lonely. She had never known another soul, but the garden was her companion, her confidante, her family. She found solace in the whispering winds, friendship in the chattering birds, and love in the blooms that reached out to caress her as she passed by. In the walled garden, surrounded by the love of nature, Jeggua was home.

It was a time of peace in both the physical and spiritual realms, and the Orishas orchestrated a grand celebration in Edin. Contentment seemed to blanket the world.. The Orishas reveled in it, frolicking and feasting, as their joy spilled into Aiye, oblivious to what lay ahead.

During the festivities in Edin, Obatala stumbled in, loosened by palm wine, his pride swelling like a sail that had caught a strong wind. He felt abandoned by the Orishas, believing they had cast him aside after he had had the idea to create mortal beings with Oris. He never considered that his excessive indulgence in palm wine had left him unreliable. To him, it seemed that the Orishas found it easier to replace him. He nurtured deep resentment toward Oduduwa, in particular, believing that Oduduwa focused solely on humans, neglecting the Orishas' own connection to Mama Onile.

The Orishas glanced at Obatala, their joy hardly disturbed, before returning to their revelry. Obatala drank from his cup, until he could no longer see straight. When his own voice became too loud in his mind, he turned to Eshu.

Eshu, known for maintaining open communication across realms and between Orishas, gravitated toward those who were ostracized and willingly lent an ear.

Obatala confided in Eshu: "Look at them," he said, pointing to the other Orishas, "blissfully unaware that they no longer hold the reins." It was now the humans who dictated the course of destiny. Obatala had designed the Children of Ori to exist in perfect harmony with Mama Onile, yet their descendants had strayed, consumed by their Osogbos. "We Orishas began to feel their pain. By mingling with the mortals, we have become burdened with their Osogbos, clinging to us like pestilence . . . yet still the Orishas never heeded my counsel. Now they are blind to the peace I brought with the barrier I created."

He had observed tears of loss, anger fueled by regret and revenge, and deep despair, all reflected in the Orishas. Obatala revealed to Eshu that, driven to ease the shared suffering, he had created a being called Jeggua who protected the Orishas from the overwhelming tide of human emotions, safeguarding their realm from collapse.

Eshu, skeptical, dismissed his words as the ramblings of a drunk. To quell Eshu's disbelief, Obatala decided to take him to the hidden garden.

Eshu was struck with wonder as Obatala led him on a hushed journey toward the place where Jeggua dwelled. He saw that Obatala hadn't deceived him, and a longing to meet her awakened within Eshu. But Obatala explained the consequences of such an encounter; if she lost her innocence, he warned, she could no longer act as a shield for the Orishas.

As Eshu peered over the wall of the garden, he was transfixed by the serene presence of Jeggua. Yet he pondered the risks of curtailed emotions. *Devoid of feeling, do we risk losing the ability to truly understand pain? Do we not become obsolete if there is no emotion to guide?* This question was not one to be dismissed lightly; it demanded deep reflection. Just as palm wine numbed Obatala's senses, Eshu saw that Jeggua was numbing the Orishas, preventing them from experiencing overwhelming human emotions. Without emotion, they risked becoming detached, unable to empathize or connect.

Despite these unsettling thoughts, Eshu made a solemn promise to Obatala. He vowed to guard the secret of Jeggua, to never speak of her existence.

Back in Edin, the grand celebration was in full swing. Shango was at the epicenter, his fingers coaxing rhythm from the Batá drums, each beat a testament to his divine prowess. Women, their eyes sparkling with admiration and desire, flocked around him, their bodies swaying.

Yet Shango wore an expression of ennui, his gaze distant, his heart untouched by the seduction surrounding him.

Eshu, forever scheming, took note. "Shango," he said, his voice weaving through the drumbeats, "why does boredom shadow your spirit amid such adoration?"

Shango, his voice gruff and lost in the music, confessed, "The allure of these flowers no longer stirs my soul. I want something new."

Seizing the moment, Eshu let slip word of a hidden world within their own—a secret garden, its beauty untouched. And in it lived a woman whose allure would make even the most stoic heart flutter. Shango was captivated, the spark in his eyes reigniting. He demanded to meet this enigma.

Eshu, aware of the dangers, made him swear an oath under Olorun to never lock eyes with the mysterious Orisha. Shango agreed, with a wave of his hand.

Guided by Eshu, Shango soon found himself climbing the walls of the garden. When he reached the top, he saw the enchanting figure of Jeggua.

From that very first glance, Shango was bewitched. Her beauty was the rarest of gems. His yearning to see her again was so potent that he returned the following dawn, his footsteps silent on the dew-kissed path to the garden.

Day after day, Shango would climb the wall and steal into the garden, concealing himself within its lush greenery, his eyes seeking out Jeggua. He studied her movements, her routines, the gentle dance of her hips as she walked, the way her voice lingered after she spoke to the budding flowers. Each day, he moved closer, his heart pounding like his Batá drums.

Finally, the day arrived when he was close enough to touch her. Nestled amid the blooms, he watched as she strolled past, oblivious to his presence. The whisper of her dress against the underbrush sent shivers down his spine, his breath hitching as he fought the urge to reach out.

Shango knew the promise he had made, the oath he had sworn. But as he gazed upon Jeggua, her beauty illuminated by the setting sun, he knew she was the most exquisite being he had ever seen. That she was unaware of him only further fueled his desire. He had to have her.

With a swift motion, Shango reached through the flowers, his fingers brushing against her shoulder. A gasp escaped her lips; she froze in place. Her eyes, wide with surprise, saw an unfamiliar figure before her.

She tilted her head, studying the stranger's face, her mind a whirlpool. Shango drank in her features, his chest thumping.

Before she could comprehend anything, Shango pulled her closer. His hand traced the small of her back, his touch gentle yet invading. And then, he kissed her. The hidden garden seemed to wilt.

The stolen kiss shattered her innocence. The kiss was a key, unlocking the cage that kept the Osogbos of humans away from the Orishas. The intensity of the moment left them both breathless and silent.

Shango, his perception irrevocably altered, saw not just a beautiful girl but

a woman who had tasted the bittersweet reality of existence. And Jeggua, her innocence lost, ushered in a new season, forever changed by a kiss that had awakened her to the complexities of life. She began to cry uncontrollably as she dropped to the ground.

The shame that enveloped her was not rooted in the act itself but in the understanding of what she had lost—and her prior ignorance of the pain across the land. Edin and the garden were no longer the same, and neither was she.

Obatala heard her cries from afar and discovered Jeggua in the ravaged garden; she was now consumed by a frenzied rage. It did not take him long to piece together what had happened, with Eshu reluctantly providing the details. Initially surprised, Obatala soon felt a wave of disappointment wash over himself. Jeggua was not only a shield herself; he had hoped to shield her from life's harsh realities. But Eshu explained to Obatala that every being must face the trials of life eventually.

As Obatala calmed the distraught Jeggua, who did not understand her own emotions, an idea formed in his mind. Jeggua, with her newfound comprehension of pain and suffering, was now uniquely suited for a task of greater importance—ushering the souls of the dead into the afterlife. It was a role that required empathy and kindness, qualities deeply rooted within Jeggua.

When Obatala shared the new purpose with her, Jeggua listened intently. Her eyes were fixed as she accepted the responsibility. No longer just a flower in a garden, she had become a bridge between life and death, guiding the souls as they transitioned into the soil, and as Orisha Obba chronicled their lives for eternity.

The Ajogun, once subdued, found their voices freed, without Jeggua to absorb them.

CHAPTER 30

The Iron Kingdom

All heads are the same, but not all thoughts are the same.

—Ghanaian proverb

Ogun emerged from the womb of creation itself, birthed by the dying breath of a star. With his first step, Onile felt her foundation tremble. With machete in hand, he forged a path for all who would follow. Ogun was the guardian of Orirun. As the Orisha of raw iron, his divine ashé served as a vital force sustaining all creation. In times when human passions flared and blood boiled in the heat of conflict, it was he who was summoned.

Ogun established his kingdom in the Garden as a monument to resilience and power. The imposing fortress was constructed from cast iron. The large gates depicted scenes of legendary battles and the triumphs of human heroes. Streets paved with dark iron slabs were so precisely aligned that not a single blade of grass dared to intrude. The gears of progress turned ceaselessly and Ogun's tireless mechanical beings vastly improved productivity, so different from their human counterparts, whose labor was often hindered by the limits of their endurance and the unpredictability of their emotions.

Ogun's ascendancy was made possible by his unparalleled command over iron, a skill that not only distinguished him among the Orishas but also reshaped the human world. His ability to transform this life sustaining raw material into tools and weapons bestowed upon humans the means to achieve their destiny. Through his divine craftsmanship, Ogun turned

Harmonia

helpless humans into warriors and hunters, and armed heroes for their epic quests.

However, Ogun's grant of his ashé to humans provoked apprehension among the Orishas. Their unchallenged reign now faced encroachments, as their authority was increasingly questioned. The mortals, who had once devoutly worshipped the Orishas, began to drift, captivated by the more tangible benefits wrought by Ogun's iron creations. Obas and Ayabas, empowered by technological marvels, exalted themselves, bypassing the Orishas' authority. This heralded a profound transformation in the relationship between Orun and Aiye.

In Edin, the Orishas gathered to deliberate on a matter of grave importance. The pantheon filled the grand hall, their number as diverse and vast as creation itself. At the front of the congregation sat the Council of Orishas: Yemayá, Shango, Oya, Eshu, Oshun, Oduduwa, and the subject of the meeting, Ogun.

The council confronted Ogun, imploring him to cease his creation of iron beasts for humans and warning that his actions would precipitate the end of their reign.

Ogun reclined, his expression contemplative. Then, leaning forward, he uttered a single word that resonated through the hushed silence: "No."

Oduduwa's response was a disgruntled huff. He assured Ogun that if he persisted in his pursuits, they would force him to stop.

Ogun's confident laughter engulfed the hall, silencing the murmurs of the crowd. He had never accepted Oduduwa's place on the council—the former mortal had taken Obatala's seat—nor forgiven him for marrying Lakange, the woman who would have been his second wife. Fixing Oduduwa with a piercing gaze, Ogun was defiant. "Force me, Oduduwa? You may sit in Obatala's chair, but you will never replace him. Orirun no longer needs your guidance . . . and it infuriates you that humans look to me, as they always have."

Yemayá rose to speak, her voice a tempest of indignation. "How dare you show such disrespect!"

Ogun met her gaze, his words a spear to the back. "Yemayá, your nurturing is no longer required. There are millions of mothers among the humans just like you."

He then turned to Oshun: "And you, Oshun, your beauty is overshadowed by my machines, which now control your rivers. Hierarchy has vanquished love. I am in the humans' veins; they rely on my creations. I am more powerful than all of you combined."

Looking out over the assembled Orishas, he declared, "In fact, I am now the judge, the leader . . . your only leader, and I will do as I please." With these words, he stormed out of the assembly, beckoning his wife Oya to follow.

Shango tried to stop her, whispering a plea, "Meet me." But Oya pulled away from his grasp, pausing only to cast a meaningful look at him before she exited the hall, leaving behind a realm on the brink of irrelevance and extinction.

Shango had observed the encounter closely. For he had awoken one day to his fire breath dwindling; it was now just smoke and coughs. He understood that his ashé was running out, as fewer offerings were being made by humans at his temples in Aiye. He had always been wary of Ogun; forging iron into weapons was an affront to the natural order.

His jealousy, coupled with his fear of losing his ashé, drove him into action. He knew he had to confront Ogun and make him submit, though the thought worried him. Shango was a powerful warrior, yet even he was dwarfed by the towering iron beasts that Ogun had built.

But he also knew that Oya held the key to Ogun's heart.

CHAPTER 31

Oya

Fear is the memory of pain. Addiction is the memory of pleasure. Freedom is beyond both.

—African proverb

Oya was an entity of ceaseless motion. Summoned from the cosmic fusion of Olorun's fiery brilliance and Olokun's deep waters, she was a balancing act, equalizing their divine ashé and ensuring they would never clash. Her partner was the volatile Jakuta, whose temper lit up the skies when their arguments erupted. Their union was a spectacle of power and passion.

In Onile's infancy, the planet was a raw canvas of dust, clay, vast sand dunes, towering mountains, sprawling ice sheets, and endless oceans. It was into this untamed world that Oya, with her wild spirit, made her dramatic entrance, captivating Ogun from the very moment of her arrival. Yet her ashé remained elusive, tantalizing yet beyond his reach, until the moment Jakuta and Oya had a thunderous fight that ended their spectacular union. .

United, Ogun and Oya became the architects of life, scattering seeds across the nascent landscape. Their combined ashé sparked a transformation, rousing Mama Onile from her slumber, awakening her to her own immense potential and powerful ashé.

Ogun found himself drawn to Oya, believing his feelings to be love. They shared countless moments together, nurturing the land and watching it flourish under their care. However, their bond was perpetually disrupted by Jakuta's interventions. Driven by jealousy and a desire to control Oya, his now-former partner in nurturing life from the skies, Jakuta stirred the lands into chaos. His bolts of ashé, hurled in fits of rage, scarred the seeds of life; he was a spirit of unrest. The other Orishas, wary of Jakuta's unpredictable nature, chose to keep their distance, recognizing the futility of trying to quell his rage.

Ogun was known for his fiery spirit, and the Council of Orishas conceived a plan to temper it: They proposed that Oya, the focus of Ogun's long-standing affection, become his consort. Ogun found in Oya a reflection of his own transformative ashé—an Orisha embodying strength and the capacity to create change.

Yet Oya had a side unknown to Ogun—she was, in fact, capable of the gentlest caresses, the softest lullabies, and the sweetest kisses. She could soothe the most troubled heart. Ogun was unacquainted with such tenderness. His ashé thrived on the boiling of blood in the heat of disputes and the clamor of battles. He saw himself as a warrior and deemed gentleness to be weakness.

Oya and Ogun's union was designed to bring tranquility to the Aiye. And for a time, their love achieved just that. Conflicts subsided and destructive forces were tamed. Yet Oya found Ogun's Iron Kingdom to be no more than an iron cage. There was no dance in iron, no freedom for the wind to swirl.

Oya was increasingly aloof, straying more often beyond the kingdom's imposing walls. Her absences, which would stretch for days, did not go unnoticed by Ogun. Within him was a simmering aggression, and he commanded her not to leave. Oya's spirit chafed against the order, yet Ogun was too strong to defy.

However, Oya was not without allies. The seeds of life that had blossomed on Earth revered her. Without her, they would not exist. She spotted a buffalo roaming free and grazing the lush land. A wave of envy surged through her, brought on by the creature's untamed spirit. Tears fell from her eyes and seeped into the soil, a heartfelt call to Oko.

Hearing Oya's silent plea, the Orisha of the soil instructed the buffalo to offer itself in an act of pure devotion. The creature complied, surrendering its life under Oya's hand.

She donned the buffalo's skin, and a transformation took place. Merged with the hide, Oya became the buffalo and experienced its inherent freedom. Cloaked in this guise, she could evade Ogun's gaze, escaping into the night whenever she pleased. Her newfound liberation was aided by the fact of Ogun's distraction as he pursued other women.

Yet Ogun was not easily beguiled when he was focused. One fateful day, he shadowed Oya, observing her as she unearthed the buffalo skin from its rock-strewn hiding place and slipped into it.

Ogun, witnessing this disobedience, felt a surge of anger. He found solace in control, in knowing each piece of his kingdom was exactly where he desired it to be. The sight of Oya's freedom disrupted this delicate balance, causing his fury to ignite like a blacksmith's forge.

Driven by rage, he seized the buffalo skin, placing it beyond her reach. He forbade her from ever wearing it again, hoping that, being stripped of her disguise, she would be forced to show him the love he so desired—a love that acknowledged his power and authority. Yet his actions and threats were akin to trying to restrict the wind, a futile endeavor that only stoked the embers of rebellion within Oya's heart.

For a time, Oya had resigned herself to her fate as Ogun's consort, finding within her heart an enduring fondness for him. Yet a piece of her heart remained unyielding, reserved exclusively for Shango. Together they danced across the skies, her intense passion for him ever growing as their ashes mingled in the clouds. But Shango's attention was ever fleeting; he reveled in his carnal exploits with mortals and Orishas alike. Still, Oya's longing remained steady, a spark awaiting a breeze to fan it back into a blaze.

Thus, when Shango unexpectedly touched her hand in the Council hall and whispered that they should meet, she was taken aback. The harder she tried to forget him, the more he occupied her thoughts. She yearned to see him but knew it would not be easy.

Oya would require a distraction potent enough to divert Ogun's attention so that she could slip away.

She knew that Ogun, a master blacksmith, was fascinated by rare metals and their properties. She recalled his particular interest in sky iron, a metal that fell from the skies and was believed to imbue any weapon created from it with unmatched power. When anointing humans as kings, he gave them weapons wrought from sky iron.

Oya crafted her plan. She started rumors of a sky iron shower that would be visible from the highest peak of the Iron Kingdom. Ogun bit. The prospect of obtaining such a rare metal was too enticing for him to ignore.

As twilight descended, Ogun, armed with his machete and an insatiable thirst for forging weapons and machines, embarked on his journey toward the land's highest summit, leaving Oya alone.

She sought out Shango. Soon enveloped in his arms, she was intoxicated by his presence, losing herself in a whirlwind of passion. She was so distracted that she didn't see the small iron creature that lurked in the shadows, observing the secret rendezvous, and reporting back to its master.

Ogun was on the highest mountaintop when he received the news of Oya's betrayal. He stormed back to his palace, his fury thundering through the silent night. Caught in the act, Oya looked to Shango but noticed something peculiar. There was no shock on his face, no surprise at Ogun's sudden appearance. Instead, he wore a smirk, displaying a grim satisfaction that sent chills through Oya. It struck her like a bolt of his lightning—it had all been planned.

Ogun lunged at Oya, attempting to seize her arm, but she pulled away. For the first time, she felt a wave of revulsion not only for Ogun but for Shango, who had used her as a pawn in his game to destabilize Ogun.

Ogun, seething with anger, threatened Shango with vengeance, promising him a battle devoid of mercy. Oya, for her part, cursed both of them and vowed to never again be imprisoned by her desire for Shango or bound by her marital ties to Ogun.

After declaring her intentions, Oya experienced a release, a purging of her emotions. She achieved new clarity. She was no longer a captive of lust or a prisoner of marriage. She was truly free.

CHAPTER 32

The Blood War

When elephants fight, the grass gets hurt.

—African proverb

Disoriented and consumed by internal turmoil, Ogun found his focus shattered. Shango seized the moment, infecting the Orisha of iron with his own Osogbo, that of wrath. He hoped to cloud Ogun's judgment and distract him from his work. As Ogun's emotional storm intensified, his production of machines that empowered humans began to falter, weakening his influence in the physical realm.

Dusk draped the world in hues of crimson and gold, and a quiet stillness enveloped the land.

Ogun, set on destroying Shango, unleashed an army of iron giants. Each was a singular marvel imbued with Ogun's wrath and power. They marched toward Shango's spirit warriors, their steps in perfect unison.

The Earth shook beneath the clash of the opposing forces. The initial engagements were marked by the sound of iron shattering wooden weaponry and of well-aimed spears bringing clockwork gears to a grinding halt.

The feud between the Orishas would come to be known as the Blood War, a conflict that echoed in the Aiye. The people of Yorubaland in Orirun found themselves in strife. Neighbor turned against neighbor, and the spiritual bonds that once unified Yorubaland weakened under the weight of the feuding Orishas, opening the way to further exploitation by foreign leaders.

The Blood War only intensified, with each skirmish surpassing the prior in brutality, and every warrior and machine becoming only more resolute in their conviction.

As destruction spread across the spiritual realm, it reached into the mortal realm as well, visiting kingdoms and villages alike. Many humans found refuge in Edin—at least those who managed to reach it. Their belief in the Orishas grew stronger in the face of adversity, their supplications becoming more impassioned. Within the Council of Orishas, it was Shango who rose as the leader of hope and strength. His name was yelled amid the haze and din of battle, invoked as a desperate cry for salvation from Ogun's iron beasts.

Wherever Ogun's war machines went, they wrought devastation. Grand empires crumbled under iron fists, lush gardens were incinerated by fiery breath, and hope withered under the unfeeling gaze of the automatons. Orirun, once known for prosperity and peace, was now crumbling. Despair settled over the kingdoms and once-mighty Obas were brought down.

As the war raged on, it appeared Ogun was on the verge of victory. Yet, in every heart that mourned a loss inflicted by his iron giants, a spark was kindled for Shango. The collective faith of the surviving humans, like a river surging toward the ocean, flowed toward Shango, empowering him and invigorating his ashé.

Once at a low ebb of devotion, Shango now found himself commanding a spiritual storm. His ashé roared back to life. Thunderous energy crackled at his fingertips, ready to be unleashed against the iron behemoths. With a war cry that shook the skies, he called forth bolts of lightning.

The bolts struck with such force that the iron giants were rendered inert, their once-terrifying forms now lying motionless, their metallic heads examining the ground. Stripped of his mechanical army, Ogun found himself alone and vulnerable.

Shango rallied his spirit warriors, and they captured the remaining mechanical beasts, turning them against Ogun. Shango and his men infiltrated Ogun's stronghold and imprisoned him within one of his own iron creations, rendering him powerless.

With Ogun in an iron cage, his once-magnificent kingdom began to decay, its vaulted structures and proud edifices showing the first signs of becoming rusted ruins. Though they had quelled the threat posed by Ogun, the Orishas wondered if Orirun—and Edin—could still thrive without their guardian.

In the absence of Ogun, the realms languished, leaving the Orishas vulnerable to their Osogbos. Humans, seeking power, led the Orishas further into the shadows. It was amid this turmoil and uncertainty that Orunmila, the Orisha of prophecy, sensed a seismic shift coming:

> *A seed of hope lies dormant. For it is written in the stars and etched in the sands of time, that from this blood-stained war . . .an Ori will be formed.*
>
> *A forgotten lineage will find its way home through the shadows. It will rise from the ashes of our fallen empire. A woman, untainted by the machinations of the divine, will be our beacon in the darkness. She will embody our salvation, our resurrection.*
>
> *From the ruins of our past, she will forge a new future. Her strength will not lie in the might of arms or the wrath of thunder, but in the purity of her spirit and the resilience of her will. She shall lead us back to the light, for in her, the promise of a new dawn resides.*

BOOK VIII

EVE

CHAPTER 33

The Fall of the Orishas

He who runs after good fortune runs away from peace.

—African proverb

The land of Orirun had long thrived under the reign of the Orishas, despite the many trials that tested both human and divine authority. Yet still winding through both realms were the serpentine paths of trade, guided by the Esin Imale. Their machinations began to transform the Garden's landscape; they molded parts of it into their own spiritual kingdom, unwittingly preparing the soil for a more threatening incursion, that of the Erankos.

The Erankos, led by the powerful Ariwa, set their sights on the Garden. These spirits, fearsome and cunning, sowed their intentions with each deliberate stride. In their wake sprouted seeds of a peculiar tree: the strangler fig. These figs latched onto the land's flora, twisting and tightening their hold with each passing moment. The figs thrived in the lush Garden and stretched their vines across the mortal realm, claiming the lands as their own.

As the Erankos entrenched themselves, the strangler figs became a permanent fixture in the Garden, casting strange shadows over the land.

In fact, Ariwa commanded these shadows, conspiring with the Ajogun, who lurked in the darkness. With a nefarious mind and golden tongue, Ariwa drew the Obas into a seductive pact, luring them with the promise of untold wealth in exchange for the ashé of their people. These rulers eagerly consented. A distinctive mark was branded on their right hands and on the right hands of each member of their families—an emblem that would protect them during the imminent hunt of the Erankos.

The fruit of the strangler fig, however, had an even darker purpose. It extracted the ashé from the Ori of those who consumed it, granting the Ajogun access to the Osogbos lurking within each mortal, sowing doubt and shame among them. The spiritual ties between many mortals and the Orishas were severed, leaving humans feeling lost. Once someone's ashé was extracted, their Ori became uprooted from their spiritual kingdom, which rendered mortals more susceptible to manipulation.

As Ariwa feasted on extracted ashé, the people of Orirun found themselves trapped in servitude. The Erankos trafficked countless souls to distant lands, even as they systematically dismantled gateways between the mortal realm and the Orishas. Devoid of refuge, Orirun lay bare. A civilization that had been nurtured by the Garden over millennia now crumbled at Ariwa's command. Yorubaland's glory and Orirun's heritage were engulfed by the tides of destruction.

The Erankos, devoted disciples of Ariwa, scoured the lands, forbidding the worship of the Orishas and capturing with ruthless efficiency those humans who still clung to the Orishas. Despite their efforts, some small villages in the jungle managed to evade the eyes of the Erankos. The chieftains of these villages guided their people deeper into the untamed wild, safeguarding their sacred connection to the Orishas and protecting their most treasured asset—their Oris.

As Ariwa's campaign of desolation advanced, the Orishas saw the specter of mortality looming before them for the first time. Like the humans who worshipped them, they sought refuge in unfamiliar territory. One by one, the Orishas faded from the mortal realm.

CHAPTER 34

Eve and the Lost Orishas

She who is destined for power does not have to fight for it.

—African proverb

Amid the ravages of the Erankos, a small village persisted, untouched within the protection of the jungle. This haven was home to the Huns, a remarkable community of weavers whose artistry was unsurpassed. The village itself was a collection of huts, each a masterpiece of weaving. The huts were connected by passageways and painted in a rich crimson.

The Huns' village was perched upon the cliff of a grand, lush mountain surrounded by towering strangler figs. With their artistry, they had carved into the figs likenesses of the Orishas, whose divine images seemed to stop the invasive vines from spreading farther. Instead, the vines wove into an imposing wall, encircling the village in a protective embrace.

There was one opening in this wall: the village was bisected by a river that cascaded into a magnificent waterfall overlooking lands as far as the eye could see.

One day, the river presented the Huns with an unexpected gift. Caught by a fallen branch and tangled within the reeds was a basket cradling a child. Her eyes, as bright as the morning sun, gleamed with pure innocence. The village women, busily washing their freshly dyed fabrics in the riverbanks, embraced the infant, took her in, and named her Eve.

As Eve grew, she was enveloped by the ease and simplicity of life within the Hun community. The people, with hearts full of warmth, nurtured her as one of their own. Eve's upbringing was shaped by care and creativity.

Yet the dark storm of the Erankos eventually arrived. They had overrun the large kingdoms of Orirun, and now Ariwa's insatiable forces stumbled upon the Huns, people with ruthless intent. They cut through the strangler figs and captured many of the villagers for sale as slaves across the seas, burning their exquisite huts to the ground.

Eve hid during the attack, surrounded by the chaos, her heart pounding against her ribs. Her once-tranquil village was ablaze, the flames devouring the memories and dreams she had shared with the others. Her eyes, wide with terror, darted around for a path of escape.

The lullaby of the river seemed to remind her of its existence, muting the cries and screams of the other villagers. To Eve, the river had always been a comfort.

She sprinted along the riverbank toward the waterfall, her feet barely kissing the earth. The horrific shouts of her pursuers trailed behind her, but she pressed on, her gaze fixed on the edge of her world.

Reaching the cliff, she felt as though time stood still. Below, the pool at the bottom of the waterfall churned furiously, a swirling vortex of uncertainty. With a courageous leap, Eve surrendered to gravity, plunging into the unknown.

The cold shock of water enveloped her, washing away the soot and sorrow, and ushering her into the spiritual realm. She was suspended in the depths when a stunning apparition emerged from the darkness, its form shimmering like quicksilver. It was a woman, intimidating yet beautiful. She turned to Eve, and her voice echoed through Eve's mind, though her lips remained still.

"Eve, you have found one of the last remaining portals to our realm," she said. "I am the Orisha Yemayá, and you must listen carefully, for time is of essence. There is an ancient, forgotten lineage destined to return home. That lineage is you, Eve. You are the daughter of Ayaba Moremi and Oonie Oranmiyan, the greatest rulers the Ife kingdom has ever known."

Eve was overcome with disbelief and awe. She remembered tales of Ife, but never knew them to be true, for the Huns never allowed anyone to travel beyond the strangler figs, worried about the dangers that lurked beyond. She could not have imagined she could be a part of such a legacy. Yemayá continued, revealing to her that when Eve was sacrificed to the river spirit Esmerian many years ago, the ibeji kept her, allowing her to grow, for her Ori held the promise of their salvation.

"You are destined to lead us from the shadows into the light," Yemayá insisted, her voice laced with urgency. "A war looms, threatening to wipe out our world. If it is not stopped, the bonds that tie Aiye and Orun will unravel entirely, casting us into nothingness. Only you can guide the Orishas to safety . . ."

From around her neck, Yemayá drew a string from which hung the Eye of Orunmila, encased in a glass amulet. Orunmila had the ashé to to see all: the past, the present, and the many paths of the future.

"Keep this with you always," Yemayá instructed. "By looking through it, you will have the power to recognize the Orishas in our Garden of shadows."

Eve emerged at the water's edge and her senses were flooded by the Garden. Here, ancient rivers coursed through the land, untouched by the passage of time, their streams meandering through the lush landscapes unmarked by human interference. This realm of natural grandeur was home to fantastical creatures long extinct in Oririun.

Despite her confusion and fear, Eve found comfort in the Eye of Orunmila, feeling its weight against her chest. The amulet was a tangible link to the prophecy and purpose that now defined her. She followed the river, its gentle murmur guiding her.

Eve's first encounter was with a seemingly ordinary young boy. Before revealing herself to him, she lifted the Eye of Orunmila from around her neck and peered through it. The world before her was thrown into an ambered hue, except for the young boy, whose youthful appearance had masked an ancient soul. He was illuminated as if glowing from within, surrounded by an aura of black and red—the unmistakable colors of Orisha Eshu! There he stood, in the middle of the river, attempting to coax fish from its depths.

Eshu had been a faithful mediator and guide for both humans and Orishas. However, with the Garden now infested with strangler figs, he had strayed far from his original purpose. Eshu turned to sinful acts, driven by pride to prove his indispensability. His actions bred discord and confusion, where there had been unity. As a result, humans were caught in perpetual indecision and conflict, their Oris lost, relationships fracturing and once-thriving communities unraveling.

Eve sought Eshu's attention, but he remained engrossed in his pursuit of fish. Determined, she drew on her upbringing among the Huns, weaving a net from the tall grass and slender branches nearby. She waded into the water, patiently waiting as Eshu threw curious glances her way. As soon as the fish began to circle, she acted, capturing them within her woven trap. She presented her catch to Eshu, asking for nothing more than to be heard. Intrigued, he agreed to listen.

Eve explained the important task Orisha Yemayá had entrusted to her: to locate the council and guide them back to Edin in preparation for a war ahead. She asked if he would help her. Eshu, however, questioned why such a task had been given to a mere human instead of him. He had heard of Ariwa and the Erankos, but was lost in his own world, having found solace in discord and in conversing with the Ajogun. With a dismissive huff, he turned his back on Eve, as he hooked the fish she had caught on his carrying rack.

Disheartened, Eve clutched the Eye of Orunmila for comfort, whispering Yemayá's words to herself: "I am the forgotten linage; this is my true home . . ."

These words caught Eshu's attention. "This is your home? Where did you come from?" he inquired, his curiosity piqued.

Eve replied, "My village is in ashes, but I was told this is where I truly belong."

As Eshu pondered her response, the prophecy came back to him: "A forgotten lineage will find her way home. She will rise from the ashes of our fallen empire . . . She shall lead us back to the light, for in her, the promise of a new dawn resides."

Eshu, recalling the responsibilities he had once embraced, recognized that Eve was the one Orunmila had foretold. He agreed to assist her, aware that his guidance would be crucial to her task. Although the whereabouts of the other Orishas was uncertain, he recalled whispers that Oya was in the bustling market of the Garden. With the fish slung over his shoulder, Eshu led Eve through an endless field of towering grass. Unbeknownst to them, a fearsome beast lay concealed along their path. It caught wind of them and gave chase. In the frenzied chaos of their escape, Eshu dropped the fish, forgotten in the urgency of survival.

Once the two of them were safe, Eve asked the Orisha about the fearsome creature. He revealed, "It is an Osogbo manifested from the Erankos that razed your village to ashes. As the Garden falls under Ariwa's shadow, our very existence is entwining with theirs."

"How can they entwine?" Eve pressed him, seeking clarity. Eshu admitted he wasn't entirely sure; the Erankos were something new to the Orishas.

"All I'm sure of is that we lost the fish." Eshu added, "Without anything to trade, we will be denied entry at the market gates." He thought about it for a moment and proposed that Eve herself could be the tradable good.

More Osogbo-Erankos were guarding the entrances to the grand market of the Garden. Eshu, wearing the disguise of a humble trader, approached the sentinels, explaining that his purpose was to trade, and nodded toward Eve. He and Eve were allowed passage, as the guards eyed her closely.

They were immediately engulfed by haggling voices, sizzling street food, and colorful textiles displayed for sale. The aroma teased Eve's empty stomach, but their pockets were as barren as their bellies. Eshu instructed Eve to steal mangoes from a blind vendor, assuring her he had done it before and had never been caught.

Driven by hunger, Eve quietly approached the blind woman. But as she reached for the plumpest mango, the woman's hand darted out with surprising speed, seizing her wrist. The vendor ran her fingers over Eve's right hand, relieved to find no mark indicating a pact with Ariwa and the Erankos. Still, she lifted a blade, the market's harsh penalty for theft looming over Eve.

Just as the blade threatened to fall, a cloaked figure intervened, pulling Eve out of harm's way. Together, they fled the market, evading the guards, until they reached a dusty road. As they caught their breath, the mysterious savior told Eve never to steal as she tossed her a mango.

Eshu, waiting by the roadside, greeted them with a knowing smile. Eve's anger flared at him; she saw that he had put her in danger. Eshu defended his actions, explaining that it was the only way to draw out Orisha Oya.

Oya had always found herself controlled by the shadow of envy, a tormenting force that drove her to convince the Orisha Obba to cut off her own ear. With Ogun's imprisonment by the other Orishas, Orirun and the Garden had lost their guardian. When Ariwa and his horde arrived, her envy deepened, fueled by the pact many Obas had entered into with the newcomer and the shift in human adoration and offerings. Oya, who commanded the winds, felt overshadowed, her contributions worth little in the eyes of those she sought to protect and guide. Her festering envy began to distort her more than ever.

The physical realm experienced the effects immediately. Crops ready to be harvested were scattered to the winds, leaving famine in their wake. Rivers, usually tamed by her hand during tumultuous weather, churned and raged, breaking ships apart and severing trade routes. The basic processes of transition and renewal were thrown off-kilter by her internal battle.

So she hid within the Garden's market, disguising herself as a beggar, receiving her ashé from the less fortunate people she protected. For, amid all the change brought on by Ariwa, humans increasingly directed their ashé not toward it but toward each other.

Standing on the dusty road, Eshu informed Oya, in a matter-of-fact way, that Eve was the prophesied one. The revelation ignited a sense of urgency within her; with a steady voice, she said, "We must move swiftly." Oya knew where to find Obatala, who was lost in the Fog of Memories. To retrieve him would demand absolute clarity of purpose.

The trio reached the edge of a jungle shrouded in mist. Oya sternly cautioned Eve to stay within arm's reach and remain focused, as the fog preyed on those who felt lost or who dwelled on the past. As they delved into the jungle, the air thickened around them, pulsating with a life of its own. Each step forward seemed to draw the mist closer, until it engulfed Eve.

Eshu and Oya had faded into shadows and then disappeared entirely, and the world around her dissolved into an unsettling quiet. Isolated in the eerie stillness, Eve tried to calm herself in the disorienting void, overwhelmed by the creeping dread of being utterly alone.

The fog started to toy with Eve's mind, a puppeteer pulling at her darkest memories. It resurrected the haunting image of her village—the warm, loving community reduced to ashes by the heartless Erankos. The horrifying vision of her home ablaze sent a shudder down her spine, paralyzing her with despair. As it fed off her ashé, the fog tightened its milky grasp, pushing her deeper into the abyss of isolation.

It was only when Oya, like a gust of wind, swept down to rescue Eve from the fog's clutches that she returned to reality. The trio emerged into a small clearing, a sanctuary amid the desolation.

There sat Obatala, whose brilliant ashé had dimmed under the weight of self-reflection and regret. His Osogbo of overindulgence had distracted him from his purpose. He had found solace alone, away from judgmental eyes, spending his days guzzling palm wine and crafting creatures from twigs and leaves. These hollow beings survived but a few fleeting hours before disintegrating, a sign of his severely weakened ashé.

The three visitors pleaded with him to join them, but Obatala dismissed their call to action, his self-imposed exile having made him indifferent to the troubles of others. He waved them off, but Oya said: "Obatala, reclaim your place and show the world who you are." She emphasized that his intervention would be crucial, and that he could once again return to the Council of Orishas.

But it was Eve who pierced his apathy. She knelt before him, her eyes full of gratitude, and said, "I was told many stories of your greatness, how you molded us from the very soil we stand upon. Knowing that I am created in your image, with an Ori capable of saving Orirun, I'm truly grateful, and I thank you." She gently bowed her head into his hands.

As Obatala read her Ori, a fog lifted from his eyes, and he felt his purpose reignite. He said, "Let us head to the city of Palm, where Shango rules."

When they arrived in Palm in disguise, they were immediately met with drunken revelry and loud song. The streets and pathways were narrow and led to either dead ends or still more sinister paths. It was a city of shattered Oris, a haven for lost souls, and a playground for the Osogbo-Erankos.

Obatala was overcome by dread, as he realized that he should not have come. For in Palm, the wine flowed like rivers through the city that bore its name. The allure proved irresistible; straying from the group, he was absorbed into the laughter and music, and joined the raucous camaraderie of those lost in their cups. When Eve, Eshu, and Oya finally tracked him down, he was in a pitiful state, and deep into a dangerous game of chance with the Osogbo-Erankos, his once-clear mind clouded by the potent brew. He had been reduced to a pawn in Shango's reckless world.

To her surprise, Oya found herself able to command the wind once more, a power she hadn't wielded in some time. Conjuring a strong gust, she scattered the other gamblers, sending them scurrying to safety. As for Obatala, she swept him into the street and forced him to purge the palm wine. Despairing, he finally acknowledged his dire state.

Meanwhile, Eve and Eshu had begun to navigate their way through the maze-like city, seeking Shango. Guided by the faint beats of a Batá drum, they finally reached the lavish abode of the drummer.

Shango was consumed by the Osogbo of greed, driven forward by an insatiable craving for power and gold. As a mortal, he had never come to terms with his Osogbo, and upon becoming an Orisha, he carried it with him. Despite this, the Orishas saw value in his immense strength and prowess. But with the council dethroned and dispersed, there was no one to monitor him, and his Osogbo took command. Now Shango received his ashé from humans' pursuit of personal gain and opulence by any means necessary.

Confronting Shango was no easy task. His ashé radiated enormous power, and his volatile nature led him to dismiss the plea from Eshu and Eve. But when Oya appeared alongside them, her presence softened his stance; he had missed her. Beneath his hardened exterior, the memory of their union, and how it ultimately had destroyed Ogun, resurfaced, filling him with remorse. He knew the path to redemption would be long and fraught with challenges, but the prospect of aiding in the restoration of their realm appealed to his long-neglected sense of duty.

He told them he would take them to Oshun, who owned an establishment where the gamblers of his city would go to end their nights and spend their winnings.

Inside the Peacock, a building of extravagant beauty, the travelers were bathed in the soft glow of orange candlelight. Eve stood mesmerized, her senses captivated by the convergence of lust and power. The establishment was renowned as a waystation for those seeking to be chosen by Obas and Ayabas for their harems.

The walls of the Peacock were adorned with glinting metals, while silk curtains danced gently as a warm breeze entered through open windows. The scent of incense filled the air. The Peacock was a playground for chieftains, warriors, and great hunters, who found delight in the seductive entertainment it provided. It was here that the growing group of travelers found Oshun, who had discovered her new ashé.

Oshun's Osogbo was lust, and after the Garden fell to the Erankos, she had played havoc with rivers and streams in the physical realm. Once flowing with abundance, nourishing the land and filling the hearts of humans with joy and gratitude, these waterways now mirrored the erratic nature of her Osogbo. The waters either swelled into destructive floods or dwindled to barren trickles. As Oshun's attention strayed, the fertility of the land waned, leaving crops to wither and die in fields that had once been bountiful.

When Oshun made her entrance, the room seemed to hold its breath. The golden streaks that Olorun had left on her skin outshone even the most dazzling of jewels. Her beauty left Eve speechless. Her every move commanded attention. She immediately spotted her fellow Orishas across the crowded room.

Their reunion was heartfelt, a moment of laughter and respite amid their arduous journeys. Yet the reprieve was cut short by a general, an Orirun convert in thrall to Ariwa. His hawkish eyes, cold and restless, scanned the group before coming to rest on Eve. He noticed that she lacked the symbol that marked her as an ally. With a wave of his hand, he commanded his accompanied men to seize her.

The Orishas, even in their diminished state, remained warriors of ancient, arcane power. As the soldiers advanced, they sprang into action, their abilities manifesting in bursts of light and force that sent the general's men reeling. In a whirlwind of divine ashé, they made sure no harm came to Eve. With the path cleared and the attackers momentarily stunned, they made their escape, leaving behind overturned tables, spilled wine, and terrified customers.

Only Oshun looked back as they fled the Peacock. The travelers threaded along hidden paths and through ancient tunnels known only to those who had once roamed the realm freely. As they neared their destination, the landscape transformed around them. The familiar gave way to the wild, and they emerged into a savanna. At its center lay Edin, a place Eve had only known from legend.

Eve and the Orishas made their way up to the Pantheon, where the calcified figure of Orunmila stood motionless. The Orisha of prophecy, whose insights had guided countless souls along their destined paths, now lay frozen, a monument to neglect.

He had been seized by the Osogbo of stillness. Fewer humans sought his prophecies, as they struggled to survive under the Erankos. The priests and priestesses who once communicated with Orunmila were hunted down by the invaders and executed, severing his connection with those few humans who still worshipped him.

Eve stepped forward and gently inserted Orunmila's missing eye into its rightful place. As she did so, the Orisha's prison crumbled away, freeing Orunmila from his long stasis.

However, the reunion of the council was still incomplete. Orunmila noted Ogun's absence, stirring displeasure among them, as bitter memories of the Blood War lingered. They feared that Ogun's release would summon his wrath.

Although he had been imprisoned for centuries, like the other Orishas Ogun was unable to avoid his Osogbo. His anger toward the gods who had consigned him to his iron-bound prison had only grown. As he lost control over his own ashé, humans exploited it for their own impulses, committing acts of violence out of spite.

The mere sight of another Orisha would unleash a fury within Ogun too wild to contain. Yet there was a glimmer of hope, after Orunmila explained that Ogun's primal instincts might recognize Eve as his granddaughter. This recognition, the travelers hoped, could thaw his heart. It was a gamble, but they had no other choice.

As Eve and the Orishas walked through the gates of the now-rusted Iron Kingdom, the air seemed to cling to their skin. Iron automatons frozen in place and vandalized surrounded them. The travelers walked carefully through this graveyard of grandeur, their eyes set on the fortified palace where the Orishas had imprisoned Ogun so long ago.

They found him where they had left him, in the deepest chamber of the palace—confined to a silent iron monolith with cords and bolts across its surface.

To awaken him from his enforced slumber, Oya and Shango united their ashé, channeling the raw energy of Earth to conjure a storm cloud. The atmosphere crackled as lightning arced toward Ogun, the bolt of electricity jolting him out of hibernation.

Upon his release, Ogun erupted, lashing out at Shango in particular. His last memory before the darkness had claimed him was of Shango and his spirit warriors coming for him. The other Orishas offered pleas and commands, yet it was Eve's voice that halted the chaos. Her words, delivered with a calm strength, sliced through Ogun's anger, reminding him of the bonds that had once united him with the other Orishas, of the battles they had fought side by side.

She raced toward Ogun, her plea for peace softening his anger. She embraced him, urging him to aid her people. As Ogun sensed her ashé, the spiritual essence that connected them, he recognized her as his granddaughter. His rage subsided, replaced by a feeling he had never experienced before: pure love.

United with the reawakened Orishas, Eve had fulfilled the prophecy and claimed her birthright, ascending to the throne as the first human Ayaba of Edin. As she took on immense authority and responsibility, the vines of Ariwa's strangler figs crept ever closer.

CHAPTER 35

The White Lion

A spider's cobweb isn't only its sleeping spring but also its food trap.

—African proverb

Mama Onile found herself stricken as Orirun was overrun by the Erankos, who had descended like a swarm of locusts. They consumed everything in sight, stripping her bare, mining her very ashé until she bled dust, and leaving her lands barren and desolate.

For a time, Mama Onile languished in her affliction. Days turned to nights and the moon waxed and waned as she endured the agony of labor. At the climax of her pain, she purged herself, bringing forth Babalu-aye.

Born from his mother's suffering, he was unlike any Orisha Edin had ever beheld. His skin was marred by sores, and each blemish oozed with anguish. He was a stark contrast to the radiant beauty of the other Orishas. There was no symmetry in his form, no grace in his movements.

The other Orishas recoiled at the very sight of him. They maintained their distance, speaking quietly among themselves, their eyes filled with a mix of pity and disdain. Babalu-aye, despite being an Orisha himself, was treated as an outcast, shunned and isolated by Edin.

His growth was rapid, and with it came a strange illness that plagued Orirun. What began as a single affliction soon multiplied, each infected mortal reflecting the visage of Babalu-aye. This illness was unlike any known before—deadly, relentless, and impervious to all remedies known to the Orishas.

Ayaba Eve, desperate to save her people, summoned the Council of Orishas, seeking their guidance. As the plague claimed more lives, the already fragile hope of Edin's people all but disappeared.

Eve recognized that Babalu-aye did not understand the effect he was having on the realms of Orishas and humans. "We must not banish him without just cause," she implored passionately, "for if he has indeed ushered in this plague, he knows not what he does." However, the majority of the council, driven by the urgent need to save Orirun's people, decided otherwise. Bereft of evidence to absolve him, Eve acquiesced to their verdict. Babalu-aye was exiled from Edin, cast out into the shadows of the fig trees, in the hope that this might bring relief to the suffering kingdom.

Although Babalu-aye had been exiled, the toll from the disease only continued to increase. Every attempted cure had failed. In private, Shango confided in Eve, "I have pondered deeply—if Babalu-aye brought this illness that knows no remedy, then perhaps he himself holds the key."

Eve felt a wave of relief wash over her as Shango voiced what she herself had begun to suspect. "However, the council will never permit his return without some sort of proof, and the proof lies in the Garden," she replied.

Eve was forbidden to venture beyond the walls of Edin, for Erankos prowled the Garden, preying upon mortals. Yet Eve was persistent, and, seeing her determination, Shango said he would protect her, and they sought Babalu-aye together.

Embarking on their journey, Shango and Eve immediately realized that the soil was no longer fertile and the plants were riddled with parasites feeding off their leaves. With caution, they steered clear of the strangler figs.

When they encountered a dark, imposing shadow, Shango sensed Babalu-aye was near. Shango instructed Eve to remain in the light as he stepped in the shadows to approach the banished Orisha, promising to return quickly.

With his fire breath, Shango ignited a thick branch to illuminate his path.

Within the shadows, he found Babalu-aye, who had been transformed from the meek Orisha that was shown no love. In the darkness among the Ajogun, Babalu-aye had discovered his true home, and the one being who cared for him was Iku, the lady of death.

Babalu-aye had learned to heal the disease that he had brought with him into the world, by embracing the shadows within himself. He now spent his time healing the sick and returning the dead back to the soil; he had no desire to return to Edin, preferring to tend to his purpose in the Garden. As Eve stood amid the death and decay of the Garden, awaiting Shango's return, a majestic white lion appeared. Its coat was so pure that it cast a haloed glow, a soft luminescence that seemed out of place against the desolation.

Eve was mesmerized by the splendid creature; she found herself inexorably drawn toward it. Her curiosity was piqued, and she was oblivious to the hidden menace that lurked beneath the lion's enchanting beauty. It lowered its massive body in an elegant bow, an invitation for her to mount its back.

Eve's breath grew shallow, her pulse quickening as her curiosity overcame her caution. She stepped closer. The beauty of the beast stripped her of reason and replaced it with wonder. Her fingers brushed the creature's fur as she climbed upon its back. She barely had the time to settle before her world shattered.

The lion sprang forward, a sudden blur of motion. Grass and roots buckled beneath its charge, and Eve had no choice but to cling tightly. The Garden dissolved into a stream of shapes and colors. It was only then that Shango emerged.

A storm heralded his approach. Dark clouds churned above the Garden, an angry sky split by bolts of lightning. Shango's voice thundered across Edin, his anguish twisting her name into a roar. "Eve!" he bellowed. He sprinted through the broken brush, his ax in hand, his ashé surging with fury. And yet, despite his power, he could not catch her.

The other Orishas appeared by his side, summoned by the threatening sky and Shango's call, which had carried to every corner of Edin. Eve was gone.

BOOK IX

OLOKUN'S OCEAN

CHAPTER 36

The Ascension of Yemayá

A bridge is repaired only when someone falls into the water.

—Somali proverb

The white lion took Eve to the west, across the great ocean. Witnessing her abduction without the power to intervene, the Orisha Yemayá understood she would have to make a sacrifice. Olokun's saltwater domain beckoned to her. It was a realm unfamiliar to her and beyond the influence of Mama Onile. By crossing its border, Yemayá would irretrievably sever her connection with the spiritual realm, anchoring herself in the flow of human existence.

Yet her unbridled devotion compelled her forward. Eve tugged at her ashé, a plea she could not ignore. Yemayá took a final glance at the spiritual realm, her home, before diving deep into Olokun's ocean. There, she embraced the world of humans, forever tying her fate to theirs.

The journey to Olokun's prison at the bottom of the ocean was arduous. In the eternal darkness, Yemayá could not gauge distance or speed, yet she pressed on, knowing that Olokun was her only hope to find a path to Eve.

As Yemayá descended to the ocean's floor, a haunting sight met her eyes: Olokun was surrounded by a blanket of lost souls. The spirits of Orirun's people, once full of life, now lingered in this watery realm where the rays of Olorun could not reach. She could not comprehend how so many had found their fate in Olokun's domain.

Yemayá wove her way through the underwater graveyard. She felt the souls' pain under the weight of Olokun. Olokun only knew how to embrace their suffering, finding comfort in those who shared her eternal sorrow. Yemayá found herself powerless to free them, for Olokun held them tightly, their anguish reflecting her own.

Yemayá approached Olokun with great caution, and momentarily set aside her search for Eve. She asked the deity where the countless souls had come from.

Olokun lifted her head slowly, and said, "The Erankos take the humans of Orirun to the western lands, chained. Many perish crossing my kingdom, while others choose the waters over bondage, hurling themselves from the vessels to find refuge with me."

A chill swept over Yemayá, for the threat posed by Ariwa and the Erankos was darker and more dire than she or the Orishas had understood. She implored Olokun for aid in locating Eve. But Olokun, wrapped in her chains of resentment, met Yemayá's plea with derision. "You come to me for help?" Olokun scoffed, her voice laced with bitterness. "Well, I desire my *freedom*!"

Olokun had been chained by the Orishas many centuries earlier, her chaotic rule deemed too dangerous after the arrival of humans. Forgotten by the lands touched by Olorun's light, she initially seethed with anger, an emotion as volatile as her crashing waves above. But as time passed, her fury transformed into a profound feeling of brokenness. This once-indomitable force of nature, who commanded the waters and harnessed Onile, left behind her old ambitions. Now humbled, she longed merely to be released, to be free.

Yemayá replied, "Olokun, it was you who called the flood upon the land. You threatened everything, every life, without thought or care . . . not even for your own daughter, Mama Onile. Your rage nearly swallowed all creation. Your chains are your own doing."

Olokun paused, her tone shifting from anger to cunning. "Tell me, Yemayá. How long will you care for them, these humans, these fleeting creatures? How long will you serve the whims of the council when your power is greater than they dare to admit?"

"What do you mean?" Yemayá asked, confused. For she had always believed her ashé was to nurture and care for mortals. Before Olokun could respond, she continued, "I rule the sweet waters, yes, but you speak of things you cannot understand. I am the mother of all, protector of life. Your chaos would undo everything we have built. The council acts for balance, for peace."

Olokun, leaning closer, her chains dragging, said, "Peace? Balance? Or is it control? They bind me because they fear me. But you . . . they have bound you in another way. You believe your duty is to protect the humans? But why else would Onile not let you return to the land once you enter my domain? You have the ashé of the moon, Yemayá. You could command the entire ocean, and the skies, too, if you only saw yourself for what you are."

Yemayá found this hard to believe, certain that Mama Onile wouldn't keep such a secret from her. Or would she? Trying to stay focused on her purpose, Yemayá replied, "You do not know what you're talking about, Olokun."

Olokun, with a sly grin, knew that she had touched something within Yemayá. "Perhaps . . ." she mused, retreating slightly, "you should ask Oya, Ogun, or Mama Onile, who has returned your ashé in crumbs. When you truly understand the depths of your power, will you still care about rules and order? You manage the waves, Yemayá. Why not free me and join forces? We could rule together, unbound by any other being."

"If I possess such power, then why should I free you?" Yemayá asked.

"Because you cannot hold the depths while you cling to the shore. Unfortunately, you still care for them," Olokun said, gesturing to the lost souls she had collected.

Yemayá's gaze swept over the endless bodies. "You choose to confine them here. For what purpose?" she asked.

Olokun was silent, her eyes never leaving Yemayá, reflecting the hopelessness that had consumed her existence.

It was in Olokun's nature to claim the countless lives cast into her domain, swallowing whole their stories, hopes, and destinies. These souls, their Oris full of potential, became her companions in the depths. Through them, she experienced the world above; they were her only window to the surface.

Olokun finally spoke again. "These souls are now part of the waters, lingering here because they are bound to me. If you wish to release them, you know what must be done." She pulled at her chains, adding, "Without my freedom, theirs will never come."

Yemayá stood on the ocean floor, lost in her thoughts. For eons she had kept to her place, that of mother. The council had told her she was the nurturer of life, that they maintained order whereas Olokun only brought chaos. But now, as she spoke with Olokun, something deep within her began to shift, something she had ignored, or perhaps forgotten.

Yemayá conceded, "You are right, Olokun. To free them, I must free you. But hear me now. If I release you, there will be no second flood, no storm of rage to drown the land."

Olokun smiled, "Is that a warning?"

"Yes," Yemayá said, her gaze cold. "The ocean is not yours alone to rule. You will not reign over this domain without me."

With a wave of her arms, Yemayá invoked her ashé, calling upon the moon's celestial pull and Aganju's dominion over Onile's fiery core to generate a powerful, synchronized force. This unleashed a tempest of tidal waves and swirling currents, crashing against Olokun's iron chains, and weakening their ancient hold. The combined energy provided just enough might to shatter them, setting Olokun free.

Olokun rose, the ocean stilled for a moment, the waves waiting for her command. The souls of the lost began to rise from the ocean floor, free to ascend. Olokun's eyes gleamed, while Yemayá's choice weighed on her.

Olokun said, "I promise you this: When you have tasted what your true power can do, the council, the land, will never look at you the same way again. The tides answer to you now, more than ever before."

As Yemayá traveled toward the surface, she knew Olokun had not misled her. Nothing would be the same.

CHAPTER 37

The Migration of the Gods

A single bracelet does not jingle.

—African proverb

As the dark tide of fate swept more of Orirun's people across Olokun's ocean to lands unknown, the Orishas found themselves unable to reach them. Each soul from Orirun that was cast upon foreign shores carried a flicker of their Ori, like a solitary star adrift in an endless night sky, bright enough to be seen, yet insufficient to chart a course for the Orishas.

But soon the lost people of Orirun began to call out in unison, and their collective ashé formed a constellation. This brilliant gathering of souls shone so brightly that it blazed a path through the darkness, reaching Edin.

Though the Garden and Edin were now beyond Yemayá's reach, her bond with them and the Orishas remained unbroken. After she had spoken with Olokun, the truth dawned upon her: she had been relegated to the role of caretaker for Obatala's creations, while Oya and Ogun concealed the truth of her strength.

With the Orishas struggling against the ever-encroaching roots and shadows of the strangler figs, Yemayá called upon the council from the ocean's depths. Her powerful voice rose with the rising tides, summoning them to gather beneath the great Baobab of Onile in Aiye, where she would seek both answers and decisive action.

Under a silver moon, Yemayá stood encircled by Obatala, Eshu, Oya, Ogun, Oshun, and Shango. Her robe shimmered with the deep blues of the ocean, her eyes serene, yet the air hummed around her. Her firm voice sliced through the thick tension. She asked why her true ashé had been hidden.

Among the others, the unspoken truth lingered like a foul scent. Oya had shielded the realms, and Yemayá herself, from her potential. The decision was born out of fear, fear of what Yemayá might become, of a power that could rival the firmament itself.

Ogun stood silent. His jaw tightened. "We were afraid of what you might do."

In disbelief, Yemayá stepped back; a laugh of incredulity escaped her lips. "Why? Did you fear I would mirror your wars for supremacy? Let us not forget, it was I who brought Eve to liberate you . . . to free you all!"

Oya, with earnestness, interjected, "Yemayá, our fear was rooted in the belief that, upon discovering your true power, you might become indifferent to the land and mortals we protect. We intended to tell you, but only after ensuring you cherished what lies beyond the waters, lest you let the world drown."

Yemayá's fierce gaze softened; she understood. "I have freed Olokun," she said, to the horror and panic of the assembled Orishas. She pressed on, "She obeys my command now. However, that is not the reason I have summoned you. The people of Orirun and Eve have been torn from their homeland, cast into bondage across the ocean. Their cries reach us, yet something blocks our way. The passage through the spiritual realm is sealed, barring us from reaching them as gods."

Shango's fists clenched, sparks of lightning flickering at his knuckles. "It's Ariwa and the Erankos, isn't it?"

Yemayá nodded.

Ogun huffed, "Then we prepare to fight!"

Yemayá cautioned, "This is no ordinary enemy, Ogun. It is a force beyond our knowledge. The chains that bind our people are forged not just from iron and wood, but seek to steal their ashé, to consume their Oris."

Obatala asked, "If the spiritual path is barred to us, how will we reach them?"

Yemayá turned to the distant horizon, where the ocean stretched endlessly toward the west. "We travel as they do. As mortals."

Eshu quickly interjected, "To travel as mortals? We will be powerless. Vulnerable. We may not survive."

Yemayá met his eyes. "I know, Eshu. But we have no choice." She turned to the rest. "This task will be the greatest of our trials, surpassing any battle or conflict we have known. It demands more than force of arms; this is a battle for the soul. Our mission is to endure, to withstand the horror and suffering, so that we may cross to the other side and set them free . . . and retrieve Eve."

The Orishas, gazing toward the western horizon, decided to heed Yemayá's call.

Bodies lay crammed together in the dim confines of the Eranko ship. The air was thick with the stench of human suffering. Chains clinked softly in the shadows. The Orishas, now bound in vessels of mortal flesh, shared the plight of their people. The oppressive heat mingled with sweat, fear, and despair. The council sat among humans, their divine strength reduced to aching bones and bruised skin as Yemayá fiercely drove the ship onward.

The beast of hunger prowled the hold, a phantom sapping their vitality as the passage of days blurred into weeks. Oshun could feel it most keenly; she felt the beast gnawing at her belly, twisting her insides as it did to those around her. The humans moaned in their sleep, some too weak to rise, their voices reduced to fragile whispers of lost hope.

Ogun, once a powerful presence, was now emaciated by hunger and bore bruises around his wrists wrought by the very iron he had once commanded. He noted the irony of his cruel struggle. Through gritted teeth, he spoke to the winds of his sadness, hoping to reach the distant ears of Yemayá. "I have

Harmonia

tried to break these shackles, but as mortals, we are no stronger than they are. I feel them slipping away, those who can no longer endure."

Ogun's words did not go unheard. Oya, whose breath was now stifled within the wooden belly of the ship, caught them. She responded, her eyes shadowed by exhaustion. "Which is worse, the beast of pain or the beast of hunger?" The pain wasn't just physical—it was spiritual. It clawed at their souls, whispering in their ears, telling them to give in, to surrender.

Shango, whose fiery spirit refused to be extinguished, answered. "The beast of pain is worse," he declared, "nourished by the despair of mortals. In the stillness of the night, I strive to sow seeds of strength in their dreams, urging them to endure. Yet pain deafens them."

"We cannot lose them," Yemayá said, her voice entering the minds of the Orishas aboard. "Bound though you are, remember you are their gods. We are their strength. We cannot allow hope to wither and die."

And then there were the lost ones.

Every few nights, there was the soft splash of a body meeting the ocean surface—another who sought release from the torment, surrendering to Olokun. As she filled their lungs in her embrace, she guided them to ascension.

Yemayá could hear the creaking of the wood, the slap of the waves against the hull. She reached out, pushing against the ocean's currents, urging the ship to move faster, to hopefully make the suffering end more quickly. The people had long called out to them in prayer and were now weak and broken. Their bodies were frail, but Yemayá could still feel the flicker of their spirits.

Yemayá implored the Orishas to sustain hope. "Though words may fail us, our presence shall speak volumes. We must show them the promise of survival. That even in this darkness, we are still with them."

Shango murmured encouragement to the weary souls beside him, urging them to clutch the fragile ropes of endurance, to hold on just a little longer, to endure the pain a little further.

Ogun, though bound by chains, straightened his back, his iron will unbroken, silently showing the others the strength of their spirit, urging them to defy the crushing gloom.

Yemayá focused on the ocean beneath. She called out to the waves, not with an Orisha's commands but with a mother's pleas. "Winds, push this ship faster. Grant them the boon of survival."

The waters responded, but only just. The winds shifted slightly, and the ship groaned as it gathered speed. Yemayá looked up at the sky and whispered softly, "Endure, my beloved children. Hold on."

But still, as the nights dragged on, more souls surrendered to the waters. Each loss etched a scar upon Yemayá's heart, yet she persevered. She continued to summon the winds, to entreat the waves; her strength wavered, but she did not stop.

IFE · ENITAN · ALKEBULAN · ASASE YAA
Harmonia

CHAPTER 38

The Dock

Tomorrow belongs to people who prepare for it today.

—African proverb

The ship approached the shores of the West Lands, the arduous voyage across the vast ocean finally nearing its end. Yemayá could still feel the familiar rhythm of the ocean, though it was now fading, and becoming something else, almost foreign. Her fingers brushed the wooden timbers as the ship approached a dock, completing its journey.

The humans, their chains clanking together, were yanked out of the hold and onto the dock by the Erankos. As the Orishas were dragged off the ship, a wave of unease washed over them; something shifted out of alignment. Oya's eyes narrowed, sensing what the others had already begun to feel—a barrier, thin yet impenetrable, separating them from the land that lay achingly close.

Oya's breath stilled, caught in her throat, as her hands began to fade, her mortal guise unraveling, pulling her away from the corporeal vessel she had donned for the journey. One by one, Ogun, Shango, and the others felt the same dissolution, their human shells dissolving into the ether, leaving them at the cusp of the new land, where the ocean met the earth.

"We cannot enter," Eshu lamented helplessly.

Ogun added, "This land turns us away."

Emerging from the waters, Yemayá knelt upon the shore, the damp sand cool beneath her palms. She watched the people of Orirun being herded into the unknown. She felt their despair, their fear, as they stepped into a new kind of darkness. "We came all this way," she said to herself, "and yet they need our presence now more than ever."

Just as hope seemed to slip away, Yemayá noticed something happening on the dock.

As the humans of Orirun who had survived the ocean crossing set foot on the dock, they carried more than just the visible scars of their tribulations. They also bore the knowledge to sustain their revered Orishas upon the foreign shore.

They dropped masks and robes, woven not from threads but from song and the potent essence of ashé. These vestments would empower the Orishas to transcend the spectral barrier, slipping unseen past the vigilant eyes of Ariwa and the Erankos.

Donning the masks and robes, the Orishas looked at one another and found themselves standing face-to-face with Awira's pantheon.

Yemayá, the nurturing matron of humans, had transformed into Mary, the revered mother of Ariwa's anointed leaders and the Erankos. Obatala, the Orisha of creation, emerged as the father of mortals. Ogun, the fierce Orisha of iron and warfare, was Saint George, a symbol of bravery and guardianship. Shango, the wielder of thunder and lightning, was altered into Saint Barbara, embodying strength and resilience.

Oshun, the personification of love and fertility, became Our Lady of Charity, who epitomized kindness and compassion. Eshu, the guardian of crossroads, was now Saint Anthony of Padua, protector of the lost souls. Orunmila, the Orisha of divination, was changed into Saint Francis of Paola, renowned for his prophetic visions. And Oya, the fierce warrior of the winds, saw herself remade into Saint Teresa, the herald of change.

Though their visages were cloaked beneath these new guises, the Orishas' ashé endured. The people of Orirun, adrift upon the West Lands, made a sacred vow to their guardians. They recognized that, while they might have taken new forms, their intrinsic and immutable ashé would persevere.

Bound by laws that silenced the Orishas' sacred names, the faithful turned to song. Through the call of music, they invoked each Orisha with their own sacred beat, strengthening their divine connection to their spiritual realm.

The Orishas were in an unfamiliar realm, one that bore no resemblance to their homeland. Each element of this land served as a stark reminder of displacement. Here, they were but wandering spirits, strangers adrift in a strange land.

They saw, in the bustling marketplaces, their people paraded and bartered for, stripped of their dignity, their worth reduced to a few gold coins. In the distance, the Orishas could see more ships arriving.

The gods of Orirun looked on in horror; their determination hardened. The West Lands stretched before them.

BOOK X

THE CHILDREN OF ORI

CHAPTER 39

The Golden Manuscript

The danger in hunting down evil is that you gradually become that which you seek to destroy.

—African proverb

The Orishas embarked on an odyssey through the vast West Lands, in search of Eve. Yet with each step that took them farther from their origins, their identities began to fade.

The border between this foreign spiritual realm and their physical existence grew indistinct, casting them in a labyrinth of uncertainty. Were they navigating spiritual corridors, or did their feet still tread upon the soil? This question lingered like a shadow upon their path, as they continued their quest.

The Orishas arrived at the edge of a great forest. They hoped that perhaps the Erankos had hidden Eve there.

In Orirun, forests were sanctuaries, places of solace and refuge. Yet here, in the West Lands, they were deemed forbidden. The Erankos spun chilling tales of monstrous beasts lurking within the depths of the forest, ready to devour any who dared to enter. Such stories instilled a paralyzing fear, binding their people to coastal cities, where safety was but an illusion of their constructed boundaries.

As the Orishas pressed deeper into the forest, they crossed over into a new plane of existence, passing through the realm of Ariwa into the original spiritual realm of the West Lands. This mysterious place, both strange and familiar, seemed to beckon them onward to its revered ruler.

They came upon a sacred grove, where none other than Mama Onile stood. Here, though, she was different; her long silver hair shimmered as it fell freely over her weathered skin, which was etched with the signs of a lifetime spent in the harsh, unpredictable elements of the West Lands. She greeted them.

"I know you have many questions," she said, her voice stern and tender, as if addressing errant children, "for you have journeyed far, learned so much. Now is the time for you to know the truth."

Mama Onile gestured to the beings among the trees. Slowly, figures emerged, their forms shifting like smoke caught in moonlight. "These guardians," she began, "are reflections of you, separated from your realm by Olokun's flood many centuries ago. When the lands split and the humans were scattered, so were your kind. Many vanished in the tides of time. But many others found new shapes and established new realms."

Mama Onile explained the mystery of Ariwa, a force not confined to any realm, but the embodiment of the Orishas in their unity. Born from the shards of their fractured selves, Ariwa was molded by human hands, sculpted from the dreams and ambitions of mortals.

"From the descendants of those who rebelled against you," she declared, "Ariwa was born. Initially, these humans sought to break free from your control, aspiring to carve out their own place in the spiritual hierarchy, where they too could wield power and influence. This rebellion sprouted not from malice but from a longing to assert their individuality. Yet this once-noble aspiration has now turned into a weapon . . . all because you defied my rule and bestowed upon them the gift of Ori."

From the folds of her garb, she pulled out a strange yet beautiful object: a golden manuscript.

She continued, "From Oah, mortals learned the power of a story preserved. They have found immortality by recording their existence within these pages, inscribing themselves as sovereigns of worlds sculpted by their hands. It is all chronicled in this book, gilded in my divine gold."

When the Orishas inquired about Eve, she tossed the manuscript at their feet. "In there she resides," she replied. "Her captivity transcends the boundaries of Aiye and Orun. It is no earthly prison, nor is it forged by chains and walls. She is bound within the tales of mortals, her essence trapped by the Erankos, who inked her fate within these gilded pages."

The golden tomb was more than just stories; it was a weapon forged to wield control over its captives indefinitely, binding souls within its gilded grasp until time itself unraveled.

The Erankos had conceived the white lion to seize Eve and deliver her to the West Lands. Once she was in their grasp, they contemplated extinguishing her Ori. However, they had settled on entombing her within the manuscript, a cunning bait to lure the Orishas into their realm.

Though Eve's Ori remained untouched, they had siphoned away her ashé, the life force that tethered her to the Orishas and the very soil from which they had sprung.

Atop her head, where once rested the crown of her lineage, they placed the seed of a strangler fig. This weapon, made not from iron but from corruption, sought to sever Eve from her roots.

As the seed germinated, it wove its vines around her being, entwining her spirit with tales that were not her own. Imposing forgetfulness on her, the strangler fig took root, pulling her into the golden manuscript. It enveloped her, suspending her above the ground she once walked with pride. The strangler fig's insidious growth represented more than physical entrapment; it was an erasure of her lineage, a silencing of the stories that had thrived among her people over generations.

With a solemn tone, Mama Onile warned the Orishas against destroying the manuscript. "Keep it bound," she implored, "for the time may yet dawn when we shall rise anew, and only then might she be free."

She continued, "I've read it. The creations of yours who oppose you have united, and they conspire to outmaneuver us. In their audacity, they have erased me from my own tales and are slowly excising you as well. As Ariwa's realm swells, ours withers, threatening to disappear entirely. I am in pain, for all that we created will be forgotten."

Yet in her lament a glimmer of possible redemption shone through. "The Erankos made one mistake, a flaw that could herald our return to power. In crafting Ariwa, they mirrored but a single visage of humanity, disregarding all the rest. Division, sown within their ranks, may be the key to our resurgence."

She grew very still. "Remember Orunmila's prophecy," she said. "*Through their toil shall they find renewal* . . . For those who have known the night most deeply carry the strength to bring the light."

The Orishas suddenly became burdened by their disguises. The masks trapped stifling heat against their faces, constricting each breath to a shallow gasp. Their robes, now heavy, clung to them like a second skin. Beads of sweat trickled down the Orishas' divine faces, seeping into the wood and clay of the masks, as if seeking to bond their spirits to the façades. Their essence shifted, their faces changing to match the masks, rendering them unrecognizable, even to themselves.

Desperation seized the Orishas as they reached for their heads, fingers clawing at the stubborn edges of the masks that seemed welded to their flesh. These visages refused to release.

Mama Onile watched as the Orishas struggled, in vain, to rid themselves of these false identities. Their efforts grew increasingly frantic, until finally they gave in to exhaustion and despair.

Once their futile attempts ceased, Mama Onile said, "These masks have become parasitic, feeding off your ashé," a hint of sorrow creeping into her tone. "They have you now, and they will not relinquish their hold. Your ashé is now barely a flicker and on the brink of dissolving into oblivion. As am I."

Mama Onile told them to return home. They could not save their people who had been taken to the West Lands until they first saved themselves and Orirun, which was in grave danger.

CHAPTER 40

The Strangler Figs

When the roots of a tree begin to decay,
it spreads death to the branches.

—Nigerian proverb

When the Council of Orishas departed Edin in their quest to reclaim Eve, chaos seeped into the land like a poison. The decay of the Garden accelerated in their absence and the strangler figs reigned, casting more shadows over Orirun's kingdoms. These silent invaders wound themselves around the mightiest kings, strangling the life from them as they reached toward the skies, spreading their suffocating canopy over the land.

The people in the Garden cowered beneath the looming trees; their crops failed, their rivers dried, and their spirits were slowly sapped of hope. In the absence of the council, humans turned inward, their faith shaken, left without guidance or consolation. They mustered what resistance they could, yet the more they struggled, the tighter the grip of the figs—twisted monuments to decay—rose.

Now Olorun's rays barely touched the Garden's ground, and Iku, the lady of death, emerged from her realm. No longer bound to the underworld, she walked freely, her presence as silent and cold as the wind that rustled the desiccated leaves. Her arrival brought fear; life itself retreated where she wandered, leaving no soul safe, no breath guaranteed.

Beside Iku stood Babalu-aye and the Ajogun warriors, his pestilence

returning humans to the soil. The Orisha of disease and decay had awaited a realm engulfed in darkness, a place where he could find belonging. Now, with his freedom, plagues swept through villages and sickness festered in the stagnant air, spreading ruin.

They did not fear the Orishas. The figs had grown too strong, their roots too deep. Even if the council returned, the land would not remember their touch. The figs had become one with Orirun's soil, spreading death to the very soul of the people who once flourished there.

Amid the despair, a strange hope could be found in the source of their suffering—the strangler figs. As the people of the Garden trod through their shadows, they noticed a curious change: the figs now bore orange, plump, ripened fruit that glistened like forbidden jewels in the dark.

The allure of the fruit was irresistible, as hunger gnawed at the people of Orirun. They fixated on the fruit, contemplating whether it could offer relief. The elders, though wary, could not ignore the pleas of their suffering people. As they gathered to deliberate, tales spread through the villages of those who had tasted the fruit, claiming it granted a brief reprieve from bottomless hunger.

Yet those who consumed the fruit found that an unusual emptiness had settled in their bones, as though a piece of themselves had been digested by the trees. The elders soon uncovered the truth: the fruit was no gift from the Orishas, but a trap devised by Ariwa and the Erankos. It offered a fleeting sense of relief in exchange for something far more precious. With each bite, the people unwittingly surrendered their ashé to Ariwa, nourishing the strangler figs and strengthening their hold on the land.

There were those who resisted the temptation. They observed the hollow look in the eyes of those who had eaten the fruit, the weakening of their bodies even as they claimed newfound vitality. These few resisters carried the stories of the Orishas, memories of a time when the land was filled with light, knowing their ashé could not be given away so easily.

CHAPTER 41

The War of the Gods

When the roots are deep, there is no reason to fear the wind.

—African proverb

The Orishas set sail once more, now carrying the golden manuscript, but this journey was not like the one that had brought them to the West. When they crossed Olokun's ocean to reach the West Lands, they had done so as mortals—enslaved, starved, and broken. Enduring silently within their fragile human vessels, they had witnessed the agonies of those they were destined to protect. Now, however, they were not returning as captives, but, still wearing their masks, they were praised as saints and guardians by the Erankos. The Erankos lavished them with praise and gave them grand accommodations; the crew was unaware of the true nature of the deities they worshipped.

After weeks at sea, the Orishas reached the shores of Orirun. The moment they touched their home soil, the masks loosened and fell to the ground. Yet they found a land that was unrecognizable; the Garden had succumbed to the darkness. Edin was now encased in the figs' parasitic vines creeping over every structure, into every sacred space. The kingdom was lost to the voracious overgrowth and the nefarious forces that had taken root in the Orishas' absence.

Heartbroken by the devastation, the Orishas found hope in Mama Onile's survival. Deep within the Earth she lay, bereft of her former splendor, her gold and jewels gone. She remained in a deep hibernation. They were determined to restore her ashé. But first they had to purge the land of the Erankos and their strangler figs.

The Orishas retreated to the ancient kingdom of Ife, the same kingdom Ayaba Moremi nurtured many centuries earlier, where the story of her sacrifice as well as Oranmiyan's legacy still lingered. Ife had remained untouched by the strangler figs' grasp, its boundaries protected by Esmerian's age-old promise to Moremi, that Ife would endure. Here, the Orishas found peace, but they knew that war was not only coming—it had already begun.

The war in the Garden was fierce. The Orishas found themselves battling not just a single deity but Ariwa's entire pantheon. The battles were not fought with swords or lightning, but with belief and ashé, the divine energy that was the very bedrock of existence.

In the mortal realm, the conflict was one of resistance and renewal. With every soul converted, Ariwa grew stronger, feeding off the ashé of those ensnared under its control. Yet each defiant stand, each act of rebellion against Ariwa, became a moment of rebirth.

The Orishas, guiding those who resisted the fruit of the figs, fought for the restoration of Oris. They knew that purging Ariwa and the Erankos from Orirun would cleanse the Garden of the strangler figs that stifled growth and prosperity. Even in Aiye, the war was not just for territorial dominance, but a sacred struggle to reclaim belief and to inspire hope.

Here, reader, is where I leave you. From the start of our voyage, you have walked beside me, as I guided you through the tangled narratives that have both united and divided Orishas and mortals. Listen closely, for these final words carry the weight of our shared destiny.

Our Garden reflects the scars inflicted upon human lands, tracing back to the dawn of humanity. In our kingdom of Edin, we, the Orishas, continue to witness conflicts as primordial as the soil beneath your feet and as immediate as the dawn's first light. The very ashé of your being, and Onile itself, still face assault and chaos. Factions target those devoted to us and continue to impose their rule through suppression and wars that ravage both realms.

There are disagreements over land and resources, displacing countless souls. Famines seize our kingdoms, and deceptive beliefs perpetuate division. At times, the seed of the strangler fig is placed upon humans' Oris.

Yet the prophecy of Orunmila, foretelling hardship before renewal, tells us that the current War of the Gods is just another chapter in a longer saga destined to end in our triumph.

The Osogbo within you and other humans will not allow you to find peace on Earth without sacrifice. It is humans themselves who must weave connections among creeds, confront tyrants, replace warfare with diplomacy, famine with generosity, and stark inequality with fairness.

Take solace in the knowledge that you will always have company. The Orishas are with you, in the caress of the wind, the firmness of the earth, the heat of the flame, and the nurturing waters that cradle and course through the land. Even though the Ajogun will emerge in your pursuit of your Ori, each obstacle comes with a chance for transformation, for envisioning once again a unified realm where empathy bridges the expanse between all beings, mortal and divine.

Now is the moment to answer our call. Today we rise. With each fig eradicated from an Ori, the constrictive vines wane, gradually freeing our Eve from their smothering clutch. Her awakening and liberation from the golden manuscript heralds the fulfillment of our prophecy. It tells us that the progeny of Ori shall prosper anew.

This is the promise of change, the hope for tomorrow, and the legacy we must strive to create, together. Let us, the Orishas, not fight for the present. Let us fight for future generations—and a promise that light will arrive to end the darkness.

Imole de, okunkun parada.

EFA · VOORAAND · EVE · HAWWA · EFA ·

Harmonia

Epilogue

From the tangled wilderness, a figure emerged, her skin a rich luminous brown. Her hair, thick and naturally loc'd, was interwoven with a living vine. She strode barefoot into a clearing where a once-vibrant jungle had once stood, its remains jutting from the earth like the bones of a dead giant. The acrid scent of sawdust filled the air as she knelt, her fingertips grazing the raw stumps of the severed trees.

The woman wept, her tears carving trails through the dried clay that clung to her body like a second skin. "Redemption," she began, her voice carrying in the wind, "lies not in conquest but in mending, and through their toil shall they find renewal."

As she rose, the brittle remnants of a once-mighty river shifted. She walked across a barren land of sand and dust. Her steps did not falter. Her eyes were fixed on the horizon. ". . . for those who have known the night most deeply," she said softly, "carry the strength to bring the light."

At last she came to a solitary baobab, captured in the suffocating grip of a strangler fig. It stood defiant in the center of the desert. Beneath its roots, hidden from the figs' reach, lay Mama Onile, in deep slumber. Her hands cradled her belly, within her a promise of the land's rebirth.

The woman knelt before the sacred tree, her hands brushing the dust from its roots. She spoke to the tree itself. "A seed of hope lies dormant. For it is written in the stars and etched in the sands of time, that from this blood-stained war, an Ori is formed . . . She shall lead us back to the light, for in them," she said, referring not to Eve but to Mama Onile and her seed, "the promise of a new dawn resides."

The woman rested her hand against its weathered bark, then turned away, her vine-bound locs sweeping over her shoulders as she disappeared into the infinite landscape.

It is known that true prophecies are tangled. To grasp a prophecy is to hold a prism to the light; every facet reveals a new perspective, though all are linked by the same eternal radiance.

CHARACTERS

Gods

ODUA	The god of creation who birthed Onile (Earth) from the seeds of life.
OLODUMARE	The god of creation who held the seeds of life. Ruler of the Kingdom of Orun—the galaxy.

Spirits of Earth

IKU	The great spirit of death.
ONILE	The great female spirit of Earth and ruler of the land. Called "Mama Onile" by the Orishas.
MAWU	The great moon spirit.
OLOKUN	The great spirit of the primordial seas who was once Odua; mother of the giants and Aje.
OLORUN	The great sun ruler in the Kingdom of Olodumare.

Other Spirits

ABIKU	A spirit who claims a child in the womb ("A child born to die").

ESMRIAN	A river spirit.
BIDA	The seven-headed serpent of trade and the seven shadows.
AJOGUN	Warrior spirts of darkness that awaken the Osogbos.
BABALU-AYE	Aligned with the Ajogun warriors, the deity of disease and illness.

Orishas (born when Earth was created)

AGANJU	The deity of fire who controls Earth's core. Father of Jakuta.
AJE	The deity of wealth and Olokun's daughter.
AJALA	The creator of the Ori/Destinies.
JAKUTA	The primordial deity of lightning and thunder. Father of Shango.
OBBA NANI	The deity of matrimony and record keeper of the dead. Wife of Shango.
OGUN	The deity of iron and war.
OKO	The deity of the soil.
OYA	The deity of winds and storms.
OSHUMARE	The serpent deity of transformation and obstacles.
OSHUN	The deity of rivers, fertility, and love.
YEMAYÁ	The deity of the surface of the ocean and spiritual mother to humanity.

Irunmole (existed before Earth was created)

ESHU	The deity of crossroads and messenger between spirits, gods, and mortals.
OBATALA	The deity and creator of humanity.
ORUNMILA	The deity of prophecy and wisdom.

Mortals who become Orishas (after Earth was created)

ERINLE	The deity of the in-between space where the river meets the sea.
EVE	The mother to the African diaspora in the west. Oranmiyan and Moremi's daughter.
JEGGUA	The deity of chastity, loneliness, and the mysteries of death.
OSHOSI	The deity of justice and the hunt.
SHANGO	The deity of thunder, lightning, and fire. Third king of Oyo. Son of Jakuta and Torosi.
TAIWO	One half of the deity of balance and duality. Nubian Pharaoh. Oshun's son.
KHENDE	One half of the deity of balance and duality. General of the Romeyetu Empire. Oshun's son.

Mortals

ABRONOMA	Princess of Wågådu.
ADENIYI	A chief of Ife and husband to Okanbi.
ADEBISI	Moremi's mother.
ADZO	Ogiso of Wågådu. Abronoma's mother.
AJAKA	Second and fourth Alaafin of Oyo, son of Oranmiyan. Shango's half brother.
BADIAKO	Ogiso of Wågådu. Abronoma's father.
BANKOLE	Chief of the palm berries in Òkè Òrà.
DADA	Enk who helped fight the giants with Oah.
ERINMEDEA	Mother of Eweka.
EWEKA	First Oba of the new Igodomigodo (Benin). Son of Oranmiyan and Erinmedea.
GBONA	General of the Katunga army.
HABEN	Son of Oah.

JAIYESIMI	Ife soldier and friend of Oranmiyan.
KUSH	Son of Haben.
KOFI	A prince within the Wågådu Empire.
KOSOKO	Oba of Nupe Kingdom. Brother of Torosi. Uncle to Ajaka and Shango.
LAMURADU	Descendant of Oah, king of the Tower of the Gods, father of Oduduwa.
LAKANGE	Wife of Oduduwa. Mother of Oranmiyan and Okanbi.
LAUIS	Emperor of the Romeyetu Empire.
LEO	Adopted son of Lauis.
MOREMI	Ayaba of Ife kingdom, wife of Oranmiyan, mother of Eve.
MURAT	Half brother to the king of Troy.
OAH	Hero of the ancient world. Killed the giants.
OBAMARI	The chief of the yams in Òkè Òrà.
ODUDUWA	Founder of Ife, son of Lamuradu, stepfather of Oranmiyan. Father of Okanbi.
OGIAMWEN	Last Ogiso of Igodomigodo.
OKANBI	Priestess of Ifé. Daughter of Oduduwa and Lakange.
ORANMIYAN	Founder of the Oyo Empire, Son of Ogun, father of Eve, Eweke, Ajaka.
SAHIBU	Warrior tasked with eliminating the Oonie of Ife.
SALEH	Royal family and followers of the Esin Imale.
TIMI	Second General of Katunga army.
TIWA	Mother of Haben, descendent of a Child of Ori and the first wife of Oah.
TOROSI	Nupe princess, wife of Oranmiyan, mother of Ajaka and Shango.

GLOSSARY

AIYE	The physical realm of Earth.
ALAAFIN	Emperor.
ARIWA	The weaponized spirit of the Christian god.
ASHÉ	The life force and energy that is within everything, living or inanimate.
AYABA	Queen.
DA'WAH	The warriors of the Esin Imale.
EBO	A sacrifice.
EDIN	The kingdom of the Orishas in the Garden.
ENKS	Original inhabitants of Earth. With no destiny, a spirit of servitude.
ERANKOS	The hunters who represent the seven European powers that colonized Africa.
ESIN IMALE	Leaders of the Muslim religion intent on expanding their spiritual realm into Africa, causing conflict with the Orishas.
THE GARDEN	The land under the Orishas' influence in the Kingdom of Olodumare.
IRUNMOLE	Deities who existed before Earth was created.
IYALÁWO	A priestess. Helps the humans connect with the spiritual realm.

OBA	King, made only through heredity or by Orisha Ogun.
OGISO	The mortal descendants of the Orishas chosen to lead: "rulers of the sky."
OKUNKUN	The darkness and shadows that take over one's mind, spirit, and purpose.
OONIE	Priest or priestess of a kingdom.
ORI	Literally "head," but represents destiny, a spirit's guiding compass.
ORISHAS	Deities, each an aspect of Olodumare.
ORUN	The universe, Spiritual realm.
OSOGBO	The sources of misfortune that plague humans and pull them away from their Ori.

BACKGROUND AND SOURCES

In Western societies, ancient Greek gods such as Zeus, Aphrodite, and Poseidon are widely known, though no longer worshipped. Yet mention the names Shango, Yemayá, or Oya—African gods still venerated today—and many people in the West will draw a blank. In the words of renowned jazz singer Abbey Lincoln, "Where are the African Gods? Did they leave us on our journey over here . . . will we know them when they suddenly appear?"

They never left, of course. This book is a personal retelling of West African myths, filtered through my own family and its diasporic experiences. The book has its origins in my late Afro-Cuban grandmother, who carried these stories with her from Cuba. The eastern regions of the island are a rich blend of African, indigenous, and rural cultures. They have long served as a sanctuary for Afro-Cuban communities; the relative isolation allowed them to preserve African cultural traditions, religions, and social practices.

My grandmother, like many in her community, was a descendant of enslaved Africans brought to Cuba during the transatlantic slave trade to toil on sugar and coffee plantations. Following the abolition of slavery in 1886, numerous Afro-Cubans sought refuge in the hills, during the earlier rebellions of the enslaved, forming maroon communities known as palenques, where they could resist colonial control.

It was in one of these communities that my grandmother was raised, steeped in African influences and the Yoruba spirituality, protected by the hills. Preserving her cherished traditions, she passed down the Yoruba religion and these storied histories to my father. Both shared them with me.

In my youth, the stories were like many others I loved, fairy tales and Greek mythology, all stored within the library of my imagination. It was during this time that my mother, an artist, fostered my passion for the visual arts. She opened the door to one of the most pivotal experiences of my life: visiting the Art Institute of Chicago. I recall being utterly amazed by the beauty of the European masters' works, aspiring to one day paint my own tales with such skill. Time and time again I would return to those paintings and imagine my own narratives tied to them.

The life I had in Chicago with my grandparents was the perfect environment for my Ori to thrive. However, everything changed when my parents decided to move us to a small town. With this sudden shift, I was thrown off balance. I found myself lost for years in a society indifferent to the deities and spiritual beliefs I had been raised with. Over time, my connections to the Orishas faded, along with pieces of my own identity.

It wasn't until the arrival of my children that my life shifted once again. This time motherhood became my new axis. I wanted to share the joys of my own childhood with my kids. With my son still a toddler, I decided to take my five-year-old daughter to the Art Institute, a place to fuel the imagination. She too fell in love, just like I had. But as we neared the European masterpieces, her excitement dwindled. Curious, I asked why she wasn't drawn to the woman in one particular painting, celebrated for her glowing perfection. Her simple response, "Because she doesn't look like me," struck something deep within me, revealing how far I'd drifted from the little girl I once was.

I realized I never wanted my daughter to feel anything less than, nor for her brown skin and coily hair to be seen as anything but beautiful. I set out to paint a world where she would feel a sense of belonging, surrounded by gods that mirrored her beauty. It became a healing process, connecting to my roots. I began painting the stories I knew well and researching and painting those unfamiliar to me. This not only led to my career as an artist but revealed an eager audience, diverse in background and color, yearning for these tales.

I found myself reviving the oral tradition of my ancestors with each art exhibition, and fielding inquiries about where the stories my paintings depicted could be found. Thus the writing of *Chronicles of Ori* began. This book takes the reader through the West African spiritual world, narrating the mythology and folklore that are still part of the spiritual practices of millions of African-descended people on the continent and in the diaspora.

The oral patakis—the ancient stories of the Orishas—were not designed to be woven together into a cohesive, overarching tale. Instead, each story stands as an individual lesson in morality. Each story has also evolved over time, mirroring the transformative essence of life. Each has been adapted by the teller to offer guidance tailored to those seeking it.

I have taken a different approach in this book. In creating a linear epic, I strived to connect ancient folklore to the African forced migration to the West in the early modern and modern eras. My process started with recalling the patakis shared by my grandmother and father. I explored various iterations of those stories and selected versions that aligned with the mostly linear narrative I aimed to assemble; oral narratives change and evolve over time. As I gathered and wrote them down, Yorubaland began to expand beyond its current geographical confines. I noticed intriguing connections to and similarities with other African folktales, and even religious narratives from different parts of the world.

For me, coming from such a colorful background, this made sense. To tell the story of the Orishas from their own perspective, it had to encompass the world in its entirety, acknowledging ancient migrations and cultural exchanges long before these were documented. Mythologies and folktales, regardless of their origins, are both specific and universal. While this book ends with the story of a people's forced migration, it strives at the same time to reveal humanity's collective journey.

To write this book, I also consulted the work of scholars such as Reverend Samuel Johnson's *The History of the Yorubas*, David H. Brown's *Patakin*, Robin Walker's *When We Ruled*, Chancellor Williams's *The Destruction Of Black Civilization*, Walter Rodney's *How Europe Underdeveloped Africa*, and many more. By combining oral traditions and history, I have sought to restore authenticity to the West African gods and their patakis. At the same time, I have offered my own, personal retelling. I do not claim that my retelling of these myths is definitive or authoritative. It is simply mine.

Although *Chronicles of Ori* does not include every tale, hero, or kingdom in the vast corpus of African myth, I have attempted to tell an alternative history of Africa, starting well before the era of the slave ships, docks, and auction houses, for our strength and resilience did not begin from enduring slavery but with the building of empires—spiritual and physical. I hope this book plays a small role in embedding these stories within our collective consciousness.

I truly believe in the power of storytelling, in all forms, to unify us and foster pure love and understanding.

ACKNOWLEDGMENTS

If it truly takes a village to raise a book, then my village might just be a city. To start, a standing ovation to my parents, who armed me with the tools for creativity and the courage to embrace being different.

To my children, who add purpose to the chaos and remind me daily why I do what I do.

To Maurice Smith, my incredibly loving and patient husband, you have been my sounding board for countless late-night ideas, even when they strayed into confusion. Your support is as unwavering as it is invaluable.

A huge thank-you to the ever-thoughtful and supportive Arthur Lewis, your constant excitement, support, and encouragement for my grandiose plans make you my ultimate creative cheerleader, pom-poms and all.

To Mara Tatevosian, my studio manager and right hand, your tireless dedication day and night goes above and beyond. Thank you for being by my side every step of the way.

To my agents, Christy Fletcher, Duvall Osteen, and my UTA family, your expertise ensured my manuscript landed in its perfect home.

Dan Gerstle, your editing magic transformed my initial drafts into polished perfection, and your enthusiasm has been a powerful motivator. A heartfelt thank-you to the team at W. W. Norton for believing in a first-time author and taking this journey with me.

To all the collectors and institutions who have supported me throughout the years, your faith in my work has truly been the fuel to my expanding practice.

Here's to everyone who has been part of this adventure—I couldn't have done it without you.

IMAGE CREDITS

212 *The Taking of Oya's Freedom,* Harmonia Rosales, 2023, 48 × 60 in.
236 *White Lion,* Harmonia Rosales, 2022, 48 × 60 in.
248 *Migration of the Gods,* Harmonia Rosales, 2021, 36 × 72 in.
252 *Harvest,* Harmonia Rosales, 2018, 46 × 27 in.
258 *Portrait of Eve,* Harmonia Rosales, 2021, 36 × 36 in.
264 *Obedience,* Harmonia Rosales, 2022, 48 × 72 in.
270 *Eve and the Orishas,* Harmonia Rosales, 2023, 48 × 60 in.